To Margo,

Love,

Tom

Murdered Sleep

Thomas D. Davis

Suffer Little Children

Murdered Sleep

A Dave Strickland Mystery

Thomas D. Davis

Walker and Company
New York

All the characters and events portrayed in this work are fictitious.

First published in the United States of America in 1994
by Walker Publishing Company, Inc.

Published simultaneously in Canada by Thomas Allen & Son
Canada, Limited, Markham, Ontario

Library of Congress Cataloging-in-Publication Data
Davis, Thomas D., 1941–
Murdered sleep / Thomas D. Davis.
p. cm.
"A Dave Strickland mystery."
ISBN 0-8027-3177-5
I. Title.
PS3554.A937774M87 1994
813'.54 – dc20 93-6298
CIP

Printed in the United States of America
2 4 6 8 10 9 7 5 3 1

To
my wife, Diane,
and
my daughter, Virginia,
with love

Methought I heard a voice cry 'Sleep no more!'
Macbeth does murder sleep, the innocent sleep

—Shakespeare, *Macbeth*

Murdered Sleep

▽

1

I KNEW I was dying.

Nothing on the right side of my body would move. Somewhere up on the left side of my head a piece of skull had been crushed inward, as if a boiled egg had been rapped with a spoon. There were splinters inside the skull; blood was pooling against the covering of the brain. I was lying on a gurney, waiting for the surgery I knew would be hopeless. And trying to fight the awful panic. My mind wasn't helping: It kept imagining the sound of a saw blade whirring against bone.

To distract myself, I asked, "The girl . . . you're sure she's all right?"

"Yes," said the disembodied voice. Actually I had seen the body once, of the orderly or nurse or whoever he was, with the rough beard and the gentle eyes. He was sitting somewhere in back of me, keeping watch.

"You're not . . ." It was hard to get words out. Fear had congested my chest, making it difficult to speak or breathe. ". . . not just . . . saying that?"

"No, Mr. Strickland. She's out in the waiting room right now. I saw her myself. She's not hurt."

"Good."

I tried to picture the girl, but I had so little to go on. I had first seen her from a distance in the cemetery at dusk, then on the beach, in greater darkness, struggling against her assailant. I hadn't seen her face; I never would. It was hard to die for an abstraction.

"What's she . . . look like?" I asked.

"Sort of skinny. Long dark hair. I didn't get a real good look at her. She was curled up asleep against her mother. I think they gave her a sedative. She looked real helpless—you know, the way kids do when they're asleep. Made me feel grateful to you for saving her life. You should be very proud."

"Mostly I . . . feel stupid. For getting hurt." Moving too fast into the dark spaces between the rocks, feeling the shove, teetering on the edge of the small cliff, not able to balance, sick at the sight of the hard shadows below. "One lousy . . . mistake. Hadn't been . . . so careless . . . I wouldn't be dying."

"Please don't say that, Mr. Strickland. I told you the prognosis is good."

"Don't believe you."

"Then try. You've got to think good thoughts. They make all the difference." I felt a slight pressure on my head and assumed he had put his hand there. "You'd better lie still now. Save your strength. They'll be coming for us any minute."

Reluctantly I turned back to my solitude. I braced myself against the return of panic, then slowly realized it was gone. Depression had taken its place, dulling my nerves like some dismal anesthetic.

I looked around the emergency room cubicle with its bare white ceiling and its gray, rubber-curtain walls. A hospital was a miserable place to die. In the past, when I had tried to form an image of death that would offer a little comfort to one who believed that death was the end, the image had been of night, stars, soft breezes, silence. But this place: It was like dying in a giant trash can.

The only possible escape was into the past. I looked up at the bare ceiling and tried to project my memory images there. They came, but so weakly, like old home movies shown in daylight on a makeshift screen. Worse, no feelings came with the memories, no stirrings of love, or pride, or pleasure. The feelings must have been buried beneath my depression;

without them I felt no connection to my past. It was as if life had already been stripped away from me, and like one of those dead in the Greek myths, I was left with nothing but longing.

I felt my depression deepen. *Please,* I whispered, *give me something to hold on to.* And then, perhaps because the wish had sounded like a kind of prayer, I had it.

I hadn't given in.

I had won the battle with the God of my childhood, the God who had haunted me throughout my life. "There's no atheist in a foxhole," my mother had been fond of saying, with her Christian cynicism. Well, this was my foxhole, and I still didn't believe, I wouldn't believe—not in that so-called God of love who could let his creatures suffer and die. Who could let my wife and baby die. My bitterness had won out against my need. No doubt it was a sad sort of victory, but it was all I had. It would have to be enough.

Suddenly there was a commotion, then motion, as the gurney was propelled down a hallway, surrounded by figures in white. I felt the pricks of needles, saw a mounted bottle of liquid dripping into my arm. A nurse leaned over, sprayed something down my throat, and then began feeding a stomach pump tube into my nose. I gagged and had an intimation of terror, but the tube slid down easily and the terror never took effect, perhaps because of some sedative they had given me.

I grew sleepy and began to wonder what dreams might lie ahead. I had always hoped that at the end, when the fear of death had become pointless, the mind would relinquish its savage will to live and give itself some comfort—perhaps reliving joyful moments of the past, or simply infusing itself with a feeling of peace.

I cast my mind back in search of my own best moments and felt a dull stab of alarm. Many of those moments had been when I was a Christian. What if they became the stuff of my operating table dreams. What if the last few minutes of my life were spent walking with my Savior, glorying in the

Lord. What a cruel trick that would be. What a mockery of everything I believed.

I began to summon all my will against the possibility, then realized how pointless that was. The dreams would come from somewhere far beyond consciousness, far beyond my reach. All I could do was beg.

Please, I whispered. Don't betray me.

Don't let me dream of Jesus.

▽

2

THERE WAS A blinding white light, and a face within the light, and the words, "oh, no" forming in my anesthetized brain. Then the face came into focus. It was too plain to be either angel or devil, and anyway, it wore a nurse's cap.

"I'll be damned," I said. "I made it."

"We won't know for sure until morning."

"Thanks a lot," I said, and fell back asleep.

When I woke again it was night. I felt a sedated surge of joy at being alive until I remembered the words of the nurse. I couldn't afford hope. Not yet.

I glanced around the dark room. It was as if I were alone in the cockpit of a plane on a night flight, with a panorama of sky above a bank of instruments with lighted dials. For all I knew this flight was about to crash, but even so, I felt grateful for being here: If I had to die, better this dim solitude than the blare and glare of the emergency room.

I was amazed at how peaceful I felt. What I had gone through earlier had been horrible, and there were bound to be bad days ahead—if there were any days at all. But tonight, through some trick of shock or anesthesia, I had escaped all that. There was no pain. My body, except for the still numb and motionless right side, was marked only by a pleasant warmth. There was no fear, no anger, no sadness—all emotion had been stilled. It was as if part of a mind had woken in a creature otherwise asleep. My thoughts were clear, my only feeling a kind of benign detachment. It was wonderful.

I turned toward the windows and stared out at the night sky with its pale stars. When I'd been a Christian, the world had been a place of light, the dark things a kind of illusion that would one day be dispelled. Now that God was gone, light was the illusion. Reality was the darkness beyond the stars—silent, infinite, empty. Sometimes I found that darkness frightening, but tonight it seemed so peaceful, seemed to touch in me something that beneath the frantic struggling of life longed for rest. I had the feeling that it wouldn't be so hard to let go, to let myself drift off into the darkness. I almost wished it.

After a time I turned my head away from the windows, preparing to sleep. But sleep wouldn't come. Instead an image formed against the dim ceiling, an image of Katie's face. As I felt myself smile at her, I realized that this was the first time since her death that I was able to think of her without a large measure of anger and pain. Such was my intensive-care calm. It occurred to me that this would be a good night for making peace.

I turned my memory toward that terrible Sunday when I found Katie in her bath, the water red with the blood from her razor-cut wrists. For the first time since Katie's death, my mind was able to go back into that room. The scream was gone now from my throat, the urge to vomit from my gut, as I knelt down next to the tub and touched Katie's bare shoulder. Her skin was so pale it was almost translucent, as if her flesh had begun to lose its materiality. The waxen peace of her face held no traces of the grief that she had clung to so tightly since that Sunday, a year before, when we'd found our infant daughter dead in her crib. Katie had let go of her pain; tonight, at least through the illusion of anesthesia, I felt I could let go of mine as well.

Since this seemed to be a night for unfinished business, I let my mind drift back farther in time, to those three people with whom I had shared so much pain in my earliest years—to my separate images of each.

My father. I'm four years old, and it's night, and my

parents are yelling at each other in slurred voices. I'm lying in bed listening, hoping he won't come for me, but he does come, and faking sleep doesn't help: He forces me up, into my clothes, and out the door. We go down into the apartment basement that's like a cement maze, the incessant, clanging machinery like some beast trapped within it. We make it to the underground garage, then we drive off into a night that feels like something out of a bad dream, a night infused with my own fright and my father's fury. We end up at some all-night eatery where we stay for what seems like hours, the two of us sitting across from each other but saying nothing, his face numbed with drink. He toys with his food for a time, then his eyelids droop toward sleep, his head nodding downward toward the full plate of food in front of him. My memory of those times is of enormous effort: of holding back tears, of willing his head to stay upright, of never letting myself look at the eyes of the others, eyes I know must be watching and mocking us.

My mother. After months of periodic crying as her husband, her life, and her self have become unbearable to her, the strange day comes when she announces that she has been "born again," that everything has changed. In a way it has. Once she was cold and self-absorbed, using the word "love" only as a weapon; now she is cold and Christ-absorbed, God's love her new and more powerful weapon. Before her conversion, everything I did was wrong because it irritated her; now everything I do is wrong because it irritates Jesus, and the full force of the universe comes to bear on my failings. I must be saved, she says. For a few years I hold out against her home crusade. But then, in a sixth-grade paper clip fight, I almost cost a girl her sight, and all resistance crumbles beneath the weight of my guilt. I give myself to Jesus, giving up the few things in my life that bring me joy.

Amy. She was such a cute child, whose wide-eyed, little-sister love for me was one of the few things that got me through the earliest years. I was taught as far back as I could remember that it is a brother's job to protect his sister, but there was no protecting her from her own parents, from herself, from the accidents of a life. There must have been things missing in her that she needed to survive, the anger and the dreams that give life some meaning in the worst of times. It didn't help that my parents almost totally ignored her, my father because a daughter wasn't of interest, my mother because without my father's interest, there was no contest there. Since Amy didn't exist for them, how could she exist for herself? She crippled her leg in a fall when she was very young, and that deprived her of the possible salvation of school-age friends, making her an outsider, a figure of fun. She drifted through life with increasing invisibility, and when she died of pneumonia at age thirty, the event seemed almost incidental.

Staring up at the ceiling, I turned off my mental projector and let the screen go dark. There was no hope of making peace with those three, not now, not ever. My earliest years were mostly vacant from memory, and what images survived were mostly awful. There was too much pain there; I wouldn't know where to begin. The only way to deal with it was as I always had: by forgetting.

▽

3

MY EYES WERE like doors beyond which lay a world of pain. I'd make a move to go out, feel the shock of the light, then pull back into the darkness. Things would happen around me, and to me, but I tried to observe these things from a distance, from the safety of my cave. The pain outside was blunt, feverish, dreary, and it seemed to encompass everything. I was determined to stay in the darkness as long as possible, curl up, wait it out.

I had a vague memory of last night and of a man who'd been grateful for life, philosophical about death, and at peace with the world. Whoever that had been, it wasn't me. I felt grouchy as hell and grateful for nothing. As for being at peace, if there'd been anything to hit, I would have put my fist through it. That is, if I'd had enough energy. And if I could have moved my right arm.

"Strickland."

The voice seemed to come from a long way off. It sounded vaguely familiar, but I didn't want to recognize it. All I wanted to do was hide from it.

"Strickland," came the voice again. "It's Sergeant Deffinger—Ocean Point police. Can you hear me?"

I squeezed my eyelids shut, as if they were also doors to my hearing and could block out the noise of his voice. I would just ignore him. Eventually he'd get tired and go away.

"Come on, Strickland. I know you're awake. I see your eyelids moving. I know you can talk—the doctor said he talked to you before. I need to ask you some questions."

I moved back farther into the darkness, searching for escape. The voice kept growing louder, following me.

"Strickland, talk to me. It won't take long. And it's the only way to get rid of me."

So there would be no escape.

"Come on, Strickland, what do you say?"

"Shit," I said.

He laughed. "Well, that's a start."

Since he wouldn't go away, the thing was to stay in a half doze, speak to him from just inside it, try to get rid of him as soon as possible. But to speak I'd have to do something about my mouth: It felt glued together.

"Water," I muttered, and waited. In a moment water started dripping toward my open mouth. Some of it got in. Most of it dribbled down the sides of my jaw.

"Great aim," I said as Deffinger patted at my face with some kind of cloth.

"Can you shift up a little?"

"Help me."

I felt his hands move under my back as I pushed up with my left hand and foot, trying to get my head and shoulders higher on the pillows. The movement wrenched at a dozen hurts all at once, causing one huge shock of pain. The pain jarred me awake, forcing a groan. The curses that followed were all voluntary.

"Goddamn it. Why the fuck couldn't this have waited till tomorrow?"

"Sorry, Strickland. I need to know what you saw."

"Bullshit. I didn't see anything. It was too damn dark."

"I need to hear it anyway." Deffinger picked up the bedside pitcher and poured water into a small corrugated paper cup. "Come on. Let's try this again."

As Deffinger dribbled the water into my mouth, I watched him with something less than kindness. He was a slender man, his hair slicked back like a fifties rock singer's. His otherwise average face had skin that was coarse and pocked, as if whoever had sculpted that face had decided it wasn't worth finishing. In contrast to all that roughness, he was wearing thick-framed glasses and an old brown corduroy sport jacket, which, along with something rather deliberate in his gestures, suggested someone stuffy and academic. It was an odd combination. He looked like a truck driver who'd had a make-over by Miss Manners.

Deffinger crumpled the cup and dropped it into the wastebasket. "The doctor says you're a very lucky man. He says they almost lost you."

"Maybe I'll care when I feel better. Come on, Deffinger, I don't want to be rude, but let's get this the hell over with so I can get back to sleep."

"All right. Just tell me what happened."

I sighed. It seemed like such a long way to the end of that story. Also, the ache in my head was beginning to throb, and it wasn't going to get any better as I went along. But there was no help for it. I might as well try to get it over with, taking whatever shortcuts I could.

"I came to Monterey yesterday to go over a final report with a client," I said. "I finished up in the early afternoon. It was a nice day for February. I figured I'd hang around for a while."

I closed my eyes as I started talking. Submerged in darkness, I felt myself relax a little. The thing to do was to take the story a few sentences at a time, trying not to think about how much more there was to go.

"I had a late lunch at the Wharf, took a drive along the peninsula, parked at the point. Walked around. Ended up at the cemetery."

It seemed I often ended up in cemeteries. Part of what drew me, of course, was the hurt of Katie and the baby. I'd sit there massaging that hurt like some badly strained muscle, telling myself that the fresh pain was a necessary part of getting well. But I wasn't so sure about my motives anymore. Sometimes it seemed that there was something in the pain itself that I craved.

But it wasn't only memories of Katie and the baby that

drew me to cemeteries. Of the few people I'd really cared about in my life, most were no longer alive. Those other memories were there for me too. Beyond all that, I sensed something in myself that made me feel so at home in cemeteries. Something dead.

"I must have gotten to the cemetery about five o'clock. I sat on a rock among some trees on the east side of the cemetery. I started thinking and just lost track of time."

An image of the cemetery formed behind my closed eyes. It was like a small park, the gravestones flat and sunken and only visible up close. The place seemed isolated, surrounded as it was by trees and bushes on all sides. But the isolation was something of an illusion. A closer look showed glimpses of a golf course fairway to the north and east, glimpses of houses to the south, a glimpse of sand dunes to the west.

"At dusk, I noticed the girl. She was at the opposite end of the cemetery—the side nearest the dunes—visiting a grave."

She'd made a sad little figure there in the dusk. She'd been sitting on the ground, bent over the grave as if over a hospital bed, her hand moving slowly over the gravestone as if she were soothing someone's face. Once she'd put her other hand over her eyes, and I'd wondered if she was crying. I had watched her for a little while, then drawn back into my own thoughts.

"It got darker, and I started to leave. Then I saw that the girl was still there. It was so stupid—her being there alone in that dark, isolated place. I wanted to say something—offer to walk her home—but I knew I'd only frighten her. So I watched. A few minutes later, she left. Walked away through some bushes at the southwest corner of the cemetery. I figured she was heading toward one of those houses to the south."

"You followed her?" asked Deffinger.

I nodded. My mouth was beginning to stick again. I asked Deffinger for more water, and he helped me drink three minuscule cupfuls. I swished each sip of water around in my mouth, trying to get some effect. It was as if I were trying to irrigate a patch of sand; the water just seemed to disappear. Finally some of it stuck.

"Just after she disappeared into the bushes, there was this funny shaking in the leaves. More than just from someone passing through. It gave me a funny feeling. I thought I'd better check."

The image of the park was vivid now, even to the damp coolness of the air and the wisps of fog. I remembered how in the growing darkness the world had seemed to take on a greater solidity, becoming a massive, threatening presence. But even as I'd felt that sudden foreboding, my mind had been telling me that I was being stupid, that nothing was wrong, that my time in the cemetery had made me morbid.

"I went over to the place where the girl had left. There was a path leading toward some houses. A street lamp in the distance formed a backdrop light, and I wondered why I couldn't see the girl up ahead, against it. On impulse I went through the trees to my right and climbed the dune.

"At the top, I saw two figures on the beach. I assumed the other was a man, though I'm not completely sure it was. He was dressed in black, and he was holding the girl against him. The impression was confusing. The man was wearing something like a poncho, and he'd wrapped part of it around the girl's upper body—all I could really see of her were her white sneakers below the coat. She looked like she was struggling, but I wasn't absolutely certain. It was awfully dark. The man could have been someone like her father, come to get her; they could have been joking around; he could have been shielding her from the wind. For that matter I wasn't absolutely sure it was the same girl, but they were the only people on that beach, and I had to know.

"When I first saw them, they were already across the beach, near some huge rocks. I called and ran after them. I didn't know if they could hear me—the wind was coming in pretty hard from their direction. They went behind the rocks, disappearing from my view. I got to the rocks and started scrambling over them. Suddenly I was on this small cliff, and the girl was below me on another stretch of beach, by herself, running away. For a second I just stood there, confused, thinking it had all been a mistake. Then I felt the shove."

The memory came rushing back in a conspiracy of senses: the damp chill, the image of dark rocks, the sensation of helpless teetering, the sudden inhalation of terror. I felt my left arm and foot brace convulsively against the bed, as if to stop it all from happening again.

"Jesus," I muttered, and suddenly my whole body was shaking.

I felt Deffinger's hand on my arm, saw his face leaning in toward mine.

"It's all right," he said. "You're all right." His voice was that of the professional soother, kind and concerned, and a little detached. "Take some deep breaths. Try to relax."

I obeyed his instructions, but deep breathing was a pathetic weapon against such a fierce onrush of fear. At most it offered a kind of distraction, keeping me from compounding the fear with added-on panic.

"Any better?" asked Deffinger after a few moments.

"No."

"You got some pills or something you can take?"

I motioned my head toward the nightstand. "In that cup there."

Deffinger put the pills on my tongue, then poured the water I needed to swallow.

"Must have been really rough," said Deffinger, his sympathy sounding less professional, more natural, this time.

I nodded, taking up the deep breathing again to sustain me until the pills kicked in. Through the continued panic, I kept monitoring myself, urging the medication on. After a few minutes I got the impression that my skin was being coated with a calming layer of warmth. The warmth began seeping inward toward the source of the fear and the tremors. After a few more minutes, I became calm enough to unclench my fists and return to normal breathing.

I nodded to Deffinger. "I'm okay now. Thanks."

"You sure?"

"Yes."

"Good," he said. Then, after a moment: "Look, I'm sorry, but I just need one more thing. Then I'll let you go."

"You don't have any choice about letting me go, Deffinger. In a few minutes, I'm going to be sound asleep."

"Describe the assailant for me."

"I can't," I said. "With that poncho he was wearing—part of it wrapped around the girl, and the other part whipped around by the wind—I didn't really get a sense of his build. With the hood up, I couldn't see his face, or even the shape of his head. Like I said, I got the impression of a man, but I can't swear to that. I suppose it could have been a woman."

"The girl is five-three. If you picture her against the assailant, do you get a definite impression of height?"

I closed my eyes, calling back the images of the dark beach. Thanks to the pills, it was just a picture now, stripped of sinister feeling.

"The girl was on his right side," I said, trying to peer through the amorphous night that filled my head. "I think his right arm was around her upper body, and I get the impression that his left hand was reaching over, maybe grabbing her hair. What I don't know is whether he had her head partially bent or not. And with that loose poncho or hood, I could be off an inch or more on picturing the top of his shoulders, or head." I opened my eyes. "I'm pretty sure that whoever grabbed her would be in the five-eight to six-one range, but I know that's not much help." I yawned, feeling myself getting sleepy. "You get anything helpful from the girl?"

Deffinger shook his head. "She says whoever it was grabbed her from behind, wrapped 'something rubbery' around her face so she couldn't see, and started pushing her forward. She tried resisting, but he was too strong, and he hurt her when she resisted too hard. The only thing she can add to your description is that the person was wearing gloves.

When I talked to her I tried to find out if she had gotten any physical impressions that might indicate gender, size, or any other physical characteristics, but she didn't come up with anything. I think she was too panicked to be noticing much. I'll try her again later, but I don't have a lot of hope in that direction. She did say that the person was 'very strong,' but how strong do you have to be to drag along a skinny eleven-year-old girl? If your five-eight-minimum guess is correct, I guess we can rule out any women who aren't both tall and fit. As for men, I guess we can rule out pro basketball players and dwarfs." Deffinger sighed. "I've had more to go on."

The warmth from the pills had worked its way down to the center of me. My eyelids were feeling very heavy. This conversation had taken on a purely abstract interest.

"How'd she get away?" I asked.

"She says she heard someone yelling—presumably you. Says she felt the assailant's grip loosen, and she pulled away. She's not sure if he was letting her go or if he got distracted. She started running and never looked back. Apparently she didn't see you get pushed. In fact, she never saw you at all."

I couldn't remember ever having felt more deeply relaxed than I did at that moment. I felt as if I could sleep for a week.

"How'd you find me?" I asked. The words sounded slightly slurred to my ears. I was beginning to feel kind of goofy.

"When she got home, her aunt called the police, and they went to check on where it happened. And there you were."

"And there I was," I said, happily, like a kid repeating the ending of his favorite bedtime story.

Anything Deffinger had to say after that he had to say to himself.

▽

4

I HAD A dream of Charlie and Julie. The dream was like one of those sentimental commercials portraying dreams as they're supposed to be but rarely are—set on a spring day with sunshine and wildflowers, all images softened and blurred as if filtered through gauze. I had my arm around Charlie and was looking down at her red-brown hair, at that freckled face both tomboyish and womanly, at the soft curves of her breasts beneath a silky white blouse. Julie was ahead of us, moving well in spite of her leg brace, exploring everything the way kids do. I said, "I was afraid it was over, that I'd never see you again," and Charlie said, "No, we're here now; everything's going to be all right."

When I opened my eyes, there was a girl's face just above mine. For a moment I thought the girl was Julie. Then I saw that she wasn't.

This girl was about twelve. She was looking down at me with an expression of intense curiosity and slight repulsion, as if she were studying some bug. When she saw my eyes open, she stepped back quickly, the curiosity gone, the repulsion still in place. I just stared at her, my half-asleep mind not grasping the meaning of this creature.

A woman's voice said, "We won't stay long. We just wanted to thank you."

I glanced toward the voice. As I blinked, a film of moisture seeped over my eyes, making the woman look as if she were an inch or two underwater. I got a blurred image of a tall female form, dark hair, red blazer, white blouse.

I felt my jaw opening in a cavernous yawn. By reflex I tried to cover it with my right hand and, of course, nothing happened. By the time I got my left hand there, the woman could have counted my fillings.

"I'm sorry," I said through another yawn, this one covered. "I took a couple of pills. I'm sort of out of it."

"I'm sorry we woke you," said the woman. "The nurse told us you were awake."

"I probably was when she saw me. I keep drifting in and out."

"Maybe we should go."

"No, please, it's okay," I said, trying to dredge up some manners from beneath my lethargy. "Have a seat."

I noticed that the air around us had that yellowish cast of purely artificial light. I twisted my head toward the window. All I saw there was a vague patch of darkness.

"What time is it?" I asked, turning back.

"Almost eight."

"I must have really slept," I said, covering another yawn.

The yawning had added to the blurriness of my eyes. I blinked a few times, trying to clear my vision, but didn't quite make it. I saw that the woman had pulled a metal chair up to the bedside and was sitting on the edge of the seat, leaning toward me. I just couldn't quite get her face into focus.

"Is there a cloth or towel on the table there?" I asked.

"Yes," said the woman.

"Would you mind pouring some water on it and handing it to me. If I rub it over my face, it might wake me up a little."

"Certainly."

I had a slightly fuzzy peripheral image of red blazer, metal pitcher, and white cloth in motion. When the cloth appeared closer to the center of my vision, I lifted up my left hand to take it.

"No," she said. "Let me."

The cloth in her hand felt cool against my face. As the cloth moved down from my forehead and eyes to my jaw and neck, I felt my mind and body waking up. And my sight finally cleared so I could see the woman.

She seemed to be in her early thirties. She had large dark brown eyes, features that were fine but not delicate, a face that would have been oval except for the slight distortion of a prominent jawline. She wore no makeup, but she had obviously fussed a bit with her dark, mid-neck-length hair, curling it up and out in a style that struck me as somewhat out-of-date and inappropriate for her age, suggesting a middle-aged woman going to church. She had an intelligent face and a direct, unselfconscious gaze. She had a serious look about her, even when she smiled, and when she wasn't smiling, her face seemed a bit stern. She gave the impression of strength and moral force. The word "feminist" would have come immediately to mind if it hadn't been for the oddly old-fashioned hairstyle. Instead I got an image of an earlier era, of a pleasant but proper and rather strict schoolmarm who wouldn't mind rapping your knuckles with the ruler if you got out of line.

"Better?" she asked.

"Much," I said. "Thanks."

"You . . ." She stopped and gave a self-conscious laugh that softened and brightened her face. "I just realized you don't know who we are."

"I can guess who you are. I just don't know your names."

"This is Becky, Mr. Strickland," she said, gesturing toward the girl. "And I'm Janet Kendall. Becky's aunt."

That the woman was not the girl's mother surprised me. Even through groggy eyes, the two of them seemed a match—both slender, with the same dark brown color in the hair and eyes, the same slight olive tinge to the skin. The girl's face had that slightly two-dimensional look that young faces often do—a matter, I suppose, of unformed bones and baby fat. Yet one could see that, when time had given more definition to the girl's face, the finer features that emerged would be much like the woman's.

Of course, an aunt and a niece would share many of the

same genes. Maybe the similarity between them wasn't odd after all.

"Nice to meet you both," I said.

"We wanted to tell you how grateful we are to you for helping Becky," said Ms. Kendall. "And how sorry we are that you're hurt."

I liked the way she said it. Her tone sounded genuine, had none of the usual add-on artifice by which people try to convince you of more gratitude or sympathy than they actually feel. And there was none of that curious note of pleading you often find in people's voices when they're thanking you for something vital. The pleading seems to be for some sort of absolution, though from what I'm not quite sure. Probably from owing you more than they'd ever care to pay.

"Becky?" prompted the woman.

The girl was standing next to the metal nightstand, picking nervously at the rubber edging. I took a closer look at her. Her overall appearance should have been appealing: She had beautiful long, dark hair, combed straight and smooth to her shoulder blades, and an awkward, coltish body that seemed mostly legs. Her face could have been cute, with the large eyes, the full cheeks, and the slightly upturned nose. But her expression spoiled everything. The face she showed me seemed rigid, self-absorbed, and sullen.

The girl gave me a slight nod.

"What do you *say*?" prompted the woman again.

"Thank you," said the girl in a whisper, looking not even remotely grateful.

I felt a sudden stab of anger: I had gone through hell for *this* kid? But then sense and sympathy took over. The girl had had a bad scare; she must still feel frightened. She hadn't seen me get hurt; I was just some story she'd heard later. On top of that, my bruised and bandaged face would hardly put her at ease.

"Oh, Becky," said Ms. Kendall, in a soft moan of disappointment. "I'm sorry, Mr. Strickland. Becky's still pretty upset. I hope you'll understand."

I was still looking at the girl. "You must have been pretty scared, huh?"

She nodded again. This time her eyes met mine, seeming to appraise me. For an instant something seemed to open up in those eyes, something small and faraway. Suddenly, for no reason I could name, I felt sad.

"Maybe we should go," said Ms. Kendall, getting up from her chair. "I think we could all use some rest. We'll be back tomorrow." She seemed to hesitate. "I mean, I assume that would be all right."

"Sure," I said, half my attention still absorbed by my odd reaction to the girl.

"What can we bring you?"

"What? Oh, something to read, I guess. Maybe *Newsweek* or *Time*."

"Do you read novels?"

"Yes. But I can't think offhand . . ."

"I've got some paperbacks at home. I'll bring them in and let you pick. And we'll get you some toiletries."

"Thanks," I said, "but you don't really have to—"

"Yes, I do," she said firmly. "But I also want to. Come on, Becky, let's go."

As I watched the girl leave, I felt a sudden sense of loss. I had the strange feeling that I ought to call her back, that there was something vital I should say to her. I couldn't for the life of me figure out what.

In the dream it was night.

Amy and I were running toward the steps that led down to the basement of the huge apartment building where we'd lived as small children. Something was behind us, coming after us, something dark, amorphous, and menacing.

I had Amy by the hand, pulling her with me. But as we descended the stairs, she began to slow, became harder to move, as if her body were slowly turning to stone. I sensed that whatever was behind us was slowing as well, but not as much as we, and so was gradually gaining on us. As the thing got closer, the air began to fill with an awful stench.

I could hear the caged machinery of the apartment building clacking and clanging on the landing below us. The sound of it frightened me, but there was no choice but to go on. Across that landing was another set of stairs leading down to passageways that would take us outside; I was sure that if we could just make it down those other stairs we would be safe. But Amy was getting harder and harder to move. I kept yanking on her arm, crying, "It's farther, Amy, please run."

As we struggled down the stairs, I became aware that the sound of the machinery was changing: It was as if the machinery were starting to come apart, throwing off pieces of itself within its metal cage. By the time we reached the landing, the look and sound of the machinery had become horrible: The thing was spewing out red-and-yellow flame, hurling chunks of itself against the metal screen with a terrible banging and clanging. Terrified, I pulled at Amy with all my strength, screaming at her to help me, but it was no good, we weren't moving at all. I knew I could let go of her hand and save myself—I wanted to—I was so angry she wouldn't help—but I knew I could never do that, never leave her that way.

The machinery exploded in slow but deadly motion, hunks of metal hurtling through the screen, everything around us shaking as in some enormous earthquake. Something knocked me to the ground, dazing me, and it was a moment before I could look for Amy. I saw that she was across the landing, near the far stairs, a huge fissure beginning to open in the ground beneath her. She cried out for me to help her, but I must have been hurt, it was so hard for me to move now.

As I struggled to get up, my body began to grow dark, began to give off that same stench. By the time I'd gotten to my feet, I had become large and clumsy, so that I stumbled as I tried to walk. I finally made my way to Amy, but just as I reached out my hand, the earth opened up beneath her, and she fell away into terrible darkness. She continued to call to me as she fell. Finally I couldn't stand it anymore. I closed my eyes and covered my ears and began to scream.

I woke in darkness, trembling. My surroundings seemed so strange that for a time I had trouble believing I wasn't still dreaming. Then my eyes began to adjust to the dark, the shadows became more distinct, and I recognized the shapes of my hospital room. I lay back on the pillow, waiting for my heart to stop racing, my nerves to calm. There was no need to think about the dream. I'd had that same dream on and off since I was a child, knew every detail of it. The meaning of it was obvious enough. I'd been afraid as a child that in that madhouse of ours, neither Amy nor I would survive, had felt responsible to help my little sister through. I'd made it, she hadn't, and some small, frightened part of me was trying, hopelessly, to save her still. There was no point thinking about the dream; thought would only add pain to pain. I'd made it; she hadn't. There was no help for it.

I lay there for a time, old misery sitting in my stomach like poisoned food. Then drowsiness returned, working its way through me, quieting all feeling.

"I'm sorry, Amy," I whispered as I drifted toward sleep, "I did all I could do."

▽

5

AN ELDERLY HISPANIC man—a stroke victim who couldn't speak—was in the bed next to me now. Behind the curtains that surrounded his bed, the man's wife was speaking Spanish in mournful, incantatory tones—whether to her husband or God, I didn't know. Outside the window to my right, a heavy late-afternoon fog was rolling in, giving everything the color of winter sludge. I was dividing my attention between a four-month-old *U.S. News & World Report* and a large spider scaling the blank wall in front of me. Whenever I let my attention lapse, an assortment of aches and pains would occupy my mind. I was not in a good mood.

I was thumbing through the magazine, cursing it for not carrying the kind of features that might still be of interest after all this time, when I heard someone whisper my name. I glanced up. Off to the left, Janet Kendall was peering around the foot of the curtained bed. The moment I saw her I felt my mood brighten.

"May I come in?" she asked.

"Please," I said.

Ms. Kendall emerged from behind the curtain carrying a large Mervyn's shopping bag. I noticed, more than I had the other day, what a pretty face she had, what a slender, attractive figure. I also noticed how little she was doing to enhance her natural good looks. Her hair had been freshly curled in that same ladies-auxiliary style. Her beige blazer, rust-colored turtleneck, and charcoal slacks, though pleasant enough, showed the slight fading and slackness of older clothes; her outfit combined with her hairstyle to give her a mildly dowdy look. She brought to mind movies in which a director tries to make a beautiful actress look plain and sexually uninteresting by means of less stylish clothes, large glasses, a serious expression, and an odd hairdo. Ms. Kendall was managing just fine without the glasses. I found myself wondering in passing whether she ever let down her hair, whether that look I was seeing ever came off.

She walked over to the chair and put the Mervyn's bag on the floor next to it. She slipped a large purse off her shoulder and placed it on the floor as well. I glanced behind her in the direction of the door, which was now hidden by the curtained bed.

"No Becky today?"

"She's here. She stopped off at the bathroom. She'll be along in a minute."

"How's she doing?"

"Much better than I ever would have believed," she said. "I was afraid that with everything . . ." She hesitated, then discarded the rest of the sentence. "Becky's doing all right. Thank you." Ms. Kendall pulled the gray metal chair a little closer to the bed and sat down. "I'm sorry we couldn't get here earlier. We had to talk to the police."

"Have they found out anything?"

"I think so," she said. There was an edge of excitement in her voice. "I have some real hope that this is going to get resolved in the next few days. And maybe a lot of other things as well."

"You're being pretty enigmatic today."

She gave me an apologetic smile. "I'm sorry. I don't mean to be. It's just that I don't feel it would be right to say anything until the police have had a chance to do their work."

"All right."

"Anyway," she said, with a small clap of her hands, "you've got enough to worry about just getting well." She straightened up in her chair, giving me a brisk cheer-up-the-patient smile. "How are you feeling, Mr. Strickland? You're certainly looking better."

"I'm feeling better, thanks. But I'd feel better yet if you'd stop calling me Mr. Strickland. How about Dave?"

"All right. If you call me Janet. I see you've found something to read."

"Of sorts." I showed her the cover.

"I think we can do better than that." She reached down into her shopping bag. "Here's *Time* . . . and *People* . . . ," she said as she pulled out the magazines and put them on the bedcovers. ". . . and some paperbacks of mine." She put a small stack of books on the nightstand, frowned, and took *Rabbit at Rest* off the stack. "I don't know how that got in there. You don't want to read that one."

"Maybe five hundred pages about a depressed man dying wouldn't be the best way to cheer me up," I agreed. "Actually, I've already read it." I glanced at the remaining books, which included an Anne Tyler and a couple of adventure novels. "I'm glad to see you didn't get me *Coma*."

She ignored the joke. "Have you read any of those others?"

"No."

"That's good," she said, dipping into her bag again. "Here's a toilet kit for you. I hope it has what you need."

She handed me the kit. It was one of those that are sold with preselected toiletries inside. I opened it, sorting through the items with my index finger, finding shaving cream, disposable razors, toothbrush, toothpaste, deodorant, mouthwash, and comb. I pulled up a thin plastic bottle from the bottom of the kit.

"Mousse. Just what I need. I can polish my head with it."

Janet glanced at my bandages. "They shaved your whole head?"

"Every last hair."

"It'll all grow back."

"It won't have much of a chance. They're going to shave my head again in three or four months."

"Why?" She looked concerned.

"More surgery. They've got to put in a plate to cover the missing bone."

"Why didn't they just put the plate in during the last surgery?"

"I asked them the same thing. It seems they can't put in the plate until the swelling in the bone goes down."

"So you come back in a few months, and they put in the plate?"

"Yes." I made a face.

"And they use some kind of metal?"

"A lot of doctors do. These guys are going to use plastic. It doesn't pick up radio signals. It's better for heat and cold, too."

"Are there any side effects with the plastic?"

"Just a craving for Tupperware."

Janet gave an involuntary laugh, accompanied by an inhibiting frown and head shake. Either she didn't think skull surgery was a fit subject for humor or felt the joke hadn't earned her laughter. I didn't know why I was feeling kind of silly. Maybe after staring at spiders and four-month-old news, having company felt like a party. Also, there was something determinedly serious about Janet that made me want to act up. She looked as if she'd be fun to tease.

"I thought you might like to borrow my Walkman," said Janet, pulling a small radio with earphones out of her shopping bag. "It should be perfect for the hospital. I also got you these. . . ."

She pulled out a plastic pouch containing a pair of solid blue pajamas. I was really pleased. I was going to be in this place for a couple more weeks and wasn't looking forward to spending the time with half of me hanging out of a hospital gown.

" 'Large,' " I said, inspecting the label. "You even got the right size."

"I guessed," she said, looking down into her bag. "And one more thing . . ."

She pulled out another pouch containing a maroon robe.

"Terrific," I said. "A little color around here is going to be great. With all this hospital white, and all this regimen, I keep feeling as if I'm in the middle of some play about the evils of socialism."

"Now you can be the rebel."

"In spirit, anyway. It doesn't look as if I'm going to break out of this place anytime soon." I looked down at the items spread out on the bed. "How much do I owe you?"

She waved away the suggestion. "They're presents."

"Are you sure?"

"Yes."

"Well, thank you. This feels like Christmas. I should get my head bashed in more often."

"Hardly," she said, with a small laugh.

As Janet leaned over to put the Updike book back in her shopping bag, I noticed Becky coming toward me. She was wearing jeans, purple-and-white running shoes, and a bulky white sweater imprinted with a figure of someone skiing. She was shuffling slowly by the foot of the curtained bed, craning her neck to see what was behind the curtain.

"Hi, Becky," I said.

She turned her head toward me, a hint of embarrassment in her face. Then she glared at me, as if I were the one doing the prying.

As Becky approached the bed, Janet reached out her hands, her face softening as she said, "Hi, hon, come here." Becky didn't resist: She moved close enough so that Janet could put a hand on each of her upper arms. But Becky's face remained passive the whole time, showing no sign of warmth. When Janet asked her if she wanted to sit down, the girl just shook her head.

"How're you doing, Becky?" I asked.

"Okay," she said with a shrug.

"Mr. Strickland is feeling a lot better today," said Janet. "Isn't that nice?"

"Uh-huh."

There was definitely something wrong with this kid that

went far beyond any possible effects from that frightening incident the other day. Fright might have caused a lot of things, but not what I now saw to be a peculiar rigidity of the face. It was a bit like what you see in women who've had too much cosmetic facial surgery: At first glance the face looks normal, but then you notice that it doesn't fully register changes of expression, that it is a kind of mask. What had fixed this girl's face was not a surgeon, but something inside her. Unlike cosmetically altered faces, the girl's face was set in what was beginning to look like an expression of permanent sourness. Also, there was a tension to this mask, as if there were something behind the skin that was trying to burst through.

I tried to engage Becky in conversation. For my trouble I found out that she was eleven years old and in fifth grade, and that she thought living in Ocean Point was "okay." Janet prodded her a bit, eliciting the further information that the kids in her class were "pretty okay" and the teacher "sort of okay." After that the three of us just kind of stared at each other until the girl decided she'd had enough. She stuck out her hand, asking her aunt to give her money for a Pepsi.

Janet's face had shown her growing frustration at the girl's behavior, and now it showed the impulse to anger. She seemed to hesitate, glancing first at me, then at the curtained bed, perhaps wondering if she was willing to risk a scene. Finally she let out a small sigh and put the money in Becky's hand.

As I watched the girl leave the room, I felt puzzled by my own mild reaction. Sullen teens usually get my stomach churning. It's true my mind was thinking some predictably nasty thoughts, but my emotions just weren't going along. Perhaps what I had seen in Becky's face made me suspect that there was more to her than the usual teenage obnoxiousness. But there was some other factor as well, something I couldn't quite identify.

"I'm really sorry, Dave," said Janet, obviously distressed. "And very embarrassed. After what you did, you shouldn't have to put up with that." She gestured toward the door. "I wouldn't blame you if you were really angry."

I shrugged.

"I don't know if this will help," said Janet, "but there's a really sweet kid under all that moodiness."

Something seemed to occur to Janet, and she glanced back self-consciously toward the curtained bed.

"They don't speak any English, if that's what you're worried about," I said. "The nurse told me."

"Good," said Janet, visibly relaxing. "I was going to say that there's a sweet kid under all that moodiness, all that rudeness. I used to see her sweetness a lot; I still see it some. But Becky's been having a really bad time for almost a year now. I think it's really tough for her to control the way she is. Still . . . I wish she'd try harder."

"What kind of bad time?" I asked.

She hesitated. "I want to say 'emotional,' or 'psychological,' but I'm not sure how you'll react to those terms. A lot of people take them as synonyms for whining and making excuses."

"I don't," I said. "My wife died a few years ago, and afterwards I went through a long period of anxiety and depression. It was awful. I know that the physical effects of those states are as real as any physical illness. And as difficult to control."

Janet looked relieved. "Then you can understand. Becky's fighting those things now. As well as terrible nightmares. I hope your knowing will help you forgive the awful way she's acting. At least a little, anyway. I know you can't see it, but there's a lot of pain under that sometimes obnoxious exterior."

Suddenly I had it, the full reason why I'd reacted so mildly to Becky's sullenness, why looking at her had saddened me so.

I had already toyed with the possibility that my mind might be making some association between Becky and Amy. But the only connection I'd been able to find had seemed too superficial to be meaningful—the fact that both girls had had serious troubles. Certainly there wasn't much physical similarity between Becky now and Amy at about the same age. Becky was slender; Amy had been of average build. Becky's hair was soft and long; Amy's hair, too curly to be easily managed, had been worn short. Becky's skin had a slight olive tinge; Amy's skin had been pale.

I now realized where the similarity lay. When things had first started going wrong for Amy, her hurt had showed as hurt; it had made her more lovable, even as it had made loving her more painful. But over time, it was as if the hurt had congealed inside her heart, turning into something sour that had leaked into her face. It was hard to love that sour look, hard to sympathize with pain one never saw. Loving became a kind of abstract obligation or a forced memory of what she'd once been, and might still be, somewhere under all that bitterness. Becky's pain seemed to be turning sour in just the same way.

"Dave?" I heard Janet asking. "Are you all right? You look kind of distracted."

"I'm sorry," I said. "I didn't mean to be rude. It's just that I've been getting a strange reaction to Becky. I just realized what it was. Becky reminds me of my sister. She had a lot of psychological problems too."

"How's your sister now?"

"She died some years ago."

"I'm sorry."

"She never did get any better. Maybe she would have if she'd ever gotten any decent help. I hope Becky is seeing someone—someone good."

"Yes. She's seeing a very good psychiatrist, who's also a very nice guy. But he says it's a tough case."

"It must be tough on you too."

She shrugged. "I love her very much. Taking care of her is one of the things I do."

"What else do you do?"

"I'm a high school English teacher."

"Where do you teach?" I asked.

"In Ocean Point," she said. "Sergeant Deffinger tells me you're a private investigator from San Jose."

"That's right."

"I feel so lucky that you happened by. And so awful about your getting hurt."

"Thanks. But it was my choice. Don't start feeling responsible."

"That's nice of you to say. But I do anyway."

"I keep wondering why I never see Becky's mother and father. The orderly mentioned seeing her mother in the emergency room."

"I was the one there with her. The man must have gotten confused." Janet's eyes turned sad. "Becky's mother is dead. She was my sister."

"I'm sorry. She's buried in that cemetery?"

"Yes."

An image came back to me of the girl's grief and tenderness as she'd sat by the grave. Suddenly that image gained new meaning.

"The poor kid," I said. "How long's her mother been dead?"

"Six years."

Just as suddenly, the image lost all sense. I felt myself frown.

"What's the matter?" asked Janet.

"Maybe that wasn't her mother's grave Becky was visiting."

"It was. What's wrong?"

"What's wrong is, when I saw Becky in the cemetery, she was grieving as if her mother had died a few weeks ago. Now you tell me it's been six years."

"It's kind of complicated," said Janet. Her eyes made small darting motions as if she were tracing out the complications in her head. "Let me just say that Becky had a terrible reaction to Ann's death. It's as if that reaction is reoccurring now. A lot of her nightmares are about her mother, and they just keep dredging up the old grief. Also, she's feeling pretty lost right now. Dr. Blake says it's natural she'd be feeling the lack of a mother pretty deeply."

"What about Becky's father? Is he dead too?"

She gave a thin, inward-directed laugh, as if at some private and not very happy joke. "No . . . he's very much alive. He just doesn't like to be tied down. We see him occasionally. Not often. He's in Australia right now."

"So he sticks you with raising his child."

"I don't think of it that way. Ann and I were very close. I feel I owe it to her. Not that it feels like owing. I shared in the raising of Becky from the beginning. I don't have any children of my own, and Becky has helped fill that void. She almost feels like my own now. If Corky tried to take her back, I'd fight him. Very hard."

"Corky? That's the father's name?"

"His real name's Bill Schrader. Corky's his nickname. He's a professional surfer. If it can be called a profession when you don't make any money at it. Actually he does make a little in tournaments. And a little more selling boards. Just enough to keep him going."

"So Becky's mother died early, and her father isn't interested in her. I guess that would make anyone feel depressed."

"Yes," she said. Her face took on a look of concern, and she glanced toward the door. "Maybe I'd better go. I should see about Becky."

But Janet didn't get up. She looked at me, started to speak, then didn't. She appeared uncomfortable. Finally, she seemed to compel her body upright in the chair, as she was also, perhaps, compelling her will.

"There's one other thing," she said. "I'm going to make you an offer. I want you to know that it's sincerely meant. But I don't want you to feel any pressure to accept if it doesn't fit what you need."

"Go ahead," I said.

"I was talking to Sergeant Deffinger the other day," she said. "He tells me that you live alone in the Santa Cruz mountains—in an out-of-the-way spot. It occurred to me that's going to make things kind of tough for you for the first couple of weeks after you get out of here—until you get your . . . strength back."

"I'll manage somehow. I'm sure I can find someone to come in and help."

Janet gave me a reflex look of frustration, as if I were some passerby who'd gotten in her way. Her arm moved as if she were pushing something aside.

"Maybe you could. But you'd also have a problem getting to your doctor, who'll be fifty miles away. Anyway, what I was going to offer is this: Becky and I have a modest house, but it's got a fair amount of room. There's one room that we rent out—usually to older women—but we're between renters right now. The room is pleasant, has its own bath, access to the kitchen, a separate entrance. What I'm offering you is that room for a couple of weeks—plus help with your meals, rides to the doctor, that sort of thing."

I watched Janet's face as she spoke, intrigued by changes I saw there. Before this she had seemed strong, straightforward, and self-assured. Now I saw a piece of armor go up, designed, I supposed, to make sure that I didn't read anything extra into her offer. Behind the armor I could see her vulnerability—her fear that I might after all mistake her intentions, the effort that making this offer was costing her. I sensed that she was determinedly acting on some principle here, and it wasn't easy for her. More than anything else I had seen of her, that moment made me like her.

"You don't know me," I said. "Aren't you worried about taking a strange man into your home?"

"I know you saved Becky from . . . something awful. And at great cost to yourself. That's all I need to know. But also . . ." Here she got a slightly sheepish look. ". . . I asked Sergeant Deffinger a lot of questions about you."

I grinned. "Pretty sneaky. He didn't scare you off?"

"No. Actually, he said a lot of nice things about you."

"I'm amazed. But wouldn't it be a lot of work for you, having me there?"

"I'd insist you do whatever you could for yourself—everyone does his share around our house. Yes, it would be some work, but I can certainly manage, and I feel it's the least we can do. Anyway it would only be for a couple of weeks."

"What about Becky? You must have your hands full with

her already. And from what I've seen, she not going to be real enthusiastic about my being there."

"She can just live with that," said Janet firmly. "Yes, Becky does take a lot of time. But I'm assuming you're not the kind of person who needs to be constantly entertained."

"Hardly," I said. "Just the opposite."

"There will be times when Becky needs to be alone with me—and alone with herself, for that matter. But it's not like we're all going to be clustered together. We should all be able to have our privacy. Anyway, it's only for—"

"—a couple of weeks?"

She glanced at me, saw, I guess, that she was being needled, and blushed slightly.

"Do I keep saying that?" she asked. "I'm sorry. I don't mean to sound stingy."

"No. I understand. You want to be nice, but you're afraid of what you might be letting yourself in for. And it's hard to have a stranger in the house."

"I really do mean the offer sincerely."

"I believe you," I said. "And I think your offer is very generous."

I looked away from her, considering. On the plus side, Janet would be a lot more pleasant company than anyone I might hire to take care of me. It would be nice to put off the hassle of that first trip home, the hassle of making arrangements for the help I'd need once I was there. It would certainly make return trips to the doctor easier—though I'd have to find out just how often I'd need to see the doctor once I was out of the hospital. On the negative side, there were Becky's problems, which could make my living with them difficult for all of us. And I was already missing my house in the mountains—the privacy, the peacefulness, the feeling of being home. I sensed that I would decide, finally, not to take Janet's offer. But I might as well think about it a little. Anyway, I wouldn't want to seem as if I were rejecting the offer out of hand, not after the obvious effort it had taken her to make it.

"Can I have a little time to consider?" I asked.

"Of course."

"I want you to know how much I appreciate what you're doing—the generous offer you just made, all those nice things you brought me. But it's not only that. I was sitting around this morning thinking how dreary this place would be without visitors. I really appreciate the company."

"That sounds like an invitation to come back."

"*Yes*," I said, letting my enthusiasm show.

Janet smiled. "I'm glad the visits help. I want to do what I can. Is there anything I can bring you tomorrow?"

"Do you play gin rummy?" I asked.

"I used to. Do you want me to bring some cards?"

"Please."

She cocked her head at me, pretending caution. "This isn't going to get expensive, is it?"

"Not for you," I said. "I always lose."

▽

6

I WAS LYING in bed, earphones in, listening to country music. It had been good at first, getting lost in the music, but soon the songs had called up painful memories that had taken shape against the February drizzle, and I'd started feeling awful. Like a morose drunk who keeps ordering another round, even though he knows it will just make things worse, I'd kept hanging in there for one more hurtin' song. After a while, with the music and the memories, the bad weather and the bare walls, I'd begun to inhabit the kind of world that depressives know, where misery seems woven into the very fabric of the world. It was as if I could see what some poet had called "the tears in things."

I was relieved when I saw Janet coming toward me, expecting her to pull me out of my funk. Then she came into focus, and I knew it wasn't going to happen. She looked as if she'd been listening to that same country station: Her shoulders were slumped, her face pale, her eyes puffy. Not that her mood was all that blatant: I sensed that she was trying hard to control her emotions. But something was obviously wrong.

"What is it?" I asked as I pulled off the earphones.

Janet gave a quick shake of her head, her eyes not meeting mine.

"Is there something wrong with Becky?"

She shook her head again.

"Why don't you sit down," I said, gesturing toward the chair.

Janet sat, but on the edge of the seat, as if she wasn't relaxed enough to settle. From behind her came the labored breathing of the old man behind the curtain. He was alone now in whatever kind of prison his stroke had built for him. His wife, who'd prayed by his bed for hours in her black dress and scarf, had been forced away to eat and rest by a cluster of relatives.

"I shouldn't have come today," said Janet, her voice whispery and hoarse. She coughed into her fingers, trying to clear her throat. It wasn't much of a cough, and it didn't get much of a result. "But I wanted to see . . ." She coughed again. ". . . I wanted to see how you were doing, and I figured you were counting on me, and I didn't want—"

"Easy," I said, holding up a hand to slow the acceleration of her words. "Don't worry about me. What's wrong?"

"I just thought . . ." A teary frustration bubbled just beneath her words, and she bit down to hold it in. "I thought . . . finally the police . . ."

A few tears spilled out of her eyes. Janet swiped at the tears with a rough motion of her hand, as if she were punishing herself.

"This is so stupid," she said angrily. "I don't do this."

"It's okay."

"No, it's not okay." Frustration seemed to be building in her against the effort of holding back. Her face took on a slightly frantic look. "I'm sorry. I've got to . . ."

"Janet . . ."

She got up from the chair, almost tripping as she moved.

"Janet!"

I didn't yell it, out of consideration for the old man, but there was enough aggressive emphasis in the half whisper to startle her. She hesitated, blinking at me.

"Damn it, sit down for a minute," I said. "You don't have to talk to me if you don't want to. Just try to collect yourself. You're so wound up you look as if you could walk through a wall."

She sat back down but looked at me fiercely, as if she were

fighting me in some way. Then her face bunched up, and she covered it with her hands. There were three quick exhalations of breath in rhythm with three quick jerks of her shoulders—what I took to be a controlled sob. Then there was quiet. Her fingertips pressed hard against her forehead, as if she were literally getting a grip on herself; her teeth bit down on her lip. She sat that way for almost a minute. Then she let out a long, slow breath and began steady, purposeful breathing.

In the near silence I became aware of a faint, sad music leaking from the earphones of the radio lying beside me on the bed. I reached over and switched the radio off.

"Feeling a little better?" I asked.

There was a quick nodding of head and hands. I grabbed several tissues out of the box on my nightstand and held them out to her.

"Here," I said. "Maybe you could use these."

The fingers of one of her hands opened just far enough for her to locate the tissues. Then the other hand darted out quickly and brought the tissues to her face.

"I'm sorry," she said from beneath the tissues.

"There's nothing to be sorry about."

She dabbed at her eyes, then moved her hands and the tissues away from her face. Since she hadn't been wearing any makeup, there was no ghastly aftermath of mascara. The more subtle result was that her face and eyes were splotched with red. Still, I figured she'd be self-conscious enough about that.

"If you want to throw some water on your face," I said, "you're welcome to use the bathroom here in the room."

"I think I will."

When Janet returned a few minutes later, her face had a kind of pale luster to it, as if she had managed to scrub the red out. She'd had less luck with the misery, but even that seemed diminished.

"I feel stupid," she said as she sat down. "I never do that."

"There's nothing wrong with doing that," I said. "Anyway, as far as I could see, you didn't do much of it."

"I can't afford to."

Janet tilted her head forward and closed her eyes. She pressed fingertips against both temples, making small, circular, massaging motions. The gray skirt and black sweater she wore accentuated the pallor of her face. The only real color to her now were her reddened eyes and the single emerald at the center of the silver pendant she wore around her neck.

"I don't like giving in like this," she said. "I guess I'm just so tired of it going on and on: Ann . . . Becky . . . that man. I thought the police were finally . . . but they're not . . ."

Her words stopped, as did the movement of her hands. She sat very still, her eyes closed, her fingertips resting against her temples.

"I know that didn't make any sense to you," she said softly.

"No."

Her hands dropped slowly to her lap. Her eyes opened.

"My sister was murdered," she said. "The man who murdered her is trying to kill Becky, and the police won't do anything about it."

For a moment I just stared at her.

I had formed a definite impression of Janet as sensible and intelligent. I liked her; I was concerned for her. On the other hand, I don't get dramatic claims like hers thrown at me very often; when it happens, the claims usually turn out to be nonsense, the people who make them, connivers, hysterics, or outright mental cases. I found it hard to believe that Janet was nutty, she was certainly no hysteric, and what could be the point of her lying to me? Then again, how much did I really know about her and what was going on in her life? I found my mind divided between sympathy and skepticism, as busy assessing her as what she had just said.

"The other day you told me that Becky's mother had died," I said cautiously. "You didn't say anything about her being murdered."

"I didn't see any reason to. You're sick—you shouldn't

have to worry about anything but getting well. You've done so much for us already—you shouldn't have all this dumped on you. I really didn't mean to say anything today. . . . I just . . . I'm sorry . . . I know this must all sound crazy."

She made a move to get up.

"Wait," I said with a touch of annoyance. "Don't keep hopping up like that." When she had sat back down—again on the edge of the seat—I said, more gently: "Look, since you've already said something, why don't you tell me all of it. It might do you some good to talk, and it won't do me any harm to listen. Maybe I can give you some advice. Anyway, if you keep letting little remarks slip about Becky and the police and your sister's murder, and then not saying any more, you're going to drive *me* crazy."

The last part was meant to evoke a smile, and it did, however thin. What it didn't evoke was anything in the way of information.

"Janet?" I asked after a moment.

"All right," she said, in a tone of concession. "A drug dealer named Tiny murdered my sister, and now he's after Becky, and the police won't do anything about it."

"Why not?"

"Because they say it can't be him. But it's got to be. Nothing else makes any sense."

"Tell me about it."

The invitation brought her out of her slump-shouldered lethargy. She scooted her bottom back in the chair for better balance, then leaned forward toward me for better talking. She fixed her still-reddened eyes on me, her face full of earnest energy.

"Ann owed him money, and he was threatening her—she told me. I just know he killed her because she couldn't pay."

"She was on drugs, then."

A look of embarrassment flashed over Janet's face. "Yes—for a while—but she'd given them up before she died. She took it really hard when Corky ran out on her. She was crazy about that idiot. Afterwards she went pretty wild—constant parties, heavy drinking. She started playing with drugs, and it all got out of hand. But she knew she had a problem—knew what it was doing to her and to Becky—and she was determined to change. She had gotten herself treated at a hospital, was going to Cocaine Anonymous, and was seeing a psychiatrist. She was getting free of the drug, but she couldn't get free of that man, and he killed her."

"She told you she owed this man money?"

"Yes."

"Did she tell you how much?"

"No. But I could see she was worried—even more than she was letting on. She always tried to keep things like that from me—sheltering her timid little sister. And I think maybe she was ashamed, too, afraid I wouldn't love her as much. The fact that she even told me why she needed the money showed me she was really upset."

"How much did you give her?"

Janet straightened in her chair. The movement had something vaguely defensive about it.

"Five hundred dollars. It was all I could do. I had just started teaching, and I'd already borrowed what I could for school, and I'd lent her another five hundred six months before that."

"What was that first five hundred for?"

"She said she needed some things for Becky. I believed her at the time. Looking back, I think it was for drugs."

"So you gave her the second five hundred to pay Tiny. Did you get the impression she needed more than that?"

"Yes. A lot more. I could understand why she was so frightened. Tiny is a mean-looking man, like it would be nothing to him to hurt you. I told Ann she should ask Dad—we both knew he would help. I was sure she was going to. But I think in the end she was too ashamed."

"You met Tiny yourself?"

"Yes. Once. I stopped by Ann's house to drop something off. He was there. I only saw him for a moment, but he really gave me the creeps. When I asked Ann who he was, she told me he was a bill collector and everything was settled. But later on, when she was scared, she told me who he really was."

"So you think your sister couldn't get the money, and he killed her because of it."

"Yes."

"Where was she killed?" I asked.

"At home. In her bedroom." Janet seemed to hear something in her words and quickly added: "What happened didn't have anything to do with sex. I mean, the bed was made, and Ann's clothes were on. The police said there were no signs of rape. There were signs of a search—someone had looked through her dresser drawers. I know he was there looking for money."

"How was your sister killed?"

"It was kind of a freak thing. He struck her in the face, and she fell and hit her head against this big ceramic elephant she had in her bedroom—it was a planter—two or three feet tall—it was like a boulder. She was always collecting weird things like that. Hitting her head against the planter probably wouldn't have killed her, but it turned out that she had an aneurysm no one knew about in an artery near her left temple. When she struck her head against the planter, the aneurysm burst. The doctor who did the autopsy told me that Ann would have been dead within a few minutes."

Janet gave a little shiver. Her fingers brushed the left side of her face.

"Had your sister been beaten up?"

"She was struck just once that night, if that's what you mean."

"So her dying might have been an accident."

"I guess. . . . But the police found some bruises around her mouth that were at least a day old. I just know that Tiny had already beaten her once and was coming back to do it again. I don't know if he meant to kill her. I just know that he did."

A pensive sadness settled into Janet's face. After a moment she turned her eyes on me, awaiting my reaction.

My first reaction was an urge to hug her. Before this I had admired the strength with which she was handling her troubles, but that very strength had made sympathy seem inappropriate. But today she seemed forlorn; I could glimpse what her troubles had cost her. It had to be lonely and frightening trying to save a girl from demons only the girl could see, and from another demon, which everyone could see, but no one would believe in. At the very least she needed an ally, someone she could talk to, someone who could help her see what there was to be seen.

But to help her see, I needed to see for myself, and for that I needed to be a critic as well as a sympathetic ear. It was apparent to me that she had told me much that was true; certainly the statements would be easy to verify. But those truths had come all bound up in a theory that could well be false, a theory that might have led her to include certain facts, and not others, and to slant those she had included. I took her disagreement with the police as a warning light. The police can make false assessments, but they do so a lot less often than citizens, especially those who are emotionally involved. If I were going to be able to give Janet any worthwhile advice, I would need to try to separate fact from theory, to find out what other facts there might be.

"You said that the police don't agree with you about Tiny."

"No," she said. "He was the first one they went after for Ann's murder, but a few days later they said he couldn't have done it."

"Why not?"

"They say Ann died between midnight and one-thirty. They say Tiny was with a police detective part of that time, and there wasn't enough time left over for him to get to her apartment and kill her."

"And you don't accept that?"

"I don't know how it would make sense that way. Ann owes some criminal money, and he threatens her, and she's worried, and then she's killed. What would you think?"

"If he killed her, then the policeman's lying."

"It wouldn't be the first time, would it? I'm sure most policemen are honest—especially in a town like this one—but there must be some dishonest ones. You read about them in the paper all the time. But, of course, the police just get angry if you even hint about something like that."

"Yes."

"If the policeman isn't lying—if Tiny didn't kill Ann himself—maybe he hired someone to do it. That would make sense, wouldn't it?"

"It might. What do the police say to that?"

"They say there isn't any evidence of that."

"Was there any evidence pointing to Tiny other than the fact that he threatened your sister?"

"No . . . but that's a lot, isn't it, given who he is? Anyway, because of what that policeman said, I don't think they really looked for any more."

"Were there any other definite suspects?"

"No. The police talked to some of Ann's men friends, but there wasn't any evidence pointing to them."

"Is there any other possible scenario for your sister's death that would seem to you halfway plausible? I mean, can you at least imagine someone other than Tiny having killed her?"

"I guess I could *imagine* anything."

"For example, suppose someone knew your sister had gotten together some money for Tiny and tried to steal it from her. Or suppose your sister got desperate and stole some money to pay Tiny, and the person she stole it from came to get it back. Or—"

"I get the point," said Janet, in a tone of irritation. "It's the same point the police keep making. But you're just making those people up. I've got a real person who threatened my sister."

"Yeah, but unfortunately you've also got a real person with a perfect alibi."

Janet started to respond, then didn't. She gave me a lonely look.

"You're on their side, aren't you," she said. "You're talking just like them."

I shook my head. "Maybe I am talking like them, but I'm not on their side. I know you're emotionally certain that Tiny is responsible for Ann's death. I'm just trying to find out what evidence you have to back up that feeling."

"Well, what about what just happened to Becky? When the police couldn't find any evidence of who killed Ann, I thought, well, maybe I could be wrong about Tiny. Not too long after that Tiny was gone, and I thought, let's just try to forget and get on with our lives. But now there's this."

Janet held her hands out, palms up, as if she were serving me something on a platter. But I couldn't quite make out what it was.

"You think he's the one who attacked Becky?"

"Yes."

"Why? What would be the reason he'd attack her?"

"I don't know the reason. I just know there must be one."

"It's been how long since your sister was killed?"

"Almost six years."

"Why do you think he would wait this long to hurt her?"

"Because he was locked up in prison most of the time."

"What do you mean?"

"About six months after Ann died, Tiny went to jail for something else. I don't remember for what. He's been gone all this time. A week or so ago I ran into him on the street. It was the first time I'd seen him in six years. He looked at me like he was seeing a ghost. Then a few days later Becky got attacked. Don't you think that's too many coincidences?"

"Yeah, maybe I do. But I'm having trouble seeing the specific connection. Do you have any thoughts about why his seeing you might lead to the attack on Becky?"

"No, but I know there's got to be some connection."

I looked at her for a moment, considering. I knew that before I could give Janet any useful advice, I would need to get a more objective perspective on Tiny and the murder than

I could hope to get from Janet's emotion-laden account. There was one obvious place to go for what I needed.

"I'll tell you what," I said. "Why don't I talk to Deffinger and try to find out what the police have. If I think they've missed something, I'll tell you that. If I think you've missed something, maybe I can explain it to you better than they have. In either case, at least you'll get a second opinion outside the police force."

"Would you?" said Janet, relief filling her face. "That would be great." She looked me over. "This is awful of me, isn't it? You're lying there in that hospital bed all hurt after helping Becky, and instead of letting you rest and get well, I'm dumping all this on you."

" 'All this' is only a talk with Deffinger," I said. "Anyway, it's better than lying here listening to country music and getting depressed."

7

"How're you doin'?"

I looked up from my novel to see Sergeant Deffinger standing at the foot of my bed. I'd been listening to some fifties rock songs that morning, and it occurred to me how much Deffinger resembled Buddy Holly, with those thick-framed glasses perched awkwardly against that elongated face. On the other hand, Deffinger would have been a better bet for a look-alike contest if he'd fluffed his hair forward rather than slicking it back. And Holly wouldn't have been caught dead in a blue corduroy sport coat with patches on the sleeves. Deffinger certainly had an odd taste in clothes, especially for a cop; he looked as if he'd been doing all his shopping at some college salvage sale.

"I'm feeling a lot better," I said. "By the way, thanks for the good report to Janet Kendall."

Deffinger shrugged. "All I said was, you probably wouldn't steal her silverware or pee on her carpets. That seemed to satisfy her. Apparently she's pretty easy to please."

I laughed. "Thanks anyway."

"So much for chitchat. What'd you call me about? I assume it's important."

"It is to me. Sit down, would you?"

Deffinger hesitated a moment, then moved toward my bedside chair. On the way he tilted his head to get a look inside the curtained bed—probably to make sure that nothing illegal was going on in there. Nothing was, of course, unless someone had passed a law against grief and natural death.

"What have you got for me?" asked Deffinger when he was seated.

"Some questions."

"I didn't need to come all the way up here for questions. I got plenty of those already."

"Help me out with something, will you? Janet Kendall was in here the other day, and she was all upset about some guy named Tiny. . . ."

Deffinger gave a groan and turned his eyes skyward. Still, his exasperation seemed mild and possibly mixed with something resembling humor.

"Has she been giving you trouble?" I asked.

"*Yes*. Look, I like Mrs. Kendall. She's a nice lady. Tough, too, in her own way. She's had a hard row to hoe, raising her sister's kid with all the problems that kid has had. I got a lot of respect for her. But she's got this one bug up her ass—if you'll pardon my French. A tiny bug."

Deffinger gave his own joke a halfhearted laugh.

"How about giving me your side of it?"

Deffinger gave me a wary look. "You representing her or something?"

"No way," I said. I pointed at my body. "Do I look like I'm in shape to represent anybody on anything? She's been nice to me, and I like her, and I feel kind of sorry for her. Where's the harm? Anyway, if what you've got sounds good, maybe I can help you with her."

Deffinger considered a moment. "Why not?" he said. "It might save me a lot of aggravation."

Deffinger removed his sport jacket like a man getting ready for physical labor. Or, better, for a tough lecture. No one would have been doing any physical labor in a beige V-neck sweater, white shirt, and light blue tie, even with the tie loosened just a bit.

I said, "Janet claims that her sister owed this guy Tiny

some money and that he was threatening her—this just before her sister got killed and her room searched."

"She also tell you that Tiny was with one of our guys when the sister was killed?"

"She mentioned something about that," I said. "She seemed kind of . . . skeptical."

Deffinger's face flushed just slightly. "Skeptical, huh? Look, Strickland, unlike some of the guys, I don't go ballistic when someone wonders whether a cop could be dirty. There are dirty cops; everyone knows that. But not the cop in this case. Not Frankie. Tiny is a mean bastard and a third-rate sleaze, and if I could put him away for this or anything else, I would in a minute. We liked him a lot for Ann Schrader's murder, and unlike what Mrs. Kendall seems to think, we tried hard to make him for it. But with what Douche had to say, there was no way. And when Douche said something, it was true."

"Who?"

Deffinger laughed. "Frank Bigelow—the cop I'm talking about. His nickname was Douche. He liked to tell people he got the nickname because it was his job to clean up the assholes in town. But I found out from a friend he got the name when he was a patrolman in L.A. and was cleaner than some of the older cops wanted him to be. Douche was a straight guy—big Catholic, big family man. No one was going to turn him—and sure as hell not a guy like Tiny. I mean, we're not talking about some Mafia big shot here. We're talking about a guy who hustles a little of this and peddles a little of that, and is usually on the edge himself. If anybody could have turned Douche, it would have to have been someone with more money than Tiny ever dreamed of."

"So where does Douche say that Tiny was?"

"Said. Douche died a couple of years ago."

"On the job?"

"No. At least not the way you mean. He was getting up there in years; he was close to retirement. He'd just made lieutenant, and he spent half the time at his desk trying to figure out where he was going to retire. He keeled over from a heart attack at his desk one day after eating at home. What the bad guys couldn't do, his old lady's pot roast did." Deffinger laughed. "Go figure, huh?"

"Yeah."

"Anyway, what happened was, Douche was cruising a few of the bars before going off duty. We'd had a report that a couple of places were serving minors. We were also keeping an eye out for a guy who hadn't checked in with his parole officer. About twelve-fifteen A.M., Douche was between bars when he saw Tiny walking the street. Douche knew Tiny was a friend of the guy we were looking for, and he'd heard from somewhere that Tiny had been seen hanging out near one of the junior highs, so Douche picked up Tiny and they drove somewhere for a chat. After the chat, Douche dropped Tiny off at his apartment. That was about one-twenty. Later it comes out that Tiny was walking home from his girlfriend's place when Douche picked him up, and that Tiny had a few drinks at home with his roommate after Douche dropped him off. The girlfriend and the roommate both confirmed his story. Let's suppose those two were lying—an easy supposition since they're both sleazeballs themselves. It's a twenty-five-minute drive minimum to Ann Schrader's place from where Tiny was picked up, thirty from where he was dropped off. Even if we imagine Tiny racing in from killing the Schrader woman just before Douche picked him up, or racing off to kill her just after Douche dropped him off, the timing would be what the coroner called 'implausible.' Plus the racing idea seems pretty implausible itself."

"Did any of the things that Bigelow and Tiny talked about have to do with Ann Schrader?"

"Douche said they didn't talk about her. We couldn't find any connection between Mrs. Schrader and the parole violator. As for the junior high school Tiny was supposed to be hanging around, what could that connection be? She was a user, not a pusher, her daughter was five years old, they lived on the other side of town, and her sister taught at the high school, which was also on the other side of town."

"But the woman did owe Tiny some money?"

"So Mrs. Kendall says, and I'm willing to believe her. We didn't find anyone else to confirm it—certainly not Tiny or his attorney—but it could well be true. We know that Mrs. Schrader was on crack pretty heavy, and that she was doing some of her buying from Tiny."

"What about the possibility that Tiny had someone else do the killing for him?"

Deffinger's face formed a grimace, the kind that shows temptation parading alongside skepticism. "I don't see that as Tiny's style. Anyway, if had done that, wouldn't he have set up a better alibi? Given what Tiny told Douche, Tiny had to be walking alone for at least fifteen minutes: That's the time it would take to walk from the girlfriend's house to his apartment. The alibis he's got for the rest of the time are a woman who's done a little hustling and looks it, and an ex-con who also looks it. Why not pick the most crowded bar in town and start buying drinks? It doesn't make sense."

"I got the impression that Ann Schrader's death might have been an accident."

Deffinger nodded. "Probably was. There's no telling what the guy intended to do next, but it's doubtful the blow was intended to kill her. Her having that aneurysm was a freak thing."

"So why worry about an alibi if you're just going to have a friend rough her up and pick up some money?"

"It's possible, and we tried to cover that angle too. All I can say is we shook the tree around here pretty hard, and nothing fell out."

"Did you have any other suspects?"

"We checked out some friends and acquaintances. Nothing turned up that looked promising."

"What about the husband?"

Deffinger snorted. "He skipped out on his old lady and his kid, and he was shacked up in a beach house with two—count 'em, two—Norwegian blonds, who were supporting him for services rendered. If there was any killing to do, it should have gone the other way around. Anyway, that beach house is in Australia, and we can place him there close enough so that he'd have to be James Bond to have gotten here and back in time."

"What about this business of Becky getting attacked just after Tiny gets out of prison and sees Janet? By the way, this nickname of his: Does it mean he's a giant or dwarf who couldn't be the guy I saw?"

"Naw. He grew up fast and fat and picked up the nickname as a kid before the others caught up. He's always had a gut on him, but it don't qualify him for the circus. And he's just about six foot."

"So what about him and this latest attack?"

"Mrs. Kendall's got that all wrong. Tiny went up on a manslaughter charge a few months after Ann Schrader was killed. He served four of—"

"Wait a minute. Any chance the manslaughter had some connection with Ann Schrader's death?"

"No," said Deffinger. "We checked that out pretty carefully. Tiny killed a man in a bar fight. The man was a plumbing contractor from King City who was in town to visit some relatives. Reputable enough guy, but liked to tie one on now and then. Fancied himself something of a bar fighter. That night he picked the wrong guy. Tiny was tanked up and ticked off about some broad who'd just dumped him. Once Tiny started in on the guy, he was in no mood to stop. Tiny was convicted of voluntary manslaughter, served four of six, and spent his first year of parole living right next door in Salinas, working at a factory job his parole officer got him. When the factory went belly-up, he came back here. He's been back in Ocean Point for several months. Mrs. Kendall just didn't happen to see him until the other day. If Tiny had wanted to do something to her or the kid, he's had a year and a half or so to do it."

"What about the fact that the attack on Becky happened a few days after Janet saw him?"

"What about it? Mrs. Kendall tried to make a big deal out

of that. But what's supposed to be the connection? What do you figure here?"

"I don't 'figure' anything. I'm just asking for Janet. Everything you've said about Tiny makes sense. There are just a couple of coincidences that don't sit too well—Tiny threatening Ann Schrader just before she was killed, and now his seeing Janet just before Becky was attacked."

"Yeah, well, I'm not too crazy about coincidences either. But I can't make any sense out of connecting Tiny with this attack on the kid. Let's assume for the sake of argument that Tiny was responsible for Ann Schrader's death, and either we missed the something, or Douche lied, or Tiny got someone else to do it and we missed the someone else. If we assume all that, Tiny's gotten away clean, and nobody, except maybe Janet Kendall, is much interested in him or the case anymore. What would be the point of going after the kid? Unless Mrs. Kendall had something on him, or was pushing him in some way. In which case she's not quite what she seems, and we're both getting used here."

"Did you question Tiny about the attack on Becky?"

"You bet."

"Does he have an alibi for the time the attack took place?"

"Nothing I couldn't break down pretty easy if I had some reason to. You got one for me?"

I thought back over the things that Deffinger had said. I shook my head. "No. I agree with you that Tiny looks pretty implausible."

"So talk to the lady for me, will you? Not just for me—for her sake too. She's a nice lady, and I hate to see her get worked up over this thing the way she has. Especially when she has so many other things to worry about. I'll tell you what. Since you like what I had to say, talk to her, see if you can get her to see it the same way. If she wants, I'll go back, lean on Tiny a little bit, tell him we're watching him, tell him if he doesn't want any trouble he'd better stay as far away from Mrs. Kendall and the kid as he can."

"I'll see what I can do. So you're figuring the attack on Becky as just a sexual thing—some stranger?"

"Last night a report came in from Santa Cruz about a guy who tried to grab a twelve-year-old girl on a deserted street just after dark. Fortunately a car just happened by, and the guy took off. Now I can't guarantee you it was our guy, but it wouldn't surprise me if it was him. Anyway, we got plenty of those guys around."

"And how do you figure Ann Schrader?"

Deffinger shrugged. "Drugs, or money for drugs. It could have happened a dozen ways. It could have been a friend, or a guy she just met, or someone who spotted her at a party. It could have been some local we missed, or a stranger passing through. Maybe the guy's at her place because he knows she's got drugs or money, or maybe he's there for some other reason and there's a fight, and he figures that while she's out he might as well see what he can find. I'd bet it happened one of those ways. I wish I'd found the guy who did it, and when I think about it, I still wish I could find him. But if I never do—if I never know—well, it won't be the first time."

▽

8

I WAS SITTING up in bed, glaring at my right foot, commanding it to move. I'd been doing this, on and off, for a couple of days now. Absolutely nothing had happened. The foot seemed as foreign to me as the bed frame behind it. I felt like a psychic trying to bend a spoon.

As I slapped at my leg in frustration, I realized that I was becoming a prime example of the old saw that people are never satisfied. That first night, feeling claustrophobic terror as I lay trapped in my inert body, a part of my mind had wanted to bargain, to say, "Please, just get me through this, and I'll accept whatever else comes." Well, I had gotten through that, and more, here late in the second week of my hospital stay. I was alive; my mind was clear, my memory intact, my speech unimpaired; most of my discomfort was gone; there were as yet no signs of the seizures that sometimes occur after serious head injuries; my skull was healing nicely under the fresh bandages; and, though my right arm was weak and occasionally numb, the control I had of it was close to normal. But after all those gains, I wasn't feeling grateful or happy. What I was feeling was angry at having gotten hurt, bored by my hospital confinement, and frustrated by the bad leg. That same part of my mind was now saying, "Damn it, just get this leg working and get me out of here, and I'll . . ."

I wasn't able to work my right leg at all, except to swing it from the hip. I'd had no physical therapy as yet: Because of my head injury and the surgery and the length of time I'd spent in bed, my blood pressure was so low that anytime I got to my feet, I was in danger of fainting. So far I'd only been up for trips to the bathroom, and then with help. But over the last couple of days I'd been getting drops to raise my blood pressure, and I was finally going to try my first real walk today.

I looked up to see Janet enter the room, followed by a dawdling Becky. I had a clear view of the door now: The old man had been taken to surgery, and his bed was vacant, the curtain pulled back.

Janet and Becky were wearing "mother-daughter" outfits today: jeans, running shoes, and blouses of the same forest green, though of different styles, with Becky's having puffy sleeves. Janet was carrying the usual bag of games and other items, which she put down on the floor next to the night-stand. She glanced toward my right leg, which was stretched out by itself on top of the covers.

"What are you doing?" she asked.

"Trying to get my foot to move."

Becky went around to the lower right side of the bed to get a better look. She cocked her head, studying the bare foot as if it were some assignment she'd been given for zoology class. If the foot had been functional, I'm sure it would have twitched self-consciously.

"Can you feel anything?" asked Becky, indicating the foot.

"Yes."

"That?" She pressed a fingernail hard against my instep.

"Ouch," I said.

"Becky!" said Janet, astonished.

Becky looked at us both without apology. In fact, there was a hint of malicious delight in her eyes.

"Becky," I said. "Working on this foot's getting me exhausted. Why don't you take over for a while. Just keep staring at my foot and telling it to move."

Becky rolled her eyes and shook her head and gave me a dramatic look of exasperation. Given all that effort, I wondered if there could be a smile buried under there somewhere.

Becky and I had done a lot of sparring during the last week and a half. After the first couple of days, she'd moved from sullen silence to a hostility that I'd been more than willing to match. Whatever romantic associations my mind might have made between Becky and Amy, and however hard I might try to sympathize with Becky's problems, I had found much of her behavior during that first week really irritating. Our mutual hostility had been mostly covert. Fortunately there were limits to what Janet would tolerate from Becky. As for me, I was trying to be relatively adult; also, I didn't want to risk losing Janet's visits through open warfare with Becky.

Toward the end of the first week, Becky's hostility began to abate, diluted by familiarity and interrupted by other moods. The biggest help had been the games. After Janet had beaten me at gin rummy a couple of times, Becky had been invited, then ordered, to play. After some initial moodiness, Becky had become absorbed in the games, not wanting to quit when the time came for them to leave. Since then there had been other games—Hearts, Tripoley, Yahtzee—with Becky almost always a willing participant. Playing together had made Becky and me friendlier enemies.

The less sullenness and hostility Becky showed, the better glimpse I got of those psychological problems that Janet had mentioned. Becky seemed to be at her best when she was totally distracted, totally outside herself, so lost in a game that she wasn't really feeling anything but intense interest. I'd seen a few flashes of genuine happiness in her, but they never lasted long, and even seemed in some strange way to bring on an opposite mood: It was as if her happiness were a small creature that, the moment it moved into the open, attracted some predatory part of her nature.

There had been two visits during which Becky seemed subdued, sluggish, and miserable, as if she'd had a case of the flu. During another visit she'd been so nervous she could barely sit still. Those visits hadn't lasted very long.

Becky seemed well enough today, if not exactly charming.

She decided on a game of Yahtzee, and in a moment the dice and the score pads and the pencils were spread around the large tray that was affixed to my bed. We set the tray parallel to the bed so that the women could reach it easily. Janet sat on the edge of the bed; Becky stood.

"What have you guys been up to?" I asked, watching Becky throw two threes, two fours, and a five, then think about what to do next. I'd learned not to give her advice unless she'd asked for it.

"We ordered a pizza last night and rented a video," said Janet.

"Sounds like fun. What video?"

"*Home Alone Two*," said Janet. "For the fifth time."

"It was not," said Becky. "It was the fourth time."

"It was the fourth time," said Janet, to me, with a wan smile. "It just seemed like the fifth time."

"You really like that movie, huh?" I asked Becky.

"Uh-huh." Becky picked up the five and rolled again. It was a six.

"I wish they'd make the parents seem a little less stupid in those things," said Janet to me. "But I guess stupid parents are part of the fun."

Becky picked up the six and took her last roll. It was a three—a full house. "Yes!" she said, with something resembling enthusiasm.

We went on playing, most of our conversation focused on the game itself, figuring out what combinations to roll for and in which categories to put the failures. In spite of making some questionable decisions, Becky rolled the right numbers—including a double Yahtzee—and won the first game. We started another.

Janet had appeared every day since my accident, usually with Becky, other times not. After my talk with Deffinger, I'd gone over with Janet everything that Deffinger and I had discussed. We had reexamined Deffinger's account, formulating objections, then trying to counter those objections. As we'd gone along, Janet had even thrown in a few thoughts supporting Deffinger's position. By the end of our talk, Janet had decided that the attack on Becky had probably been random, but that if it hadn't been random, if it had come from Tiny, Deffinger's warning would keep Tiny from trying it again; in either case Becky was safe. By the next visit, Janet had been back to her usual serious good spirits.

Janet and I had reached a kind of casual-friend comfort with each other. I felt increasingly relaxed with her; she seemed to feel the same with me. We talked easily but weren't bothered by silences. She didn't seem to mind my kidding her a little, and occasionally she kidded back. But the emotionality of that discussion we'd had about her sister's murder had not led to further conversational intimacy. I sensed in her now the same deep-down reserve that I had sensed in the beginning; her reserve, in turn, had reinforced my own natural reserve. We had been over the surface facts of each other's lives but had gone no deeper. I knew that she had been married and divorced and had no children; she knew that I had been married, that my wife had died, and that I had no children. Neither of us knew any details. We generally talked about my health, or the hospital routine, or something in the news, or some movie on television, or one of the books she had given me to read. And we played games. It was a bit superficial, but also comfortable, and I always looked forward to her visits. She gave the impression of having the same feelings toward me, though I'm sure there had to be more obligation mixed in on her side.

I still hadn't given Janet an answer to her invitation to stay with them, and she hadn't brought the subject up again. Even though I was leaving my options open, each day that I felt better edged me closer to deciding to go home. I was pretty sure that after today—after having gotten up and walked a bit—the decision to go home would become final.

Janet won the second game. We were just beginning a third game when one of the nurses came in. Her effusive greeting and her exaggerated interest in our game reminded me of a mother playing "Mother" for her child's friends. The nurse never bothered with any of that for me; it was just for the women, especially Becky.

"Sorry, ladies," said the nurse, "but you're going to have to excuse Mr. Strickland. He's going to take his first walk today."

"Should we leave?" asked Janet.

"No," I said. "Please stay. We'll only be a few minutes."

"We're just going to take a short walk in the hall," said the nurse.

I maneuvered myself to the side of the bed away from Janet and Becky and the tray. I had already put on my robe in anticipation of this walk, so there was no social awkwardness as I fumbled my way out from under the covers and into a sitting position on the side of the bed. The nurse had come around from the other side of the bed and was waiting for me.

"When you first stand up," she said, "you may feel a little light-headed. Give it a moment: It should go away. If it doesn't, we'll put you back in bed and quit for today. It'll just mean we need to give the medication more time to work."

I nodded. The nurse took hold of my right arm and gave me a boost up. As I reached my feet, there was a ringing in my ears, a slight blurring of vision, and a feeling of chill. I stood my ground, a hand on the nurse's shoulder. After a moment the dizziness subsided, though it didn't quite go away.

"Are you okay?" asked the nurse.

"Yes."

"You're sure?"

I wasn't sure of anything except that I wanted to get out of this hospital as quickly as possible. "Yes."

"Use me as a crutch," said the nurse. "We'll go very slowly. If you feel faint, tell me."

Faintness was not all I had to contend with. At this stage in my recovery, my right leg was like a peg leg with the extra complication of foot drop. Every time I'd lift the leg, the toes would tilt downward, since I had no control over the instep muscles that normally hold the foot at a right angle to the shin. Thus I had to lift the leg higher than normal to clear the toes as I stepped forward, and then swing the leg out farther than normal so that the foot, as it came down, would tilt back flat rather than pitching forward from the tips of the toes. It was not an easy maneuver, especially when I could barely stand up.

The nurse and I made our way slowly to the door and out into the corridor. Every few moments faintness would pass through me like a cold, weightless ocean wave, leaving me damp, chilled, and unsteady. I suppose I should have quit right then, but a couple of clichés about not giving in were running through my mind, and anyway I had an audience.

"You're doing great," said the nurse.

In fact, I was feeling progressively worse, but I was determined to do a little more. We were now about ten yards from the end of the corridor. I decided I would push myself to go at least that far before asking for help. But at the very moment I made the decision, all the energy seemed to drain out of me. With exhaustion came a feeling of hopelessness and a sense that something deep inside me wanted to burst into tears.

I tried to fight against my weakness, but another wave of faintness came, this one dimming my vision, throwing a thin film of darkness over everything. I felt so cold. My footing began to slip away, as on wave-sucked sand.

I started to say "help me," but I was too late. Another wave was on me, this one huge and black. It swept over me, tumbling me, pulling me down.

If there were a hell, perhaps it would be what I descended into at that moment: pure darkness, pure loneliness, pure helplessness, pure terror. There I was reduced to some small, sniveling thing, without strength, without pride.

I must have cried out, judging from the frantic tone of reassurance in the voices that began to come to me through the darkness. "You're all right, Mr. Strickland," they kept saying. "You're all right. You just fainted."

The cold emptiness turned to cold linoleum; the voices

attached themselves to white-coated figures kneeling all around me. For a few moments I couldn't make sense of who they were and what they were saying. Even when I did begin to understand, the sensation of terror remained, as if it had been imprinted on my body now, and nothing anyone said or did could take it away. As I was lifted up by orderlies, I caught a glimpse of Janet and Becky standing in the corridor, looking at me wide-eyed. As I was carried past them, I heard Janet urgently asking questions and someone, in response, trying to reassure her.

I was carried into my room and placed on my bed; covers were pulled up to my chin. I looked up at the faces above me, feeling disoriented, fearful, and vaguely amnesic. I had lost all sense of my body. I felt like a severed head taking a last look at its executioners.

I closed my eyes, escaping into the darkness inside myself. I waited, enduring. Gradually my body gained solidity and some warmth, my mind became less confused, and my fear began to diminish.

"Are you feeling all right now, Mr. Strickland?" asked a male voice.

"Yes," I said, though I was feeling far from all right. I just wanted to get rid of these white-coated people.

"In that case, we'll leave you now." The voice seemed to have a smile in it as it said: "It looks like you're in capable hands. Ring if you need anything."

I heard a group of footsteps moving away. I caught the scent of Janet's perfume and felt the mattress dip under her weight as she sat on the edge of the bed. She put her hand on top of mine. I turned the hand over so I could hold hers. I opened my eyes.

"It was awful," I said, hearing shivers in my voice. "When I fainted, it was as if all the fear I hadn't let myself feel before the surgery came flooding up. I've never been so scared in my life. And I had absolutely no control over it."

"I'm sorry it was so awful," said Janet, squeezing my hand more tightly. "Is there anything I can do?"

"Just what you're doing."

"Then close your eyes. Try to relax. We'll stay here with you as long as you need us."

The word "we" made me remember Becky. I turned quickly in her direction. The fear I saw in her eyes took me out of myself for a moment.

"Don't be frightened, Becky," I said. "It's okay. It really is."

Then I saw that fear wasn't the only thing in Becky's eyes. To my amazement, there was sympathy too. And something else. It took me a moment to figure out what it was: knowledge. The poor kid knew exactly what I was going through. Instantly, I sensed something in me soften toward Becky.

I gave Becky what I hoped was a smile, then lay back, closing my eyes, still holding Janet's hand.

After a moment I whispered in Janet's direction. "Is your offer still open?"

"Definitely."

"Then I accept."

▽

9

I WAS STRETCHED out across the backseat of the Honda Civic—or what passed for stretched. My head and shoulders were bent against the window, my bad leg was lying on the seat, and my good leg was twisted between the front and back seats, jammed in with my crutches. My cramped discomfort was a fitting conclusion to my morning.

"How's the new hair feel?" asked Janet. She was just in front of me, driving.

"It feels weird. Just the way it looks."

"It doesn't look weird," she said. "It looks good."

"Sure."

"It's too bad Becky didn't come today. She would have enjoyed it."

"She would have enjoyed laughing at me, you mean."

"Nobody's laughing at you."

"Yes, you are. I can see your face in the rearview mirror. You're grinning like crazy."

She made a noise that sounded suspiciously like a muffled giggle.

"See," I said.

"Okay, okay. So I'm laughing. But not at your hair. At the way you're acting. Your hair looks fine."

"It looks great," I said sarcastically. "Especially in the bag."

I yanked the hair off my head and tossed it like a basketball toward the open shopping bag that stood up at the other end of the seat. Part of the wig caught on the rim of the bag, so it ended up half in, half out, looking like some creature from "Sesame Street." I grabbed the ski cap I had worn leaving the hospital and crammed it back down on my bald head.

"Dave, don't . . ." Janet was saying. The rearview mirror gave a view of her shaking her head. "You're being ridiculous."

The whole thing was ridiculous.

I had just bought a wig at some "salon" called Hair Apparent, where I'd been waited on by some dwarf who called himself Mr. Otto. I'd felt pretty stupid getting a wig at all, but the alternative had seemed worse—wearing a ski cap I could never take off, half the time looking like some Siberian refugee.

There was no way I could pull a Telly Savalas or a Michael Jordan and walk around with my head shaved. Aside from the still-healing cuts, there was a really ugly indentation under the skin that would have made people squeamish. The indentation was from the shattered bone that had been removed and not yet replaced with a plate. It was the equivalent of a baby's soft spot, except that it was covered by harder, deeper bone, so that the chance of injury was pretty small. Still, I'd have to be careful.

I must have tried on ten different wigs with Mr. Otto. I'd had to admit that the quality of the hair was good—not like those patches of colored straw stores throw on their male mannequins. Nonetheless, no matter what wig I'd tried on, I'd kept imagining the word *wig* flashing in neon letters over my head. I'd wanted something like my own hair—dark brown and cut to medium length. But every wig of that length had seemed to lie oddly around the ears and so had looked fake to me. The one that looked most natural was the much longer wig I had with me now. Unfortunately it made me look like Prince Valiant. I'd started regretting my decision almost the moment I'd walked out of the store. Now I was wondering whether growing a beard would help. I might end up looking like a vagrant, but at least I wouldn't look like I had fake hair.

"Dave?"

I didn't answer.

"Dave. You're not pouting back there, are you?"

"I don't pout," I said, though at least two women I'd been associated with had accused me of that before.

"I can't believe you. You go through that terrible time at the hospital like a stoic, and now you're fussing like a baby over that wig. It doesn't make any sense."

She was right. I'm not above being a petty pain in the neck from time to time, but I knew I was outdoing myself today. I also knew, as she didn't, that this was part of something larger. I'd been getting all sorts of emotional reverberations from that fainting episode in the hospital: feelings of anxiety, depression, vulnerability, helplessness, fussiness, and self-consciousness. I didn't like those feelings, and I certainly didn't like acting them out. I'd just have to try to keep them under control as best I could and hope they would disappear soon.

"I'm sorry," I said, touching Janet's shoulder over the top of the seat. "I'm just on edge today."

"You've got every right," she said. "But try to relax. It's too beautiful a day to be in a bad mood."

It was at that. We were driving along the northern edge of the Monterey peninsula, toward the Pacific. Monterey Bay was to our right. Directly across the Bay, along Route 1, were Sand City and Fort Ord. Fifty miles farther north was a huge humpback of the Santa Cruz mountains. Somewhere up on it was my place.

It was a bright California winter day, with a moderate breeze and no haze obscuring the view. Everything seemed vivid to the eye: the gray-blue water and the powder blue sky, the caramel sand and the charcoal green hills.

We passed Monterey's version of Fisherman's Wharf, a wharf full of shops next to a marina of white sailing boats with silvery metal masts and royal blue tarps. The wharf itself was ramshackle, with weathered buildings showing lots of metal fans, vents, and tubing, much of it rusted. The only new-looking building visible from the road was a schlock copy of a lighthouse done in grotesque pink stucco. There were a couple of good restaurants there and an interesting seafood market. The rest of the stores were the usual touristy souvenir stalls and snack shops.

We passed the old Cannery Row and the new gray-bunker buildings of the Monterey Bay Aquarium. At some unmarked point beyond that we crossed from Monterey into Ocean Point and soon were on a long graceful oceanside drive. To our right, in short steps down, were a strip of low greenery, a bike path, a stretch of large gray boulders, and the waters of the Bay. To the left the drive was lined with houses—some small cottages and large frame houses, many done in white, and some tall, elaborate Queen Annes, painted in blue, or green, or beige. Ahead the road seemed to fishhook into a minipeninsula tipped with huge rocks. Above the peninsula were dark green hills, with houses suspended against them like so many tree decorations.

We circled the hill along the ocean road. On the other side, we angled inland near a marshy area and passed between the inland and ocean nines of the Ocean Point golf course. The golf course gave way to a rocky "no swimming" stretch of sand. Somewhere out there was where I'd been hurt. The sunlit rocks looked benign today, in sharp contrast to my malevolent memory.

We turned away from the beach along a road lined with trees. In a moment, through the trees, I could make out the cemetery. It, too, had a placidity that seemed unreal to me: I kept having the feeling that there'd been some cosmic cover-up.

We drove into a residential area just south of the cemetery. The area had an odd look to it, not what I would have expected to find in a California oceanside town. The vegetation seemed overlush and overgrown—trees dripping with Spanish moss, and a thick, brambly undergrowth that suggested machetes rather than hedge clippers. There were regular streets and houses, but the houses were all modest, and sometimes ramshackle, each isolated by the heavy vegetation. If I hadn't known where I was, I might have guessed some Gulf Coast town in the southeastern United States.

Janet made a left turn into the gravel driveway of a small ranch-style house with white, wood-shingled siding and a rust brown composition roof. There was virtually no backyard, the woods coming to within fifteen yards of the back of the house. The front yard, however, had a kind of backyard feel to it: It was surrounded by what might once have been a normal hedge now grown and thickened into an erratic fifteen-foot-tall thicket.

The driveway broadened into an apron next to what appeared to be the garage. Parked in the driveway was a silver Mercedes 500SL convertible, top up, with a license plate that read "4 B B." Janet made a small sound of distress and stomped down on the brake, sending the car into a short, noisy skid on the gravel.

"What is it?" I asked.

"Becky . . . I'm afraid she's . . ."

Her sentence—if, in fact, she ever finished it—was lost to me as she jumped out of the car and raced toward the house. As she was climbing the steps of the small front porch, the front door of the house opened from within. Becky emerged with a bearded man in a sport coat, who had an arm around the girl's shoulders. The man immediately made calming gestures toward Janet, who seemed to be asking frantic questions of him and of Becky at the same time. I got a quick glance at Becky's face before it was hidden behind Janet's ministrations: The glance gave me the impression that Becky was exhausted, and probably ill.

I maneuvered my way slowly across the seat, opened the door, and slid both feet out. At the sound of my shoes hitting the gravel, the two adults turned in my direction. Janet said something to the man, and the three of them started moving toward me. As they approached, I got a better look at the man. He was of average height, slightly stocky, and dark complected; he was wearing a charcoal herringbone sport jacket with black slacks and an open-neck white dress shirt. What was most vivid about him was hair—dark, curly hair—covering his head and his jaw, spilling out the neck and cuffs of his shirt.

By the time the others reached me, I was standing up, leaning against the inside of the open rear car door.

"Is Becky all right?" I asked.

"Now she is," said Janet. "She had an awful anxiety attack, and she called Dr. Blake." Her head swung toward the man. "I feel so bad that I wasn't here."

"Janet, please stop worrying about that," said Blake. "You're not obligated to be around Becky every minute; she doesn't want it, and I don't either. She's likely to have anxiety attacks now and then, and she's going to have to learn to handle them on her own. If one gets to be too much for her and you're not around, she's welcome to call me."

Blake's voice was low and gravelly, yet somehow gentle. I could imagine him being particularly appealing to children, like the good beast in fairy tales. To me his bearlike appearance, the gruff warmth of his voice, and the obvious intelligence in his eyes made him seem like a walking history of evolution. A piece of unforgettably absurd jargon came back to me from some old science class: Ontogeny recapitulates philogeny. The history of the individual reproduces the history of the race.

Janet introduced him as Dr. Barry Blake. He was the psychiatrist Janet had mentioned before.

"How do you do, Mr. Strickland?" said Blake, shaking the hand I held out to him over the car door. "It's a real pleasure to meet you. I feel very grateful to you for stopping that attack on Becky. I'm sorry it had to cost you so much."

"Thank you," I said.

"How are you feeling?"

"Not too bad. Everything seems to be healing pretty nicely—except for my right leg, which I can't move below the hip. I keep hoping it will start working one of these days."

"It's only been . . . what? . . . about three weeks. If I

remember my neurology, you've probably got a few months before your condition stabilizes. Have you got a physical therapist lined up?"

"No. The doctors at the hospital told me I should get one, but it didn't go any farther than that."

"You should start right away. I know a couple of good ones if you'd like their names."

"I would."

"I'll have my secretary call Janet with the information."

"Thank you."

There was a moment of silence. In what seemed a reflex born of mild awkwardness, the adults all looked down at Becky at the same time. She had moved from Blake to Janet and was leaning against her aunt's shoulder, her eyes drooping with sleep. She looked totally wrung out.

"I should get Becky to bed," said Janet.

Janet's eyes were on me. I could see in her face the kind of look that partygoers give drinks they can't figure out where to put down.

"Go on with Becky," I said. "I'll be fine. I'll follow along in a minute."

"Are you sure?"

"Yes. Go."

Janet said good-bye to Blake and moved off toward the house with Becky. Blake and I watched them go. As the two went inside, I heard Blake give a small sigh. He seemed to deflate, as if released from some larger role.

"That attack was the last thing Becky needed," he said with quiet bitterness as he stared toward the closed front door. "She's got far too much to handle already."

"Is she going to be all right?"

When he hesitated, I asked him if he was worried about confidentiality.

"No," he said, "just truth. You always try to talk optimistically to your patients so they'll absorb some of that optimism themselves. But at bottom you never really know. I know that I want very much for her to be all right. I know

I will try everything in my power to help her be all right. Beyond that . . ." Blake shrugged.

After a moment he turned abruptly to face me. He said:

"You realize, of course, that I wouldn't be talking to you at all about Becky if Janet hadn't told me I could confide in you and if you hadn't saved Becky. That was a brave thing to do."

"Thank you."

"Janet told me you talked to the police for her."

"Yes."

"She says you convinced her that this man Tiny she's been so worried about probably wasn't behind this. You're convinced of that yourself?"

"What I believe is that it's not likely that Tiny was responsible for the death of Becky's mother, even less likely that he was responsible for this recent attack on Becky, and highly unlikely that he will bother either of them in the future. There are a couple of coincidences I'm not real happy about, but, still, it's probably not Tiny."

"You think the attacker was some rapist?"

"That's a definite possibility. There was a police report of a man approaching a young girl in Santa Cruz the other night. No one can be sure, of course, but it just might have been the same man. If so, let's just hope he won't be coming back here."

"Yes." Blake seemed to appraise me for a moment. "Speaking of coincidences, I find it a bit coincidental that a private detective just 'happened' by when the attack on Becky took place."

"That really was a coincidence. I had finished up a case in Monterey that afternoon. I was taking a walk before I headed home."

"That was certainly lucky for Becky. I understand that you're going to be staying with Janet and Becky for a little while."

"They've offered to let me use their rental room for a

couple of weeks until I can get around a little better. Do you have any problem with that?"

"I did have—before I did a little checking on you. Which maybe I should apologize for, but I won't. I've been treating Becky for six years through some very precarious times. I've got quite an emotional as well as therapeutic investment in her."

"I assume that's a complicated way of saying you like her."

Blake grinned. "We doctors can sound awfully pompous, can't we. Yes, that's exactly what I mean."

"I'm glad she has people who care about her so much. I haven't found her particularly easy to like, but that doesn't keep me from feeling sympathy for the awful times she's been going through."

"I see Becky in a fairly limited setting, but I've seen her display moods that most people would find less than likable, and Janet has told me about other displays. Part of that may be the normal teenage thing, which is not all to the bad—no matter how annoying it is to others—since a normal developmental pattern could be a healthy sign. Partly her moodiness is an understandable response to a world she finds pretty frightening right now. Also, pain and fear have a way of wearing one down after a while. But there's still sweetness under there. I hope you get to see some of it while you're here."

"I don't know," I said. "Becky's not too crazy about my being around."

"In that, I'm afraid, she doesn't get much sympathy from me. People who have to cope with fears tend to contract their worlds too much, which they think will make them feel safer, but in the end just makes them more afraid. And they try to use the fear as an excuse not to do things they don't want to do. I think it will do Becky some good to have you around, whether she likes it or not. It might do Janet some good, too. She spends so much time focused on Becky that she gets pulled down by Becky's moods. Having another adult in the house could be a very healthy thing for her. Anyway, none of that is the main point, is it? The main point is that you need and deserve help after what you've been through, and Janet is giving it. I think that's great."

Blake glanced down at his watch. "I'd better get going. Can I help you with anything first?"

"If you wouldn't mind, just grab these crutches off the floor of the backseat. Otherwise I'll be fine."

Blake leaned over, took hold of the crutches, and lifted them out of the car. He held them up and apart for me to step into, almost as if he were helping me put on a coat backwards. Once I had the crutches, I walked with him over to the Mercedes.

"Nice present," I said.

"What?" For a moment he looked bewildered. Then his eyes swung toward the license plate. "Oh, that. Actually, not this one. We were fortunate that my wife, Cynthia, had some money before I started making mine. That plate originally came with a little red Alfa Romeo Spider Veloce she bought me when I first opened my office here." His eyes glowed. "I loved that car. Nicest present I ever had in my life. I've kept the same plate on subsequent cars for sentimental reasons. It occurs to me sometimes that the plate makes me look like a kept man. But I'm always trying to convince my patients not to be so concerned about appearances. I guess I should take the same advice myself."

"That Mercedes doesn't exactly hurt in the appearances department."

Blake smiled, coloring just slightly. "I suppose I wouldn't get anywhere trying to convince you I got the car for safety reasons."

"You get a Volvo for that."

He laughed. "Yes, you're right. Well, I suppose we're all a bundle of contradictions. The trick is to keep them under some control."

Blake walked around to the driver's door of the Mercedes,

opened the door, then looked back with a smile. "Good-bye, Mr. Strickland. It was a pleasure to meet you."

"You too."

I stood to the side, on my crutches, as Blake turned the Mercedes carefully on the gravel driveway, waved, then drove away. He was a likable man. What I particularly liked about him was that he seemed to care for Becky so much. I just hoped he was good at what he did. The more I learned about Becky, the more I came to appreciate the nightmare she'd been going through. She needed all the help she could get.

▽

10

AFTER BLAKE WAS gone, I continued to stand in the driveway, staring off at nothing in particular. Slowly I became aware of a subtle warmth on my skin. I tilted my face upward to catch the faint rays of the February sun. Clouds had formed out toward the ocean, but only the cotton-candy kind, the kind that tempt one to believe for a moment that the powers behind the world are benign, and even playful. A cloud, smaller and lower than the rest, moved visibly across the sky, like a child too exuberant to stand still among its more decorous elders. Seabirds glided lazily on the winds.

A cool wisp of breeze touched my face, and I breathed it in. It was the sort of breeze that startles you with its freshness, that, when inhaled, touches memory. Something stirred inside me, a feeling so unfamiliar it took me a moment to realize what it was: joy. Pitifully weak, pitifully tentative, it was joy nonetheless, leaking up like an ancient spring through layers of encrusted rock.

I leaned back against the car for balance and closed my eyes. I tried to open myself to the feeling, but it was too faint and too far down. It was like a small thermal spring, vaporizing in the cavernous cold, warming and soothing whatever it touched as it tried to rise. I could feel it with only the smallest part of my being; the rest of me remained outside it, as heavy, as rigid, and as cold as a stone vault. I tried to will the feeling upward, to help it break through, but it was no good; it stayed trapped within its walls. Finally even that was gone—condensing and cooling and leaking away. And then there was nothing.

But Nature abhors a vacuum. Sadness began to puddle at the center of me, dense and dismal. Anger began to stir, all shut in on itself, in a thickened churning. Exhaustion and ache settled into my heart and began spreading through my limbs like some metaphysical flu. I tried what mental tricks I knew, but they were laughably flimsy, and to no effect. I felt myself sink slowly into misery where I stood, stuck fast, until I heard Janet ask me if I was enjoying the sun.

In depression you are amazed when you see people smile. It is as if the sun were going out, and the world were slowly turning to darkness and ice, and no one else has noticed. You have to keep reminding yourself that it is not *the* world, but only *your* world, that is dying. But still you're amazed.

It didn't feel as if anything in me would move. But as usual I found enough sluggish will to get myself started, knowing that all motion would feel like slogging through wet sand for the minutes or hours it took until the way got easier again.

"Hi," I said. "How's Becky?"

"She's better. She's stretched out on the couch—she didn't want to go to bed. I told her that as soon as I got you settled, I'd fix us all a snack."

As I watched Janet speak, I noticed how soft her skin seemed. I had the absurd feeling that if I would only stretch out my hand and touch her face, some of my pain would subside.

"How's the car look?" she asked.

"What?"

"Your car—how does it look?"

She was gesturing toward the car I was resting against. Using the car for support, I slowly turned myself around to take a look. Sure enough, it was the Ford Taurus I always use for work. I had known it was there, had even glimpsed it coming into the drive, but had forgotten all about it in the commotion over Becky. I'd assumed I'd been leaning against Janet's Honda, which was almost the same maroon color.

"Thanks for getting it," I said.

"No trouble."

I'd left the car in the golf course parking lot a few hours before the attack on Becky. A couple of days into my hospital stay, I'd asked Janet to locate the car and get it out of storage. In fact, she had gotten to it ahead of the tow truck.

"I don't think anyone tampered with the car," said Janet. "I have your briefcase in the house."

I hadn't had to worry about a gun in the car because I hadn't brought one this trip. With my papers safe, the rest was just car, but it did seem to be all right. I glanced inside. On the backseat were an umbrella, a folded-up travel raincoat, and one glove. On the front seat was a Travis Tritt cassette, and another by Liona Boyd. On the floor, along with an old *San Jose Mercury News*, were a napkin from Taco Bell and an empty McDonald's drink cup, the plastic top and straw still in place. It was the usual everyday stuff that looks so eerie after a disaster.

"I noticed that the Ford's an automatic," said Janet. "That should make things easier when you start driving."

"Yeah."

Janet seemed to study my face. "Are you okay?"

"I'm just tired."

"Maybe you should take a nap after we eat."

"Maybe that would be good."

Janet went to the Honda, opened the trunk, and pulled out the small suitcase into which she had packed my few possessions from the hospital. As I waited for her, I wondered if I would be able to make it through lunch. I felt so tired. And sad. I had the sense of tears deep inside me, uncried tears that had become impacted and infected. It was an infection that, even in the best of times, never quite went away.

I hobbled after Janet as she led me toward what I now saw was a converted garage, with a small door and two windows with planter boxes where the garage door should have been. As she opened the door and let me go past her inside, I couldn't resist letting my fingers brush against her shoulder to check my earlier intuition. None of the pain subsided, but the sense of her softness intensified, along with the desire to hold her, or have her hold me.

We stopped just inside the door to look over the room. It was plain but comfortable, its decor tilting toward the feminine—beige carpeting, white walls, forest green bed and chair coverings, flowered throw pillows on the bed and chair, prints of birds and flowers on the wall. To the left, as we entered, were a chest of drawers, a double bed, and a nightstand with a small lamp. To the right was a sitting area with an easy chair, a standing lamp, an end table, and a portable TV on a wheelable metal stand. Just beyond the sitting area was a narrow desk with a table lamp and straight chair.

"I like it very much," I said. "It looks very pleasant."

Later I would probably mean it. For the moment my talking about pleasures was like a blind man talking about colors.

I was really feeling awful. I kept glancing at the bed, thinking I should beg off lunch and lie down, curling up with my misery. I remembered now what I had needed so badly and so often during the days after Katie's death: instant solitude.

"I'm glad you like the room," said Janet. She pointed toward the far wall where there were three doors. "The door to the left is the bathroom, the one in the middle's a closet, and the one to the right goes to the kitchen."

"Maybe I'll try the door to the left."

I made my way to the bathroom and locked the door quietly behind me. I propped up my crutches against a corner of the small room, then leaned my forehead against the towel rack, my palms braced above it on the wall.

I don't like to cry. It goes against everything I was taught. From my early years, it was the line not to be crossed, the final giving in, the way the other knew that you were beaten. Since age seven or eight, I hadn't cried in front of another person—not Katie, not Charlie, not even the therapist I saw after Katie's suicide, part of whose job was to find tears.

I don't like to cry, but during days and nights of depression after Katie's death, I came to realize it was cry or die. Crying was the only thing that would bring relief from those episodes of agony and lethargy that constitute depression—the equivalent of having a bad case of the flu at a good friend's funeral. Crying was such laborious work for me at first, struggling to break down my resistance, struggling to find the attitude or the image or the memory that would release some pocket of tears from within the crusted matter inside me. I got better at it after a while, but never good.

Now, leaning against the wall, I stuffed a towel against my mouth with one hand and cried soundlessly. It was arid, more air than tears, from the surface of my pain. But at least it provided some relief from the rawness in my chest and the heaviness in my limbs. After the few minutes of crying were done, I threw some water on my face, took a couple of deep breaths, and left the bathroom.

Janet was tucking the last of my clothing into a dresser drawer. She asked me if I wanted to sit with her in the kitchen while she fixed the snack, and I said I did. I followed her into the kitchen and sat down at the small dinette table, leaning my crutches against the wall behind me.

While Janet went to check on Becky, I leaned back in my chair, closed my eyes, and began taking slow, deep breaths. After a few moments I could feel the muscles in my chest and stomach relax a little, could feel the rawness and heaviness in me diminish even more. I might not feel good today, but I wasn't going to feel so bad. I was getting off easy. Sometimes that happened. You just never knew.

Janet came back to the kitchen, opened the refrigerator, and started taking out the ingredients for lunch. I brought up the subject of money, asking her if she'd let me pay rent for the room. She adamantly refused. I said if I couldn't pay rent, I'd like to pay for all the groceries while I was there. I was more stubborn, and she was less adamant, this time. After some sparring, I won. When she conceded, I sensed it was with relief.

"I'm fine for money," I said, "and you two are bound to be a little pinched. What matters to me is all the trouble you're going to. It's costing you a lot of effort; I don't want to cost you money too."

"Thank you. I appreciate that."

"And now I won't have to feel guilty if I start stuffing myself. I do have some weight to gain back."

"I'm planning to go to the store later today. Let me know if there's anything in particular you'd like me to pick up."

I took a look at what Janet was putting on the two trays she had set out on the kitchen table in front of me. There was a carton of nonfat milk, a large bottle of diet 7-UP, and a box of herb teas. There was something that looked suspiciously like baked tofu, and some kind of cheese that looked like pale yellow plastic. There were whole-wheat pita, shredded lettuce, two kinds of sprouts, low-fat mayonnaise, a small mixed salad with a lot of what looked like uncooked cauliflower, and a bottle of nonfat Italian dressing. It was not the kind of fare that would make a glum man happier, or a thin man heavier.

"Would it be possible to have you get something in the nonmeat-substitute food group?" I asked. "Maybe even the red nonmeat-substitute food group."

Janet laughed. "In other words, you'd like a steak for dinner."

"Yes!"

"I think we can manage that." Janet looked down at the food trays and smiled. "I guess this meal must look pretty Spartan to you."

"This meal looks fine," I said charitably. "It's just that I'll need something a little heavier to help me gain my weight back. In fact, in that spirit, maybe you wouldn't mind picking up some ice cream and cookies or something. And get whatever you and Becky like for dessert—yogurt with fruit, or whatever."

Janet gave me an indignant look: "We're not that Spartan."

"Good," I said. "Then get a steak for three and the richest dessert you can find, and we'll all pig out tonight."

"Sounds terrific."

"Look," I said. "I wish I could go to the store on my own to save you the trouble. If my leg starts moving soon, I will. Meanwhile, I can always go without whatever you're too tired to get or to do. Don't let me be a pain."

"Are you kidding?" said Janet. "Becky and I will be eating better tonight than we have in weeks. Becky's going to love that dessert."

"You don't even know what dessert is yet."

"Yes, I do," said Janet, her eyes twinkling. "It's got a light graham cracker crust, and gobs of mint chocolate-chip ice cream, and a heavy fudge frosting, and some whipped cream. . . ."

As Janet drifted off into her dessert fantasy, I looked around at the house. From where I sat I could see not only the kitchen but also the dining room and a small portion of the living room. It was a modest house, in terms of both size and furnishings: The small kitchen had white-painted wood cabinets that were beginning to peel here and there and a yellow checked linoleum floor that had buckled slightly near the sink; the medium-sized dining room and living room had heavy old furniture of no particular distinction sitting on worn brown carpeting.

But then there were the plants. They were everywhere—large ones growing from big pots on the floor, medium ones hung from the ceiling with beaded macramé slings, and small ones set out on table surfaces and window ledges and tucked away on shelves. The plants turned what could have been a slightly dingy house into something lush, funky, and exotic. The plants also gave the house a hideaway feeling, which I found particularly appealing in my present condition.

When Janet had finished the meal preparations, she took one of the trays out to the living room, then returned for me and the second tray. In the living room Becky was stretched out on the couch, a bed pillow behind her neck, a comforter covering her. She looked tired rather than exhausted, her color was better, and she didn't look sleepy. She was reading what appeared to be a teenage romance novel, which she tucked away with a self-conscious expression when I entered the room. Janet had Becky sit up a bit to give me some room on the couch, and I sank down into the soft cushion on the opposite end from Becky, my right leg stretched out to the side of the large coffee table. Janet covered the table with a cloth and put the food out.

"This is a nice place you have here," I said. "How long have you had it?"

"About four years," said Janet. "Actually Becky and I are buying it together."

"Becky must have quite an allowance."

Becky actually smiled. The smile was small, but genuine. I hadn't seen many smiles from her to this point, genuine or otherwise.

"Becky's contribution comes from money put in trust for her from Ann's life insurance," said Janet. "You know how things are priced in California—I never could have afforded this place on a teacher's salary. I'm so glad the court approved this joint purchase—it makes things so much nicer for Becky and me. When she's eighteen, either I'll buy her out or we'll sell and split the equity."

"Sounds like a good arrangement."

"The house isn't anything great, but it's got plenty of room for us, and some yard, and it's so much better than an apartment. And we're so close to the ocean. It's great. I just love walking along the beach in the eve—"

Janet stopped abruptly, her expression abashed, looking at Becky, then at me, then at Becky again. The room seemed suddenly very quiet.

"I like walking on the beach too," I said. "The only trouble is, you sometimes run into some real pushy people. Right, Becky?"

The lame joke was a gamble, and for a moment I thought it wasn't going to work. Becky gave me a pale, expressionless look that could have gone different ways. Maybe my smiling at her was what made the difference. In any case, she suddenly let out a small giggle.

I was getting a look at the sweeter Becky that Janet and Blake had mentioned. For the moment, anyway, anxiety seemed to have emptied her of rudeness and irritability, leaving her a pale, passive, vulnerable thing with visible need and warmth. The kid I was seeing now would be an easy kid to love, the other one, a real chore.

We fixed our sandwiches, most of our conversation directed toward passing this or that. I found that the pale, rubbery cheese (which was nonfat and so, probably, noncheese) didn't have a bad taste, since it had no taste at all. If you took a piece of cheese and the smallest piece of tofu you could find, tucked them as far down into the pita and under the lettuce and sprouts as possible, and then smeared the whole thing with the mustard I'd talked Janet into digging out from the back of the refrigerator, it was actually possible to get one of those sandwiches down. I drank a little Diet 7-Up until I was reminded of how much I disliked the aftertaste of diet drinks, and reluctantly turned to the box of herb teas to try to pick out the least objectionable flavor, choosing peppermint.

As I stretched out my right arm to reach for the thermos of hot water, I lost my balance slightly, my right leg not making the proper compensatory motions. To catch myself I had to thrust my right hand against the table edge, which didn't keep my shin from smacking against the table leg. The impact did rattle a few things on the table, though it spilled nothing. I muttered an oath and an apology in the same breath.

"You all right?" asked Janet.

"Yeah. I'm just sick of this damn . . . darn . . . leg not working." I pointed at the leg in a gesture of reprimand. "Tomorrow we get serious."

"Don't push yourself too hard," said Janet. "You lost—how many pounds did you tell me?"

"Almost thirty—down to one-fifty."

"You look skinny, you look tired, you have almost no color. You need to recuperate."

"You forgot to mention no hair among my nonattractions."

There was a glimmer of mischief in Janet's eyes.

"Oh, you've got hair all right," she said. "You've got it right in your room."

"What do you mean?" asked Becky.

"Janet—"

"Dave bought himself a wig today," said Janet, her expression openly mischievous now.

"Let me see!" exclaimed Becky, not with vigor, but with more life than I'd seen in her since I'd arrived at the house, and more enthusiasm than was usual with her.

"No," I said.

"Please!"

"Come on, Dave," said Janet. "You're about to be going into the big, wide world. You don't want to walk around with that ski cap on your head, do you? The whole point of getting the wig was so you wouldn't have to. You might as well put the wig on."

She was right, but what convinced me to put aside my self-consciousness so quickly was the open, childish enthusiasm on Becky's face. I figured she deserved any small thrill she could get, and if it took my looking like an idiot to do it for her, well, so be it.

"Oh, all right," I said, sounding more grudging than I actually felt.

"Yeah!" said Becky.

"I'll get it," said Janet quickly.

Becky and I sat together in strained silence during the short time that Janet was gone. Becky wasn't comfortable enough with me to get along without Janet for psychological and conversational protection. I suppose I felt a little bit the same way. I made a couple of jokes about the hair, to which she gave polite murmurs and nods, and then we both busied ourselves with eating.

"Ta-da," sang Janet as she entered the room behind me.

"Oh, my God," said Becky with an expression of amazed amusement.

I turned my head. Janet was carrying a blank-faced Styrofoam head. On the head was my wig: long dark hair without a wave or curl in it, flowing down to almost shoulder length, cut with bangs in front. All I needed was a broadsword and chain mail, and I'd be all set. I could share Becky's amazement that such a wig was for me, but I couldn't share her amusement.

Janet put the head down on the coffee table along with the brush and mirror she'd also been carrying. Then she came around to me.

"Okay," she said. "Off with the cap."

"You don't need to look," I said. "Nor Becky."

"I do, if I'm going to help you. Becky doesn't. Becky, turn around."

"I can see," said Becky.

"Turn," said Janet.

Becky did a half turn, her hand up to her face, the kind of position from which sneaking a peek would be easy.

"Turn."

"Oh, all right," said Becky, really turning this time.

Janet started to lift off the cap. I reached my hand to stop her.

"Don't be so silly," said Janet, pushing my hand aside and lifting the cap. "It doesn't bother me. I've seen it before. Just fuzz, some healing cuts, and a small indentation under the skin. Big deal."

"Some small indentation. It feels as big as a softball."

"I want to see," said Becky.

"No," said Janet. Then to me, as the bandage came off: "That's just your imagination. It's about the size of an egg. Here." She took my left hand, lifted it to my head, placed my fingers along the circumference of the wound, and holding the fingers in place, brought them down in front of my eyes. "See? Egg sized. And a small egg, at that."

"Hurry," said Becky. "Stop talking so much."

"Just wait."

Janet took the wig off the Styrofoam head and put it on my head. She tugged the wig down, did some adjusting and fluffing, then grabbed the hairbrush and brushed the hair.

"Okay," she said, stepping away.

Becky whirled around. She stared at me for a moment with that blank expression people have when they are slightly stunned, then pressed her lips together and brought a hand to her mouth in an unsuccessful, and probably halfhearted, attempt to stifle the giggling that followed.

"Goddamn it," I said to Janet, reaching up to grab my hair, "I told you it looked stupid."

"No," said Janet, slapping my hand away, laughing. "It looks good."

"It does," said Becky, still giggling.

"Right. That's why you're practically falling over laughing."

"Dave, stop being so silly," said Janet. "Sure, the wig looks a little strange at first, but that's only because we've only seen you with those bandages, which gave you a whole different look. And because you look so miserable and self-conscious when you have it on. But it's a great wig—it looks really natural—and you look good in it."

"You do," said Becky. "You look cool. Like a rock singer."

"Right."

"No, really," said Janet, reaching for the mirror. "Take a look at yourself."

Janet held out a mirror in front of me. Because I didn't really want to see and because I'm not really comfortable staring at myself, I kept mumbling things like, "Okay, I've seen it," and trying to turn away. But Janet kept pushing my head back. With all my fussing I had built up such a negative memory of that wig that the real thing was bound to look better to me. As I was forced to stare into the mirror, some of the strangeness diminished, and I began to adjust a bit to the look. A beard was definitely needed, but if I did grow the beard, then maybe with, say, jeans and a jacket, the wig wouldn't look so bad.

"Doesn't it look good?" asked Janet.

"Well . . ."

As I looked at their smiling, on-the-verge-of-laughing faces, I found that I wasn't quite able to hold back the smile that came in response. That was all the two of them needed to let out the laughter they'd been holding in. To play along, and get over some of my own stupidity, I turned the wig 180 degrees on my head, parted the mass of hair with my fingers, and peeked out—which brought more laughter. It felt good to see Becky looking genuinely happy for a moment. And it felt good—the three of us together like that.

▽

11

I HEARD A child screaming.

I woke with a start, frantic in my half-asleep state, not knowing where I was. Then reason filtering through my dream state and moonlight filtering through the curtains gave me a sense of my surroundings. I turned on the small bedside light, struggled my way out of bed, found my crutches, and made my way toward the kitchen. The screaming had turned into weepy bursts of words in what I now recognized as Becky's voice. As I got to the dining room, I could see Janet and Becky just ahead on the living room couch, both in their cotton nightgowns, Janet with her arms around Becky. The girl, tearful and frightened, would alternately pull herself close to Janet for comfort and push herself away in the agitation of speaking.

". . . she's so angry with me . . . and she wants to kill me. . . ."

"No, honey, she—"

"She does—she wants to kill me . . . she keeps saying she does. I say, 'No, Mama,' but it doesn't do any good. Her face is horrible with the blood all over it, and she looks at me like she really hates me. I try to get away, but no matter where I go she's always there, and she comes closer, and I know I'm going to die. . . ."

Becky's voice, which had been rising hysterically, now broke off into sobbing. She threw herself against Janet, burying her face in Janet's shoulder. Janet soothed and petted her until the sobbing began to diminish and then tightened her hug and began rocking the girl gently.

"There now, honey, there now. I know those dreams are awful—I wish I could make them stop—but they are just dreams, they're not real. Your mother loved you very much—she wouldn't have hurt you for the world. Your mind's just making all that stuff up. That's not the way your mother was at all."

"I want the dreams to stop," said Becky in a moan.

"They will, honey, they will. But until they do you have to try to remember what Dr. Blake's been telling you. The dreams come from a little girl inside you who went through some terrible things she didn't understand and couldn't face. When you wake up all frightened, you are that little girl again. But there's another part of you who's older and smarter and stronger. More and more you have to become that part of you when you wake up, so you can comfort the little girl just the way I'm comforting you now."

"I know and I try, but it's so hard, I'm so scared."

"It is hard."

"I'm so tired of being scared. It seems like I'm scared all the time. I feel like I'm going crazy, and they're going to lock me up, or I'm going to be like those people in the streets. . . ."

"Becky," said Janet firmly, "that's not going to happen. I know it feels that way, but that's not going to happen. Deep down you know it's not going to happen, and you have to tell yourself that. Come on, hon. Be still now. Try to relax."

Becky obeyed, leaning against Janet quietly while Janet continued to rock her.

I was standing just inside the dining room. I had told myself to stay still, that I might startle them if I made a move to leave, but I knew that was mostly an excuse to try to justify my own curiosity. Now, however, seemed a good time to sneak away. But as I started to turn, one of the crutches made a slight squeaking sound on the wood floor, catching Janet's attention. Her head turned toward me.

I indicated that I was sorry to have disturbed her, and she, that she was sorry they had disturbed me, and I inquired if everything was all right, and she indicated it was, and I let her know that I was leaving, and she indicated that she would meet me in the kitchen—all this with gestures and silent mouthing of words in a comiclike pantomime that had no humor to it.

In the kitchen I leaned the crutches up against the wall and made my way around the kitchen by hopping and holding on to things. I got the tea kettle on and found the tea bags and some cups, then discovered I was hungry, so I took out an apple and a box of cookies and put everything on the dinette table. When the kettle boiled, I poured myself a cup of tea and brought it over to the table. There was a copy of the day's paper, which I hadn't gotten to, and I skimmed over the sports section and the national news while I was eating my snack. I was just getting up the energy to do some cleanup when Janet came into the kitchen. She had put on a light blue terry-cloth robe over her white nightgown.

"I'm really sorry about that," said Janet. "Becky's screams must have startled you something awful."

"They did wake me up with a pretty good jolt."

"I wish I could say it won't happen again. But I can't. I'm afraid this isn't always going to be a real restful place to recuperate."

"I'll manage. It sounded pretty rough for Becky. Obviously that was one of those nightmares you mentioned."

"The worst of them. The one that keeps happening over and over." Janet glanced down at the food items in front of me, then toward the stove. "I think I could use some tea myself."

"Let me get it for you."

Janet smiled. "Your good intentions are noted. But you're on sick leave."

"I heated plenty of water, and it's pretty hot. You might want to heat it for a couple more minutes."

"You want another cup yourself?"

"Sure. Why not."

Janet reheated the kettle for about half a minute until it whistled, then fixed us both cups of tea. When she was sitting opposite me at the kitchen table, I said:

"I thought I heard Becky saying something about her mother wanting to kill her."

"That's part of the dream," said Janet. "What a terrible thing for someone to have to dream about—especially a young girl whose mother was murdered. She's been working with Dr. Blake on trying to control the dream, or at least control her reaction to it, but so far she hasn't had any luck. The dream keeps recurring, and Becky keeps getting more and more terrified."

"What does Blake say about why Becky's having that dream?"

"He says it represents a childish fantasy of guilt and punishment. In the dream, Becky wakes up in her room at night, senses that Ann is in danger, and runs to help her. She finds Ann on the floor of her room, blood all over her face. Becky shakes Ann to try to bring her around, but when Ann opens her eyes, she gives Becky this awful look and says she's going to kill her. Becky tries to run away and hide, but Ann keeps following her and finally catches up with her and starts to stab her. That's when Becky wakes up screaming."

"What's the guilt and punishment angle?"

"Dr. Blake says Becky's caught in a dilemma. On the one hand, she wants her mother alive. On the other hand, she feels responsible for her mother's death. If Ann stays dead, Becky has to live without her mother's love and with her own awful guilt. If Anne comes to life, Becky has to face terrible punishment. In the dream her unconscious is trying to work out the solution to an unsolvable problem."

"Why on earth would she feel responsible for her mother's death?"

"The usual thing about small children and repressed anger and not being able to distinguish between feelings and actions. Becky feels down deep that her childish anger toward Ann was what caused Ann's death."

"Becky says this? About the anger?"

"No. It's the doctor's theory."

"It sounds pretty hypothetical to me. Not to mention pretty pat."

"I don't think so. Not given the way Ann was acting before she died. She was awful to Becky. I don't want you to think Ann didn't love Becky; she loved her very much. One proof of that is the life insurance policy that's helping us now. Even when Ann was desperate for money, she kept her policy going."

"Even when she was desperate for money to pay Tiny?"

"Oh, it wouldn't have helped her much there: It was a term policy, with no cash value. Maybe I'm making too much of this point. What I meant was the payments. Ann could have used the payment money for drugs, but she never did. It was a point of pride with her."

"Good for her."

"She did love Becky. But it's also true that Ann wasn't that good a mother during the last year of her life. She was kind of coming apart. It was the drugs, of course, but it wasn't only that. Ann had always been . . . I don't know . . . kind of overexuberant. That was fine in high school where everybody was always yelling and squealing and trying to outdo each other: Ann was one of the most popular students. But she didn't have the kind of personality that would wear well, or hold up under stress. Being married to Corky, and then having Becky, seemed to simmer her down a bit. But after Corky left, she began turning into a kind of hysteric. That was before the drugs, though the drugs just made it worse. One minute she could be really up—though the ups never seemed all that happy—there was always a little desperation to them. The next minute she'd be down. One minute you'd be her best friend; the next you were a betrayer. And her judgment about things was awful.

"I don't think Ann really minded being out of control: It was her way of thumbing her nose at life. But it scared her where Becky was concerned, and she tried especially hard to keep herself under control around Becky. Partly she succeeded; partly she didn't. Ann could get pretty angry. Becky loved her mother and needed her, of course, but she was angry too. Becky didn't express her anger directly very often—she was a timid child, and pretty intimidated by Ann. But I could see it in her face, and sometimes she'd say something to me. The night Ann died, I was there in the house with them—they had a little rental cottage not too far from here. Ann was being awful. She got angry at Becky for something petty, and it escalated, and Ann slapped Becky across the face, hard. I hate it when people slap children like that; I remember cringing when I saw it. Becky's face dissolved in tears and she started saying she hated her mother. I think Ann might have hit her again for that if I hadn't stepped in. I put Becky to bed and—"

"Wait a minute. Becky was at home the night her mother was killed?"

"Yes. Can you imagine the impact on a five-year-old—waking up to find her mother murdered?"

"Jesus. The poor thing."

"As long as I live I'll never forget the moment I found the two of them. I was supposed to take care of Becky that morning. I got to the house about nine-thirty. I rang the bell, and no one answered, so I let myself in with my key. Ann was crumpled up on the floor, a smear of blood by her head—from the external head wound. Becky was in her nightgown, sitting on the floor near the body, her face and eyes totally blank. God knows how long she'd been sitting there. She was catatonic for a couple of weeks. When she came out of it, she was in awful shape. Gradually she starting adjusting—thanks to Dr. Blake—and for a while during elementary school she seemed to be okay. Then during this last year she started having all these terrible emotional problems. In a way, it's not a total surprise. Dr. Blake warned me years ago that Becky's troubles might recur later. I guess I kept hoping he was wrong."

"The poor kid. I knew she'd had a tough time of it. I didn't have any idea how tough."

"I hope so much that Dr. Blake can help her—and soon. It hurts so much to see her hurting the way she is."

"Does Becky remember finding her mother's body?" I asked.

"No. When she came out of her catatonia, she couldn't remember anything about that night. She was told later what had happened, of course. But the dream is the only thing resembling a memory that she's ever had, and of course it's all distorted."

"So the idea is that her unconscious is wrestling with the conflict between her wanting her mother alive again and her fear that if her mother were brought back to life, Becky would be punished for her imagined guilt."

"That's right."

"You called the problem 'unsolvable.' I assume you meant that it's unsolvable to Becky's unconscious, not unsolvable to Blake. I assume he's trying to get Becky to see that her mother's death wasn't really her fault."

"Yes. But, according to Dr. Blake, the illogical thinking that really matters is buried deep inside Becky with everything else that she's repressed. To affect that logic, Dr. Blake and Becky need to be able to access the repressed material, and that's just what Becky's mind is fighting to prevent. But Dr. Blake is hoping that the nightmares and the anxiety attacks mean that those memories are beginning to surface."

I turned my head in the direction of Becky's room. But what I was seeing was that little figure by her mother's grave, all that misery in her past and present, and another threat lurking just beyond the edge of the cemetery. Some people have too much pain.

▽

12

THE MAIN DOWNTOWN area of Ocean Point was four blocks long, built along the midsection of a hill that swept upward from the ocean like a gigantic green wave. The broad main street ran parallel to the ocean, curving up and over a huge knoll. Along the street were graceful old Victorians that had been converted to offices and stores, and brightly painted, wood-faced commercial buildings done up with Victorian cornices and windows; these were interspersed with large, plain stone buildings that looked as awkward and out of place as relatives from Minnesota. The downtown area was bracketed at one end by a Spanish-style post office trumpeting express mail, and at the other end by a Catholic church advertising three masses a day. Lying in between were a phone company office and a small storefront with a sign that said Psychic: In Ocean Point you could send a message just about anywhere and any way you wanted.

Janet was trying to get hers through to Toledo via the U.S. Postal Service. She was inside the post office mailing an overnight letter to relatives while I was outside, sitting in the backseat of her Honda. Becky had run across the street to the Benetton store where we were to meet her in a few minutes.

A passerby glancing in the car at that moment might have thought me literally an idiot: I looked like a forty-year-old baby gurgling and playing with its toes. I didn't care: I was in a great mood. Yesterday—just three days into my stay at Janet's—I'd found myself suddenly able to hinge my knee and wiggle my toes; since then I'd been working on the leg with the enthusiasm of a child for a new toy. The leg was still more crippled than not, but I knew now that it was going to be all right.

I heard a tap at the window, and I turned my head back to the left. Janet was outside the driver's window, laughing and giving me the thumbs-up sign. She opened the door and stuck her head in the car.

"You look like you're having fun," she said.

"Yes—in my own imbecilic way."

"You ready for the big wide world?"

"Yes!"

Today was going to be a big day for me. With the exception of that brief trip to the wig store, this was going to be my first day out in the world since my accident. A little later this morning it would become my first day out alone: I'd asked Janet to leave me downtown while she and Becky went over to Carmel to do some errands. I was looking forward to wandering around on my own, being among people, spending some time in the bookstore, maybe sitting in a coffee shop reading the paper, and certainly exercising the leg. It was a clear, crisp day, a good day for walking.

This would also be my first day off crutches: In a few minutes I would be trading in my crutches for a cane. Now that I could work my knee and my toes, I figured I could do without the crutches. But it would be a while before I could do without some kind of support. I hoped a cane would be enough.

My leg was still spastic, meaning that the nerves would overrespond: During a reflex test on the right knee, the lower leg would jump out and almost straighten, as if in some lewd comedy routine. If I got nervous or chilled, my right leg would seize up and become difficult to move; the smaller toes on that foot would curl under so that I'd be walking on the tips of the toenails. I still had foot drop and little control over the muscles on the right side of my ankle and foot; if I put much weight on the outside of the right foot, I would lose my balance. I was in no shape to do the tango just yet. Not that I ever was.

I got out of the car without Janet's help, boosting myself up on the open rear door, then sliding away from the door along the back fender so that Janet could grab my crutches out of the back. I tested my right leg by walking along the exterior of the car, supporting myself with fingertips that did a crab walk on the car body. I was encouraged by how the leg felt. It was nice to know, as I accepted the crutches from Janet, that this would be the last time for them.

We made our way across the broad street, past a median planted with grass and small trees, to the other side. At one point I felt a burst of giddy panic, but the feeling was gone almost at once.

After reaching the sidewalk and walking half a block, we came to a wooden building with a large sign that read Town Pharmacy. A smaller sign said John Triplett, Proprietor, and one smaller yet said Home Health Care Supplies.

I followed Janet into the store. The pharmacy was at least twice as deep as it was wide, giving the place the feel of a train car. Shelves along the left wall and standing shelves running down the middle held the usual nonprescription pharmaceutical items. There was a checkout counter front right, which seemed to be closed today, and a pharmaceutical counter mid-right.

Janet led me to the pharmacist area, which consisted of double counters. Behind the low front counter, which had its own cash register, was a young white-jacketed blond woman helping an elderly customer. Behind the elevated inner counter was a slender man with longish hair who was also wearing white; he was filling prescriptions. I saw the man's reaction as he glanced up and noticed Janet. It was much more than friendly recognition: It looked like the brightening of a teenager spotting his current crush.

"Janet," he said, rushing out from behind the two counters to greet her. When he got to Janet, he took her hand and said, "I've really been worried about you and Becky. How are you doing?"

"We're doing all right, John. Thank you."

I was watching Janet to see if her reaction would in any way match the pharmacist's. It didn't. She gave him a nice smile, but nothing electric, and her eyes held a definite reserve. She removed her hand before the man seemed inclined to let go.

Janet introduced us. He was the John Triplett listed on the sign outside—the pharmacist as well as the proprietor. He didn't look to me like a pharmacist. He looked like a sweet-tempered ex-hippie who should have been working in a day-care center. Perhaps he was making the transition from hippie to yuppie, or more likely straddling the two worlds, like so many people you run across in Northern California coastal towns. Spiritual materialism. Karma and cash.

Triplett, who seemed to be in his mid-thirties, had curly brown hair grown to the base of his neck. He wore those round, rimless spectacles that were referred to in the sixties as granny glasses, but which, when worn by a man, always make me think of early-twentieth-century revolutionaries. The lower half of his face, which was full and pale, seemed naked somehow, as if he'd just shaved off a beard. His eyes, perhaps magnified by his spectacles, were large, gentle, and sad. Even though he smiled as he shook my hand, his eyes gave me the odd impression that I had hurt him somehow.

"Dave, of course, is the man who saved Becky," said Janet, "the one who's staying with us for a couple of weeks."

That announcement didn't make Triplett's eyes any happier. I doubted that I was the cause of his sad look; I suspected it was built in. But perhaps my being with Janet had given it a little extra boost.

"Nice to meet you," said Triplett politely but without a lot of enthusiasm. He turned to Janet. "I worry about you two living out there by yourselves."

"John, that's very sweet of you, but we're not in an isolated cabin somewhere. We've got plenty of neighbors."

"Yes, but those houses are pretty hidden from each other. And there are a lot of deserted areas around there. Look what happened to Becky."

"We'll be careful," said Janet, in a tone that indicated she'd had enough of that conversation. She glanced around. "We want to turn in the rental crutches and rent Dave a cane. And I want to get a refill on Becky's prescription. Maybe you can have the young lady help us with the cane while you do the prescription."

Triplett looked reluctant, as if he'd have preferred to do both, but he let himself be left behind as his assistant took us to the back of the store. "Home health care supplies" included items like wheelchairs, walkers, crutches, canes, special pillows, bedpans, and supplies for the "incontinent." All the canes were basically the same—smooth and straight, made of mahogany-colored wood. There were some differences in length, and I tested out a few until I found the one that felt best. My leg was relaxed now, and I had no trouble getting around with the cane. It was nice getting rid of those crutches. I could sense a new feeling of freedom coming on.

Back at the counter I paid the fee on the crutches Janet had rented for me and gave a charge card number as deposit on the cane. Janet paid for Becky's prescription and stood there chatting with Triplett for a few minutes. She seemed more relaxed with him now that our business was over—and perhaps with the counter between them: A couple of times he leaned toward her with an earnest expression, and she drew back a little, leaving him pressed against the barricade.

While I was waiting for them, I put a hand up to scratch my face, then laughed to myself as I felt the growing beard: I was viewing Triplett as a kind of hippie, but I looked like twice the hippie he did.

As Janet and I were leaving the store, Triplett called after her, "See you at the Blakes' Sunday." Janet waved back a combination of acknowledgment and good-bye.

"Is he talking about Dr. Blake's house?" I asked Janet when we were outside.

"Yes. Why?"

"I thought psychiatrists weren't supposed to socialize with the families of their patients."

"This isn't really socializing. Anyway it has to do with his wife, not him. Cynthia and I are part of a group that's been trying to upgrade the drug education and counseling programs at the schools in town. We've been raising money to bring in speakers, train peer counselors, add an experienced drug counselor to the community counseling center, that sort of thing. The group wanted to put on a thank-you party for all the people that have helped us, and Cynthia offered their ranch. You should come if you have enough energy."

"Why should they want me at that kind of party?"

"We're allowed to bring guests. It should be fun. I hear their ranch is just gorgeous—it's back in the Laguna Hills, and it's supposed to have a spectacular setting. The Blakes have been building for almost a year. They haven't moved in yet—it's not quite finished—but I guess it's finished enough for an outdoor reception. It should be quite nice. There'll be music and catered hors d'oeuvres—no alcohol, but soft drinks and an espresso bar with Italian pastries."

"I appreciate the invitation. Let's see how I feel."

"Speaking of Italian pastries, the guy who's doing the portable espresso bar for us has his regular bar just a block from here. Are you in the mood for some good Italian coffee? And maybe something sweet?"

"Sure."

"Good. I'm kind of hungry. Let's get Becky and go."

Getting Becky out of the Benetton store was easier said than done. She had partially reverted to her sour self today, and her attempt to convince Janet to buy her a particular skirt and sweater was done mostly through whining. Finally Janet and Becky worked out some sort of compromise involving a slightly different sweater that would go well with some skirt Becky had at home, and we were out of there.

A half a block farther up the street, Janet steered us into a place that was supposed to be an "authentic" Italian bar, minus the hard liquor. There was a stainless steel metal counter with windows displaying slices of pizza, sandwiches made with small loaves of bread, and different types of cakes and cookies. Behind the counter was a large espresso machine, dispensers for mineral water and wine, and several small tubs of gelato served in cones or cups. There were two customers standing at the counter, and two others sitting at one of the five small tables that lined one wall. The place was decorated with reproductions of Renaissance art and posters of various Italian cities.

As we approached the counter, Janet was greeted by a handsome, thirtyish Italian male complete with open shirt front, curly dark chest hair, and dangling gold chains. The man's greeting was effusive, and I was beginning to think sarcastic thoughts about Janet having a boyfriend in every store. But after observing the greeting more closely I decided it was more the standard Italian effusiveness of the male toward a female—especially a female customer—than the serious attraction that the pharmacist had displayed. And when Janet introduced us—his name was Renzo—his greeting to me was friendly, not competitive.

Becky ordered a hot chocolate and a *mille foglie*—what seemed to be a flatter, Italian version of a napoleon. Janet ordered a cappuccino and what looked like a piece of jelly roll with chocolate pudding in place of the jelly. I ordered an espresso and a piece of a sweet one-layer cake topped with apples and syrup.

When we were seated, we sampled each other's tortes, generally to the advantage of Becky, who supervised the portioning. My apple torte was the best—at least judging from the few tastes I got of it.

Janet's cappuccino was in a soup-bowl-sized cup, brimming with foamy, steamed milk and dusted with chocolate. My espresso was in a tiny cup that looked as if it had come from some child's play set. What was inside, however, was far from childish. The coffee looked as if it had the consistency of chocolate mousse, and when I took a sip I felt my eyelids jump up like two marionettes.

"Whoo," I said.

Janet laughed. "Too much?"

"Was the atomic bomb too much? Actually, it's delicious. Maybe it could use a little sugar, though. Like about half the bowl."

I added a teaspoon and drank.

"Better," I said. I looked down at the empty thimble. "Now what do I do for the rest of the morning?"

"Order a cappuccino. Or better, maybe, move on down to the regular old coffee shop just down the street. It would be a better place to sit and sip and read the paper."

"I'll do that—after I've gotten in my exercise."

"Are you sure you want to stay in town? We could easily drop you off at home before we go shopping. You could walk around there. Or you could come with us shopping. We'd give you some exercise."

"What you'd give me would be lots of chances to stand around staring at clothing."

"We enjoy it," said Janet. "Why shouldn't you?"

"I don't know. It's a genetic mystery, I guess."

"At least let's arrange a time for us to pick you up here."

"No. I told you I'll take a cab. It'll give me more flexibility in case I get tired sooner or want to stay longer. And you guys can shop at your own pace. I'll be fine."

When Janet and Becky were finished, we paid and went outside. I wasn't ready to try the steep streets down to the ocean until I'd tested myself with the cane, and I figured that as long as I was going to walk along the main street anyway, I might as well walk Janet and Becky back to the car. It looked like a mistake when the two of them started dawdling in front of store windows, but after I made a few grumbling noises behind them, they began moving at a better pace.

We were a block away from the post office when a man came around a corner and almost bumped into us. I didn't pay attention to him so much as my balance, which it took me a moment to secure. But then I heard Becky's quick frightened intake of air, and I looked up. The man, who was wearing a blue work uniform with some sort of emblem on his upper sleeve, was heavyset, with a large gut and thick, muscled forearms showing beneath his rolled-up sleeves. He had medium-length dark hair with unruly tufts and curls jutting out here and there; his chin was covered with dark stubble; he had a silver earring through one pierced ear. His features were good, in spite of his extra weight, but his eyes were hard, and his face had what looked like permanent sneer lines around the nose and mouth.

Becky's breathing sounded awful: a rapid, panicky gasping for air. She looked as if she were having some kind of fit—her body stuck in place, rigid and trembling, her face set in a trance of terror as she stared at the man. Janet was reaching for Becky, her eyes twitching back and forth from Becky to the man, looking frightened.

The man seemed to get caught up in the women's panic, as if it were some contagion that had infected him. He was looking at Becky with what seemed a combination of fear and fascination. He raised his right hand in a way that made me think he was going to strike her, though later I realized that it was more likely a gesture of warning or even defense. I moved clumsily to put myself between him and Becky, and he shoved out at me with his left hand. The shove threw me off balance, and I tumbled backwards onto the pavement, my cane rattling up against a car. My eyes were on the man the whole time I fell. He didn't make a move toward me or the women. Instead he continued to look frightened. He yelled, "You're all crazy—leave me alone," and then was gone.

Janet was looking frantically from Becky to me, torn in her attentions. She put her arms around Becky as she asked me if I was all right.

"Yeah," I said as I sat up on the sidewalk and reached for my cane.

"That was Tiny," said Janet breathlessly. "We've got to call the police."

"No. Not for this. How's Becky?"

"I don't know."

Janet was kneeling by Becky, hugging and stroking her.

Becky's breathing had slowed down, but she was trembling and looking off in the direction that Tiny had gone. Her eyes were still fixed as if she was in a trance, and when I moved my hands in front of her eyes, I got no response. I noticed that gawkers and helpers were beginning to gather.

"Let's get her off the main street," I said. "I don't think a crowd of people is going to relax her."

We took the side street from which Tiny had come, a street of small houses, some of them homes, some, offices. Halfway up the block we found a low stone wall, easy for sitting, in front of a small office with the shades pulled down. We sat on the wall with Becky between us. Janet resumed the touching and talking, and I put a hand on the girl's back, repeating over and over that everything was all right.

For several more minutes there was no change. Then Becky began to blink and move her head around. For a moment she glanced at us both with no sign of recognition. Then she seemed to recognize Janet. She opened her mouth as if to say something, but instead began to cry. Janet held her close, petting her hair. When Becky calmed down, Janet loosened her hold on the girl and began to question her about what had happened. Becky could speak all right, knew us, knew where she was, but seemed to have no memory of Tiny or her reaction to him. When we tried to jog her memory, Becky just got confused and upset and seemed on the verge of crying again. We gave up the questioning, and Janet pulled Becky against her once more.

"I'm going to get Becky home and call Dr. Blake," said Janet.

Janet made a move as if to get up, then sat back. I noticed that her hand had been placed over Becky's right ear, the ear closest to me.

"It *is* him," she whispered. "I knew it was all the time. We've got to make the police see that. Look at Becky. This proves it, doesn't it?"

"Proves what?"

"That he's the *one,*" said Janet, with the frustrated expression of a child who has trouble making itself understood. "Don't you see? Becky *recognized* him!"

"From where? From the beach? From . . . earlier?"

"Yes . . . no . . . I don't know."

Janet was beginning to look a little frantic. Emotional certainty and mental confusion seemed to be forming an explosive mixture in her head, revving up her mind. I reached over and put a hand on her shoulder.

"It's all right. Just take it easy. Are you telling me this is the first time Becky's seen that man since her mother was murdered?"

"Yes!" said Janet. "I didn't think she'd ever seen him at all." Janet looked down at the girl in her arms. "I've got to go. But you must see what this means."

"Do you want me to talk to the police again?"

"Please."

Janet was on her feet now, Becky tucked in against her side.

"I could talk to them now unless you need me at the house," I said.

"Talk to them now," she said. "We'll be all right once I get Dr. Blake. Tell the police what happened today. Make them see what it means. I want this to be over."

Then the two of them were walking off toward the car, leaning against each other. I was supposed to make the police see, but I wasn't seeing anything clearly, and I wasn't sure Janet was either. But if I didn't know what there was to see, I did know one thing for certain: I was going to find out.

▽

13

AS JANET AND Becky disappeared from view, I became aware that I was trembling. I'd had a subliminal sense of being agitated ever since the confrontation with Tiny, but the anxiety had been masked by my concern for Becky. Now, as I sat alone on the stone wall, the mask seemed to be coming off.

Adrenaline was surging inside me, causing a sound in my ears like the faint rushing and whistling of wind. I began to feel cold. There were small chill-like spasms that started in my chest and radiated throughout my body. All my senses were on alert, my mind waiting with dreadful expectancy, as in some animal that has just heard the footsteps of a hunter.

I knew an anxiety attack was coming. I was fearful, but not worried: I'd had these before and knew I could get through the fear by gutting it out. I figured the best thing I could do was to walk off some of the energy that would feed the anxiety. If the walking around got too difficult, I would have to find some private place where I could sit and grit my teeth and wait it out. Once the nerve storm had passed, I'd go try to talk to Deffinger.

I stood up, tried to warm and relax myself with a few subtle stretches, and then limped back toward the main street.

As I turned the corner, I felt a shock go through me. The sidewalks had grown crowded with lunchtime pedestrians, and to my hyped-up nervous system it was as if I had stumbled through a wrong door onto a stage in front of thousands of people. I cursed the fear and pushed myself forward through the crowds, but my body began to seize up with stage fright, making it difficult to move.

Having a full-blown anxiety attack feels like being tossed into shark-infested waters with your wrists and ankles separately bound: Part of the ordeal is being deprived of virtually everything you need to survive it. In an anxiety attack you are being flooded with fear, and you want to stand up to it, but there's virtually no "you" anymore, just the fear. You try to understand what's happening, but it's so hard to concentrate when someone is sobbing inside your stomach and someone else is screaming inside your head. You try to reassure yourself, but you can't be heard: Your mind has splintered into a half-dozen voices carrying on a panicky debate as to whether you are dying or merely going insane. The only "you" that exists at that moment is that small particle of mind that will decide whether or not to run—into a bottle, or into a pillbox, or into a small room where the shades are always down.

This was going to be a bad one: I could feel the panic growing and taking me over, could feel myself shrinking, disappearing into it. I needed to get away from these crowds. I knew that the stores thinned about a block ahead and that the crowds would thin out with them: If I could just get that far, some of the pressure would be off, and I could think more clearly about where to go next. I just had to go a little farther.

But moving was so difficult. I was clumsy anyway with my cane and bad leg, but now the muscles throughout the rest of my body were knotted up and hard to work. It felt as if I was moving on pure willpower, but willpower wasn't making me nimble. I seemed to be always in someone's way. I kept getting jostled by the careless or the rude, having more trouble recovering each time, feeling as if I was really close to falling. Meanwhile my thoughts kept revving up until they were painful, splitting off more voices, some of which now became attached to people around me, voices that mocked and criticized.

A young boy bumped into me as he tried to squeeze his way through the crowd, knocking me off balance. To keep myself from falling, I twisted my upper body around and put my hands out, catching myself with my palms on a plate-glass window. In front of me were two male mannequins with bird's-nest hairpieces. *That man's got one too,* said one of those voices. *It's a terrible wig,* said another. *He looks so stupid,* said a third. With each word, humiliation welled up inside me, independent of rationality, independent of will. Inside the window, just past the mannequins, a woman was looking at me with disgust. Just in back of her, a man was talking at me soundlessly, making a go-away motion with the back of his hand. *You don't understand, I'm hurt,* said a very small voice, but it was a voice no one could hear.

I pushed off from the window and past some people in front of me, trying to force the right leg to step, and when it wouldn't move, to hobble, stumble, anything to get out of there. I pushed myself too hard, and I lurched forward, and I had to grab the shoulder of the man in front of me to keep from falling. Startled, the man turned quickly and pulled away, looking frightened.

He's drunk, said a voice. *It's disgusting,* said another. *Why don't they do something about people like that?* asked a third.

I'm not drunk, I'm sick, please help me, said that small voice, but again no one heard.

Along with the voices there was still the revving up, the drowning, the disappearing, the dire warnings, all provoking unbearable terror that seemed unconnected to me, yet filling me all the same.

I finally got away from the crowds. But though I had escaped them, I still felt exposed and fearful there in the open; I sensed that if I didn't find shelter and safety in a few moments, I would be lost. I thought of going to a hospital, but part of my mind was telling me that it wasn't necessary, while another part was warning me that if I went in, I might never get out.

Then I noticed the church, a large, clay-colored Spanish-style building with its doors open. Everything within me headed desperately for that doorway, the way a child, waking from a fevered nightmare, might head for the seemingly distant crack of light coming from the doorway of his room. Except that I didn't want light; I wanted darkness.

Finally I reached the doorway and stumbled in. The inside of the church seemed cool and cavernous, blessedly dark, blessedly empty.

I hobbled along a back pew, taking a seat in a corner, away from the strip of sunlight that slipped in through the door. I put my cane on the floor and gripped the back of the next pew with both hands. My whole body was shaking. It was as if some huge, dark, violent thing were inside me, trying to wrestle his way to the surface, trying to take me over. I had met this creature during the long nights after Katie's suicide and had almost been overwhelmed by him until I learned that by wrestling and enduring, I could make him go away. Though never for good.

After a while the raging began to diminish. But there was no peace in the quiet. It was as if fear and anger and sadness had solidified at the center of me, becoming impacted in a space not large enough to contain them, so that they pressed out painfully against my insides. I sensed screams somewhere deep within me, permanent and unreachable, like the contortions of the skeletons of people caught in a lava flow centuries before, their agony forever fixed in place.

I knew I had run from my fear—had not been willing to stay out on those crowded streets whatever the costs. I felt ashamed and discouraged. I knew that the fear of not being able to handle anxiety could become the trigger for more anxiety, so that instead of pressing forward, one was constantly backpedaling, until most of life was a refusal, a search for some place that was devoid of frightening things, and since all things in time became frightening, of life itself. Anxiety was an illusion, but an illusion one could get lost in, the fear of fear of fear becoming like a hall of mirrors where illusion was the only truth, and everything led infinitely to nowhere.

Exhaustion came to me eventually, dulling my fear and half dulling my misery. I might have dozed a little, because at a certain point I felt myself start, not quite certain where I was. What I had was a sense that someone was near, had spoken. I straightened up in the pew, mouth dry, eyes hot.

"Are you all right?"

I turned toward the voice. It was that of a youngish priest in clerical collar and black suit. My head was still vague and full of sleep. My first, overwhelming impression was that I had intruded.

"I'm sorry, Father. I just stopped for a minute . . . I didn't mean . . ."

I shifted on the seat and started to reach for my cane. I felt a hand touch my shoulder in a gentle gesture of restraint.

"It's all right," he said. "That's what the Lord's house is for. Are you in trouble?"

I shook my head. As I did so, I realized that my wig had turned as I'd slept. I reached up and straightened it, his eyes openly followed my hands.

"I know a mission where you can go if you are in need," he said.

Something like a laugh came out of my mouth. "I'm in a lot of need, Father. In fact, I'm a total wreck. But I'm not homeless or hungry. I'm just sick."

"Do you need a doctor?"

"I've already got a doctor. I've had a bad head injury, and I've been in the hospital for a while, and I guess I'm feeling the aftereffects of both. I tried to get around on my own for the first time today, and I just flat out got terrified."

I wondered why I was speaking so openly to this man. There was something about him that made confidences easy.

"How'd you get hurt?" he asked.

"A man was trying to grab a young girl, and I got in the way. The girl got away; I didn't."

"You're the man who saved Becky Schrader."

"You know her?"

"I used to. She and her mother. That was a long time ago. I don't see Becky much anymore. But I pray for her."

"Her mother was a Catholic?"

"Her mother was searching—or playing—or maybe a little of both." He smiled. "We were one of the options she was considering." His smile faded. "Her death was such a sad thing. I hope she found comfort in something before she died."

"Becky's mother came to this church?"

"On and off, shortly before her death."

"And she brought Becky?"

"Yes," he said. "She was such a cute and sad little girl." He looked off somewhere. "I've often wished . . ."

"Wished what?" I asked.

He shook his head. He turned back toward me, looking me over. "That was a very brave thing you did."

"Father, at the moment I'd be happy to trade in all the bravery people want to pin on me for a body that works and a head full of hair. Maybe a new nervous system while we're at it."

"Would you trade those things for Becky's life?"

"No."

He smiled. "Then you're stuck with being brave. Maybe you'd better learn to live with it."

We looked at each other for a moment, then I put out my hand: "I'm Dave Strickland."

"I'm Father Matthew," he said, shaking my hand.

The priest was a slender man, with dark hair and pale skin. His dark eyes were almost feminine with their softness and long lashes. His face seemed gentle and a little ironic. Yet deep in his eyes there was something gloomy, mysterious, and tortured, like some relic-bearing side chapel in an old cathedral. I suspected that this was no theocrat or parish social worker, but someone for whom religion cut to the bone.

"Are you a Catholic?" he asked.

"No, Father. I'm not Catholic. I'm not even a Christian. In fact, I'm not anything."

"It must be hard not to be anything."

"Not when you realize how much it costs to believe. Your intellect if you think belief goes against all reason. Your honor if you can't condone the way the world is made."

"Yes," he said, his expression solemn. "Belief does cost. God makes us pay much. Maybe too much." He looked off toward the front of the dark church. "Sometimes I think that faith is a special way of knowing, a way more profound than reason. Other times I think it is nothing but desperate, foolish hope."

We were silent a moment. Then he gestured. "Still, there's that."

His gesture was vague, but I knew instinctively its direction: the huge crucifix at the front of the church. The body of Jesus that hung there was a passionate image of suffering, the muscles contorted in agony, the body pale to the point of death. The head, with its crown of thorns, had slumped onto the left shoulder. Pain had etched exhaustion into the face—and something else as well, a pathetic and sweet kind of calm, like that of a sick child resting against its mother, as if the man had been broken down in death into some smaller, infantile self. It was that, more than anything else, that I found touching.

"Yes, there's that," I agreed. "But maybe that's simply the most desperate and foolish hope of all."

The priest kept looking at the crucifix. "Yes. That may be. But I think . . . I would rather be on the side of that passion—even if it's only a dream. It is, at the least, the most beautiful dream I know."

After a moment he said good-bye, said he hoped I would heal well, and then was gone.

I looked back at the crucifix, which was hung against a stone wall, lit by daylight that filtered through two windows high up at the sides of the church. I knew just what the priest had meant about being on the side of that passion. My love for Jesus hadn't lasted as long as his, but I believed it had been just as strong, for I had loved with that desperate, hormonal, compensatory fervor of which only the young are capable. Like a child with an imaginary friend, like a pubescent girl with her weepy, romantic stories, I made Christianity a full-time dreamworld, the escape from my misery, my awkwardness, and my solitude. I talked to Jesus, and he to me: I found in him the sympathy of a mother and the strength of a father, the wisdom of a teacher and the companionability of an old friend. He was what filled my loneliness, this gentle Savior, and when fear and confusion filled my life, he could still those waters by whispering, "I'm here."

What was so difficult later was not so much deciding that this Jesus was an illusion that I had built out of the longings of my heart and old voices in my head: There are harder things to forgive in your God than nonexistence. The hardest thing was to realize that the sacrifice of Jesus makes no sense, even as a dream. For the God on the cross is dying to save you from himself. And that makes of the crucifixion a schizophrenic sham.

Of course, it's said that God is bound by the Law, that the death of his son was the only loophole he could find. But that makes no sense either—an infinite, omnipotent God stuck with some crusty old morality like a tortoise with his shell—a loving God endorsing a justice so barbaric that half of humanity has been embarrassed to profess it for two hundred years. Push aside the magnificent tapestry of the crucifixion and you find a little man pushing the buttons and turning the wheels; he looks much like the Wizard of Oz, but he's not nearly as nice.

Yet the tapestry is beautiful. And so too the memories of that still small voice whispering love to a boy who couldn't find it anywhere else in his life.

I know he's not there. I don't want him to be there.

But still I miss him.

▽

14

DEFFINGER WAS SITTING at his desk, bent over a book the size of an encyclopedia volume. When he heard me approach, he looked up, squinting, uncertain. At the sound of my voice greeting him, he burst out laughing.

"Strickland. Jesus. I was trying to figure out whether you were a visiting vice cop or some vagrant. What the hell are you doing in disguise?"

"It's not a damn disguise. I got my head bashed, remember. They shave your head. I needed something to cover it with."

"Yeah, but why the hippie wig? And why are you growing that beard?"

I rubbed my stubble. "It's a long story," I said grumpily. "Too long."

"Christ, that's the way we used to look when we went on leave in the service. It was the only way to get laid in those days. You just had to make sure not to let those hippie chicks fondle your hair. Not till you were done, anyway."

Deffinger smiled and drifted off into some sixties sexual reverie. I took a seat on the straight chair just in front of his desk. To the side was an eight-by-ten photograph of a middle-aged woman with gray-streaked brown hair and a nice smile. The inscription on the photo read, "To Deff, Love, Alice."

I reached out and lifted the heavy book Deffinger had been reading. The title on the spine was *Criminal Investigations*.

"You taking a course?" I asked.

"Huh? No. Teaching one."

"Seriously?"

"Yeah. A few years ago one of the profs over at the JC started asking me over now and again to talk to his class. I liked it, and I guess I did all right, so they asked me to do a course. It's interesting, and a nice change. Also, I get to tell cop war stories without boring everyone to death. The students eat them up. They look at me like I'm Dirty Harry or something. I'm thinking of doing it full-time when I quit this shit."

Now I understood some of his idiosyncrasies, including those corduroy jackets. The Miss Manners make-over was really his transition to academics.

"So," he said. "What's up?"

I told him about the run-in with Tiny. When I'd finished the story, he looked at me uncertainly, like someone who's been listening to a joke and isn't sure he caught the punch line.

"I don't get it," he said. "You want to . . . what? Make some kind of complaint?"

"No," I said impatiently. "Of course I don't want to make a complaint. I want you to think about what this means. Maybe I didn't emphasize the girl's reaction enough. She was terrified. It was like she went into some kind of trance."

"So what do you think it means?"

"I'm not sure exactly. But it must mean that Tiny's involved in the Schrader case somehow."

"What it could mean instead is that Janet Kendall's so excited by her Tiny-did-it theory that she's gotten the girl scared out of her wits—which she mostly is on her own anyway, poor kid."

"Yeah, but how would Becky know him? The aunt just found out herself that he was back."

"Maybe some kid pointed out Tiny to the girl. You know how kids are: They love to know who the local hoods are. The older kids wet their pants thinking how cool they are, and the younger kids scare themselves by looking—like it's a free haunted house."

I just looked at Deffinger, feeling stupid. I'd gotten so caught up in the women's reactions and my own anxiety attack that I hadn't been thinking clearly.

"You could be right," I said. "I shouldn't have come in before I'd thought the thing through. It's just that the girl's reaction was so intense, and Janet was so upset—but that's no excuse. Sorry to waste your time. I'll talk to Becky, and I'll only come back if I think she had no conscious awareness of who Tiny was."

I reached for my cane and started to get up. Deffinger waved me back in the chair.

"Wait a minute, not so fast. What I hate a lot worse than wasting time is missing something. Let's talk about this a little." He looked at me a moment, then shook his head and laughed. " 'Conscious awareness,' huh? Thank God you're dealing with a local criminologist here and not some rube." He gave another laugh, this one, I think, at himself.

"Okay," he said, "let's suppose that the girl didn't know who Tiny was—I mean, consciousness-wise, as us academics might put it. Or let's suppose she did know who he was but this reaction of hers was something deeper. What's your idea? That she recognized him somehow? From the beach?" When I didn't answer right away, he said: "I got to tell you right off that I'd have a hell of a hard time buying that after getting absolutely nothing from the girl in the two interviews we did with her."

"I suppose it could have been something subtle, like scent. Something she hadn't consciously remembered. But now that I think about it, I don't think that's it. He never really got that close to her. And I got the impression that her reaction to him was visual—her eyes were just riveted on his face."

"So then . . . what? That she recognized him from way back? Maybe saw him kill her mother?"

"It's a thought, anyway. You'd have wondered the same thing if you'd actually seen the girl's reaction."

Deffinger thought about it. His face made those subtle wincing and squinting motions you see when people are considering something they find hard to accept. Finally, Deffinger shook his head.

"I'm certainly going to talk to the girl as soon as she's well enough—see if she can explain what happened. But I don't see how any of this can go anywhere. Tiny can't have killed Ann Schrader himself, not with that alibi: If I gotta measure Douche's honesty against some girl's trance, Douche wins hands down. We were talking last time about the possibility of Tiny getting someone else to kill the woman, but that doesn't fit with what you're talking about now."

"So, since there's *no* possibility that your friend was lying, there's *no* possibility that Tiny could have done it."

Deffinger gave me an angry look. He seemed about to lash out, but didn't. He looked away, staring at the wall. As I watched the slow changes in his face, it seemed to me that his anger turned to reflection, which then became blended with something like sympathy. Eventually he let out a breath and turned back to me.

"Strickland, you're getting close to really pissing me off—the way you're pushing me on this thing about Douche," he said. "Half of me wants to tell you to go fuck off. But I know you're concerned about the girl. I am too. I saw that five-year-old sitting next to her mother's dead body. I'll never forget it: It was like her mind had just . . . disappeared. I'd feel really shitty about myself if something happened to her now because I was pigheaded and didn't do my job right. Actually, at the time I wanted to keep the investigation going, see if I could force something, but the higher-ups figured we'd done enough, had other priorities."

Deffinger shifted around in his chair.

"I'll tell you what, Strickland. If I don't get some obvious, innocent explanation for what happened today, I'll rethink Douche and his report, talk with a few people, see if there could be something I missed. I will not do or say anything that could put Douche's reputation in jeopardy—not unless something really suspicious smacks me in the face. But I will look into it."

"Thank you."

"Don't get your hopes up. I can see that just because I'm convinced of Douche's honesty, why should you be. But it's not just that. There are plenty of ways a cop can make money around here if he's willing to cross the line, but one of the last people he'd go to would be Tiny. Tiny's just a small-time hood, with no connections: He couldn't afford to pay you shit. If Douche was going to fall, he wouldn't have fallen for Tiny. I told you that before. It just isn't going to go that way, Strickland. But I'll look into it anyway."

"With an open mind."

"Don't push."

"Okay, let's suppose that what Douche said about being with Tiny was true. How sure are you about the time of death? Janet said she found the body the next morning; she said the police told her the time of death was between midnight and one-thirty. I don't see how the coroner could figure it that close."

"Hmmm . . . let's take a look." Deffinger reached down and lifted a huge manila file folder off the floor. "I had this pulled when the girl got attacked on the beach." He opened the folder and began flipping pages. "I'm trying to remember how that went. Here we go . . . deputy coroner checked the victim's body at the scene at ten-thirty A.M. At that time the body was not yet in full rigor mortis . . . it was more stiff up top than below . . . body achieved full rigor at about twelve-thirty P.M. As we all know, it takes approximately twelve hours to achieve full rigor, which indicates a time of death of around twelve-thirty A.M. What else? . . . body temperature. Rectal temperature of the victim's body at ten-thirty A.M. was eighty-four degrees Fahrenheit and assuming the rate of cooling at a degree and a half for the first twelve hours, that would indicate the victim had been dead for nine and a half to ten hours, putting the time of death at twelve-thirty to one A.M."

I shook my head. "Come on, Sergeant. You know those indicators are notoriously inexact. What were those times again when Douche said Tiny was with him?"

"Twelve-fifteen to one-twenty."

"And what were the time-of-driving estimates again?"

"Minimum of twenty-five minutes from the point where Tiny was picked up to the victim's house, minimum of thirty from his apartment."

"Assuming the alibi is valid, that covers Tiny from . . . what? . . . eleven-fifty to . . . one-forty-five. Come on. There's no chance that Ann Schrader died at one-forty-six? Either your coroner is overstepping his evidence or he had something else."

"Let's see . . . no . . . yeah, here. I remember now. Stomach contents. Janet Kendall called her sister at eleven-thirty, just after the eleven o'clock news was over. Mrs. Kendall had been at the house earlier that evening and was calling back as promised to say when she could come take care of the daughter the next day. Mrs. Kendall said her sister was chewing when she got on the phone and apologized, saying she'd just finished eating a tuna sandwich. Coroner found small bits of tuna fish among the stomach contents. He says that sandwiches, light snacks are digested within two hours max. Most studies, he says, indicate that the minimum is an hour, but to be safe he went with one that said a half an hour. Hence time of death was estimated at between midnight and one-thirty."

My disappointment leaked out in a small sigh. "Okay, so we're back to the validity of the alibi. Suppose we go with the alibi. Suppose it isn't Tiny. Your theory is what? She was killed by someone from the local dope scene looking for money or drugs?"

Deffinger shook his head in a gesture of uncertainty.

"I don't have anything as definite as a theory," he said. "We ruled out certain possibilities, and checked out a bunch of others, and found nothing. When I'd gone back over it all again, the result was the same. I tried to understand how it might have happened so that we couldn't find the guy. I was guessing maybe some crackhead the victim met at one of her parties—maybe someone from out of town who was just wandering through. But there are problems even with that idea."

"What problems?"

Deffinger hesitated, then said, "Hell, what's the harm in going over it? You got something to say, I'd better have enough ego by now to listen." He laughed. "Listen to me. All this teaching is turning me into a damn liberal. Either that or I think I'm in class taking questions."

"I'm all ears, Herr Professor."

He looked down at the file again. "Ann Schrader, age twenty-nine, born Ann Walsh, January twentieth, 1958. Female, Caucasian. Height: five-six. Weight: one twenty-five. Eyes: brown. Hair: brown. Skin: fair. Married: June fifth, 1980, to William DeWitt Schrader. Children: Rebecca Ann Schrader, age five, born August twelfth, 1982."

"What date was the Schrader woman killed?" I asked.

"November fourteenth, 1987."

Deffinger looked up from the file, moving to recollection and paraphrase. As he spoke, he glanced down at his file from time to time when his memory needed refreshing.

"By all accounts Ann Schrader was a beauty, and a bit of a pistol. Straight sexually, as far as we can tell. Tended to hang out with boys as friends as well as dating them. Was a tomboy when young, and tended to keep some of that, even when the boys were getting other ideas. Minor scrapes with the law—fake ID, a couple of speeding violations, destruction of school property—threw a rock through the window of the principal's office. Apparently bright, but had no great love of books or authority. School records show some disciplinary action for pranks and playing hooky. In spite of all that she was popular with teachers as well as students. In the school records the teachers talk about an excess of high spirits, which they thought would diminish in time. Apparently she did settle down a lot when she got married.

"After graduation from high school, she took a few courses at the JC, worked part-time jobs at the Wherehouse and The Gap, and partied a lot. Her husband-to-be, William Schrader, aka Corky, was a few years older than Ann, dropped out of high school senior year to follow some friends who were following the surf around the Pacific. When he and Ann met, he was hanging out in Ocean Point, working in a friend's surf shop, trying to get together enough bread to take off again. He was apparently one of those Adonis guys who get all the girls breathing hard when they walk across the beach and make all the other guys wish they'd kept their clothes on.

"The two of them fell in love hard, stayed that way for a few years, got married, and had Becky. About a year after the girl was born, Ann Schrader started making the usual noises about financial security. Corky tried on a coat and tie, but decided they didn't fit too well—especially given the jobs he could get with charm and no high school diploma. He got restless and took off on his wife and kid. After six months he came back to try it again, but that only lasted a few weeks, and he was off again. That was late 1985.

"Apparently Ann Schrader was still in love, and the breakup hit her hard. Little by little she started partying hard, but, by most accounts, was not having much fun. She seemed angry and kind of jittery. She had some affairs, but according to her girl friends, never let herself get close, never let them go on long, and always did the dumping.

"She started smoking crack for weekend recreation and eventually worked up to smoking every day. Apparently her behavior became more and more erratic, and her employer—a woman who owned a local clothing store and who genuinely liked her—threatened to fire her unless she got help. Apparently she got scared about her job and what she might be doing to her daughter and what the drugs might be doing to her head, and one day she went into the local emergency room asking for help. A psychiatrist named Blake was on duty—"

"Becky's psychiatrist?"

"Yeah. That's how he got to be Becky's psychiatrist. Because he was her mother's, I mean. When the little girl went out of her head after her mother's death, Janet Kendall called in Blake to treat her.

"Now Blake's got a good practice, but at the time he was

just opening an office here, and making most of his money on staff at the hospital. Blake put Ann Schrader in the hospital for a couple of days, got her to start CA meetings, and saw her a few times himself for a reduced fee to help her over the transition."

"Of course you checked Blake out."

"Of course," said Deffinger with a smile. "Shrink sleeping with patient is a possibility that always bears checking these days. But we found no evidence of that. Someone we talked to had seen him stop and say hello to the Schrader woman and her daughter downtown one day, but that's as racy as it got. Blake claims that the night Ann Schrader was killed, he was home asleep with his wife. I pressed the wife just a bit on a second interview when the case started hitting a dead end, and she seemed real at ease with her story."

"Janet Kendall told me she thought her sister had gotten off coke."

Deffinger gave a sour laugh. "People think what they want to think. Blake thought the same thing."

"She was back on?"

"That's what the blood tests showed, according to the coroner's office. The people at CA said they hadn't seen her in a couple of weeks; her sponsor tried to call her and got the brush-off. A couple of people who knew her said they'd seen her smoking at a party two days before she died."

"I understand she was killed in her bedroom at home."

"Yeah. Marks on the right cheekbone and the right side of the nose indicate that she was hit on the right side of her face, probably a glancing blow. There weren't enough to the marks to tell whether it was a punch or a backhand blow, or to tell anything interesting about the height of the assailant. Apparently the victim fell to her left and struck the left side of her head, near the temple, on a large ceramic planter. Death was from a cerebral hemorrhage of a previously undetected aneurysm in the middle meningeal artery. Coroner says that death would very likely have occurred within ten or fifteen minutes."

"Janet indicated that you ruled out rape."

"That's right. A sexual assault evidence kit was turned in and showed no signs of sexual assault. Of course, you don't know what the intentions were of the person who hit her—it's possible he could have gotten scared off when he hit her too hard. But if we're talking intended rape, it's doubtful the guy was a stranger. There were no signs of B and E. The victim had a chain lock on the door. It's a little hard to believe she would have admitted a stranger at one A.M."

"What about burglary? Janet said the dresser drawers looked as if they had been searched. But you're saying there were no signs of breaking and entering."

"It could be that the person who killed her was looking for something; it could be that he was only trying to make it look that way. But if it's the first, I don't see it as a standard burglary. The house the victim and her daughter were renting was a small cottage; the car was in the driveway. Her sister was there until about nine P.M. and, as I said, spoke to her on the phone about eleven-thirty. What burglar would be idiot enough to go into a small house where the people are so obviously home? Plus there were some obvious things that should have been taken but weren't: a piece of jewelry that was fake but didn't look it, and a couple of hundred dollars in her purse."

"So it's likely it was someone she knew."

"Once we ruled out Tiny, we started in on the people close to her. Blake. Janet Kendall. We wondered a lot about an on-and-off boyfriend of the victim's. He's a pharmacist in town."

"His name wouldn't be Triplett, would it?"

"Yeah. You know him?"

"I just met him, that's all."

"We ran into some talk that he'd done designer drugs in pharmacy school, so we looked at him pretty hard. But as far as we could tell he'd been straight for years. Also, the word we got was that some of the off parts of the on-and-off relationship had to do with him disapproving of the victim taking drugs. In any case, we didn't find any evidence against him."

"Did he have an alibi?"

Deffinger shook his head. "No. Claims he was asleep in his apartment—alone. In addition to Triplett, we checked out a few old friends, a couple dates, a few of the people in CA, and some of the people the victim had partied with. Nothing. The only other serious possibility was a guy we could never find."

"What do you mean?"

"A guy Mrs. Schrader mentioned to her shrink. At Janet Kendall's request, Dr. Blake gave us a summary, and later a full copy, of his notes on the victim. In her last therapy session, just before she died, the victim talked about some mystery man she was getting involved with—someone she called 'Angel.' She talked a lot of stuff about how sweet and gentle he was, and how different he was from any other men she'd been with."

"That's it? No specifics?"

"No. It came up at the end of the session. Blake had the feeling that the victim was playing some kind of game with him—purposely holding things back. We looked for this Angel from every angle we could think of. The first thing we looked for was a Hispanic male, but Hispanic males didn't figure much in the victim's life, certainly none with that name. We looked at all the males she'd been associated with and looked for names, nicknames, name associations—anything that might connect with Angel. I even had an English teacher friend from the JC go over them with me. No luck."

"You said before that you were guessing some doper killed her."

"Yeah. And it could fit with the Angel thing, in a way. I don't know about you, but one of the things 'Angel' conjures up for me is some sixties leftover, all world peace and Eastern philosophy and needle tracks in his arm. Maybe he's the sweetest guy in the world when he's high, but he gets mean, maybe even schizo, when he's out of stuff."

"Janet said there were some day-old bruises on her sister's face."

"Yeah. It looked like she'd gotten smacked a couple of times. Maybe that's when the relationship started getting rough."

"So why does this guy kill her?"

"Who knows? Maybe he freaks out and thinks she's the Wicked Witch of the North. Maybe they were arguing over love. Or money. Or maybe that she wouldn't share her crack with him."

"That would fit with the search."

Deffinger dodged his head a bit. "Yes and no. There was that two hundred in her purse. And there were some prescription drugs in the medicine cabinet. You could argue that a doper would have taken those. But it's possible he was looking for some particular stash or bundle of cash she had—something attractive enough to make him forget the little stuff. Plus you tend to get a little antsy hanging around a dead body. Maybe he heard something that scared him."

"Like, say, the daughter waking up?"

"It's possible. It's also possible that he heard a backfire, or a couple of drunks walking by—it could have been a million things."

"Including the daughter waking up."

"You mean, like—maybe she got out of bed, and maybe she saw him, and maybe now she's having trances because she suddenly remembers him, and maybe it turns out that the police have been wrong all along because they put too much trust in one of their own?"

"It's a thought."

"I told you I'd look into it, Strickland. That's all I can do."

▽

15

I FOUND JANET sitting alone on the couch, her shoulders bent, her hands covering her face, her body shaking in silent sobs. I spoke her name. Her head jerked up, her tear-reddened face growing redder with embarrassment.

"Oh . . . you're . . . home," she said. She made little brushing motions at her eyes, like someone who has just walked into a cobweb. "I . . . uh . . . didn't hear the cab."

"I had him drop me off out on the street. What's wrong? Has Becky gotten worse?"

"No." Janet's voice was whispery and hoarse, her manner disconcerted and distracted. "She's . . . okay. She's asleep. Did you . . . uh . . . talk to the police?"

"Yes. They're going to take another look at Tiny."

"I'm . . . glad."

Janet had looked so pert and starched that morning, dressed in a beige blouse, dark green fitted skirt, and pearl earrings, her hair freshly washed and curled. Now her blouse and skirt seemed damp and deflated, as if her tearful misery had seeped out her pores into her clothing. Her hair shared in the collapse, and one of her earrings was missing. She looked exhausted.

"Becky's really doing okay?" I asked as I eased myself down onto the couch next to Janet.

"Uh-huh. She . . . uh . . . seemed to feel better once we . . . got home." Janet's fingertips flicked intermittently at her eyes and nose as if she were searching out a few last strands of web. "Especially after Dr. Blake came."

"Does she remember what happened today?"

"No. But she . . . seems clear about everything else."

"Did Dr. Blake try to jog her memory?"

Janet shook her head. "He wants her to . . . rest first."

"I'm glad you got hold of Blake okay."

"He came right over—canceled two patients. Don't know . . . what we'd do without him."

"How're you doing? You don't look like you're feeling so good."

"I'm okay," she said, in words I could barely hear. "I'm just . . . kind of tired."

She gave me a small smile that seemed somehow to bring forth from inside her an opposite reaction, spilling tears out of her eyes. Immediately she turned her face away from me.

"I'm sorry," she said. "Sometimes I just . . . get so afraid . . . that Becky's not going to make it."

She put a hand quickly to her face. I reached out my hand and put it on her shoulder. She leaned against the hand, so I opened up my arms, and she leaned against me. I put my arms around her as she began to cry. I could feel her body relax as she gave in to the tears, but almost at once it began to stiffen again, and she pulled away.

"I don't think this . . . is . . . such a good idea," she whispered, her eyes not meeting mine.

"All right."

"We're in such close quarters here. I wouldn't want you to . . . I mean I couldn't handle any kind of a relationship right now. Not that you . . . I'm sorry . . . I'm just not putting this—"

"It's okay, Janet. You don't have to explain yourself to me. Is there a box of tissues I can get for you?"

"There," she whispered, gesturing vaguely in what I took to be the direction of the bathroom just ahead of us. But as I started to get up, she put a restraining hand on my arm. "No . . . better wash my face."

When Janet returned a few minutes later, with only vague improvements in her face and hair, I said, "Janet, I don't want to do anything that will make you feel uncomfortable having me here. But for the record, that hug was meant to be friendship, nothing more. Look at me: I'm thirty pounds underweight, my right leg's weak and spastic, I've got a hole in my skull, my head's shaved, I'm wearing a ridiculous wig, and I've got a face full of stubble. It never occurred to me that I would be taken for a seducer."

Janet gave me a small smile. "You don't look that—"

"Wait," I said, holding up a hand. "Maybe I put it wrong. I'm not fishing for compliments. I wouldn't believe one if I got it. Let me put it another way: I feel like shit. Half the time I'm like a cranky, crippled old man. I feel like I have no energy, no physical strength, no coordination, no . . . resources inside me. The world feels threatening to me, and I feel like I have no way to fight it off. I'm keyed up all the time and sometimes downright scared. I'm fussy and self-conscious, and I don't like myself a whole lot. The absolute last thing I expect or want right now is a physical relationship with anyone. I'm grateful for your help, and I've enjoyed your company. I'm sorry for all your troubles, and if I can help by listening or giving advice, I'm happy to. I'd like to be friends, or at least friendly. But that's all."

As I spoke I could see Janet relaxing, softening. I realized that inadvertently, in spite of my sincerity, or perhaps partly because of it, I was engaging in several of the world's more effective seduction techniques—the sympathy ploy, the expression of noninterest, and the promise to keep a respectful distance. I knew the latter well because I had used it, not so inadvertently, with my wife Katie when we were first dating. She'd been a little nervous about my wanting to touch her, feeling as if I might be trying to push her into bed. I told her I didn't think that's what I was doing, but in any case, I'd agree not to push sex on her if she'd relax a bit about more casual physical contact. She relaxed all right: About six hours later we ended up in bed together, she having "seduced" me. It was a memory we had laughed about a lot when we were first married. Before we stopped laughing altogether.

I was sure I didn't want a sexual relationship in my current physical and mental condition. I was also certain that Janet wouldn't want such a relationship with a wreck like me. But in case I had misjudged all that, in case that expression on her face was any more than sympathy, it might be better to put a more definite obstacle in the path.

"Also," I said, "I'm kind of waiting on someone."

"What do you mean?"

I told her a bit about Charlie—how we'd met not too long ago while I was on a case in central California, how she'd been the first woman I'd really been attracted to since my wife's death. I found myself struggling to convey the attraction Charlie had for me: how she seemed at once to be both a mature woman and a freckle-faced tomboy, how she combined sensitivity and intelligence with a hillbilly earthiness and a sometimes crude sense of humor. I told her too about Charlie's daughter, Julie, with her pigtail and leg brace, about how gutsy she was—told about her beating the boys at bike races and beating me at cards. I don't know if I described the two of them well, but I could feel myself smiling as I tried.

I felt the smile die, though, as I told Janet about the struggles Charlie and I had had together—trying to keep our long-distance relationship going, trying to free ourselves from our pasts and find something new with each other. More than anything, the fault had been mine: I'd had so much trouble shaking those dark moods that seemed to be a hangover from my wife's death, and when the moods had come, I hadn't been able to respond to Charlie as I should have.

"We've been fighting awfully hard to make it work, and maybe we both got kind of tired. We decided—well, actually, she decided—that we ought to cool it for a while, see how we felt about the whole of it. I don't know what's going to happen. I'm kind of waiting to see."

"You should have called her after you were hurt," said Janet.

"I didn't want her coming to see me for that reason," I said. I paused, hearing some critic in the back of my mind. "Maybe I would have given in if it had been just that. But right now Charlie and Julie are back in Detroit, because Charlie's favorite grandfather is dying. It just would have been too much of a mess if I'd called."

"They sound like nice people," said Janet. "I hope it works out for you."

"Thank you. What about you? Any romantic interest in your life right now?"

"No. With Becky to take care of, there just doesn't seem to be time." She seemed to hear her own mental critic, then said: "That's not really the truth. Or at least it's not the whole of it. My divorce was really hurtful; even though it was a long time ago, it's knocked most of the interest out of me. Actually I did date some, after the worst of the mourning for Ann and the worst of Becky's troubles were over—before Becky's troubles started up again. But the dates didn't go very well, and I guess they just confirmed my lack of interest. Now . . ." She shrugged.

"What happened with the divorce? Or is that too personal?"

"It is kind of personal, but . . . it wouldn't seem right not to tell you after the kinds of things you told me. My husband's name was John Kendall the Third. To me that name sounds strong and sophisticated, but John wasn't either of those things. His father was—his mother too, in her way. They're a pretty prominent family here in Ocean Point—the kind of people who make a big fuss over family. John was shy, kind of weak, I guess, but cute, gentle, kind. And interesting, at least to me. He read a lot; he wanted to teach some day. I was a bookworm myself, the shy, awkward sister of the beautiful, wild, and popular Ann Walsh. John was even shyer than I was, and that made me bolder than I would have been normally. He was the first boy I had ever approached. We became friends first, then fell very much in love. We were the kind of out-of-it couple that people tease a bit, but can also afford to be happy for, since neither one of the couple is someone anyone else wants. His parents weren't happy for us, though. I wasn't the kind of girl they wanted John to marry: They wanted someone prettier and more sophisticated—someone they could show off to their friends, someone who would fit into their circle."

"They gave you a rough time, huh?"

"Not at first. I guess they figured we weren't going to last as a couple. But as John and I continued dating exclusively throughout college, as we talked about getting married, they put a lot of pressure on John, then later, openly, on me, to break up the relationship. John wasn't strong enough to stand up to them the way he should have, but he loved me, and didn't want to give me up, and as a matter of fact, he wasn't strong enough to stand up to me either. It became a contest between me and his family, and on the marriage issue I won. It bothered me that John couldn't stand up for me on his own, but he was a sweet guy, and I figured that he'd mature in time, and that once we were married, everything would be all right. In fact, when his parents found out that John wouldn't give in, they seemed to give in enough to make the best of it, concentrating on fixing me up so I would be more acceptable. I guess I went along out of gratitude that they had conceded the marriage and in the hope that everything would turn out all right.

"Maybe it would have, except for one thing. We found out after a year and a half that I couldn't have children. When John's parents found out, they had a fit. They pulled out all the guns—inheritance threats, made-up stories about me, and not-so-subtle insults that made me uncomfortable enough to bite back."

"Why didn't you just adopt?"

Janet gave an unhappy laugh. "No way. Kendalls are made, not adopted: The sacred name of 'John Kendall the Fourth' was not about to be bestowed on some foundling. They were pretty rough. I tried to fight back but just ended up looking bad, partly because their provocations were more subtle than my retaliations, partly because, without John standing up for me, I was made to look like the troublemaker in the group. John and I got to arguing, which was just what his parents wanted, and eventually the marriage fell apart.

"I tried to tell myself that it was all for the good—that if John didn't want me that badly, or if he wasn't strong enough to be a good partner, that I was well rid of him. But none of that helped much. We'd been a couple for almost ten years: He was the closest friend I'd ever had, and the only lover. He was very special to me, and losing him just kind of took the heart out of me. Then, about a year later, Ann was killed and Becky became ill, and the whole world just seemed to go to hell. Caring for Becky is the one thing that got me through. I've always considered myself a fairly strong person, even a fairly optimistic one. But I'll tell you: If Becky doesn't make it, being alive isn't going to hold a lot of interest for me."

Janet gave me a bleak look, then almost immediately shook her head and forced a laugh.

"Just listen to me. I can't believe myself—whining this way. I guess I really am tired."

"Everyone else whines," I said. "Why shouldn't you take your turn? It might do you some good."

She gave me a wan smile. "Maybe because I figure that if I really started, I might never stop. What would you say to some tea? Or some coffee, if you'd like—I picked up some."

"Coffee'd be good."

"And I'll bring out some fruit and cookies. Suddenly I'm starving."

"Can I help?"

"No, just sit."

Janet got up from the couch, then turned to face me.

"Thanks for listening to me," she said. "And talking with me."

"My pleasure."

"It really is nice to have some adult company. Especially such good company. I think maybe I've cut myself off too much. Maybe I should try to get out more, meet some people—not just the same old coworkers at school who I can't really talk to for fear that what I say will get around."

"It must be hard to be a single parent whose only focus is a child. Especially a sick child. I'd think the energy would keep draining out of you and never get renewed."

"I didn't think that was so before," she said. "But maybe now my energy's on empty." She hesitated a moment. "Friends?"

She held out a hand to me in an uncertain, quasi-handshake gesture. I reached up and squeezed her hand gently—just once. "Friends," I said, and then she turned and went into the kitchen.

Just as she returned a few minutes later with a tray, the phone rang. She put the tray down and went to answer the phone. When she came back to the living room, she was looking at me with concern.

"Did something happen to you today?" she asked. "Did you get sick?"

"Why?"

"That was Father Matthew on the phone. He said you'd gotten sick earlier. He was calling to find out how you were."

"That was nice of him. I hope you told him I was fine."

"I told him that you looked fine, but that you hadn't said anything at all about it." She looked at me with mild reproach. "Why didn't you tell me? For that matter, why didn't you call me when it happened?"

"Because next to Becky's problem, it was nothing, and you had all you could handle. Besides, I was okay."

"You felt sick?"

"It was just an anxiety attack. I've had them before. The accident seems to have brought them on again."

"That's understandable. You know, if you ever feel you need any help, you could go see Dr. Blake. Or ask him to recommend someone."

"Thanks, but I've got a therapist in Santa Cruz—also a nice guy—who helped me before. If things get rough, I'll go back and see him."

"Just let me know. I'd be happy to give you a ride to Santa Cruz. I've taken some sick leave to be with Becky more, so I'll have free time."

"I don't think it will be necessary for me to see him, but I appreciate the offer."

I drank some coffee and then asked Janet if she knew Father Matthew well.

"Not real well. I met him through Ann years ago, and I run into him now and then. He's nice: He always asks about Becky. He and Ann were sort of friends: They'd been to high school together."

"Did you know him in high school?"

"Just a little bit—through Ann. He was a strange young man. It was as if he'd stepped out of the Middle Ages—all that darkness and intensity—renouncing the flesh for the world of the spirit. He was a real oddity among all those California sun-and-fun airheads. He was nice, though, and really bright. Ann had a class with him, and he helped her with some homework problems, and she got kind of intrigued by him. She liked to talk to him sometimes, especially when she'd get a little down. I think she felt safe with him because he wasn't after her the way the other boys were. I remember thinking, though, that she was being a little too casual with him. He was a boy after all, with the usual hormones, and I couldn't believe he didn't have just a little bit of a crush on her. Anyway, he went on to become a priest, and they remained friends of sorts and would talk now and again."

"Was your sister religious?"

"Not in high school. But when she was younger. She and I were both raised Catholics. That was my mother's doing: My father wasn't religious, but he agreed to let my mother raise us Catholics. My mother was one of those liberal Catholics who disagree with this and disagree with that: Finally she disagreed with so much that she lost the point. We all stopped going to church by the time Ann and I were in late elementary school. I don't know: Maybe more of it stuck with Ann—if only in a kind of emotional way. Maybe that was part of the reason that she and Matthew became friendly in high school."

"Father Matthew said that your sister and Becky started coming to church some time before your sister died. He said she was 'searching.' He didn't seem to know if she was serious or not."

"I doubt if she knew either," said Janet. "She was starting to fall apart before she gave up the drugs, and she was looking for anything she could find to hold herself together. It depended on her mood, and her moods were pretty erratic. One minute it would be the church, the next minute some Eastern thing, the next minute romance, and the next minute her drugs. She was doing what she had to do. I just wish she hadn't gotten Becky involved."

"What do you mean?"

"I mean taking the child to church. Not that that would have been bad in itself—just the opposite. But Ann could get into such morbid moods, and Catholicism can really feed that—the bleeding heart of Jesus and that sort of thing. And I can imagine how intense and dark her talks with Father Matthew could have gotten. I don't think a five-year-old needed anything like that."

"While we're talking about your sister, I wanted to ask you about that pharmacist—Triplett."

"John. What about him?"

"Deffinger mentioned today that he was your sister's boyfriend just before she died."

"He was and he wasn't. They dated. They were intimate. But it was a lopsided relationship. He was crazy about her. He had been for a long time. But Ann wasn't about to commit herself to anyone. I think she'd be with him when she felt she needed a safe place, and then when she'd get 'up' again she'd be off partying with someone else. I know it hurt him, the way Ann treated him. I also know it hurt him to see what the drugs were doing to her. They had a lot of arguments over that. I was hoping that with Ann finally off drugs, she'd come to her senses about a lot of things, and she and John could work things out. He would have been good for her."

"You think he's a good person, then?"

"Yes. He's a sweet guy. And very responsible."

"He seems to be in love with you."

Janet flushed slightly. "I know. I wish he wouldn't be. A while back I wondered if I could feel romantically about him. Maybe I even tried to make myself feel that way. But I don't think I can. Also—I don't know—maybe in the back of my mind it feels kind of creepy—the idea of being with someone my sister was with. And maybe wondering too if he's just trying to find her in me."

Janet and I were silent for a moment. Then I said:

"Well, look, if we can't get you fixed up with the pharmacist, at least we can make sure that you get out of this house and have a little fun. You owe it to yourself, and you owe it to Becky: If you keep pushing yourself toward depression by focusing on nothing but her illness, you're not going to be in much shape to help her."

"That's not necessary. I'll be fine. I just—"

"It *is* necessary. I'll tell you what. Why don't you and I go out on a friendly date this week—grab a bite to eat, maybe catch a movie. It might do us both some good. That is, if you don't mind taking a date from Rent-A-Wreck."

Janet laughed. "I don't mind at all. Okay. Sounds like fun."

"How about tomorrow evening?"

"Tomorrow evening won't work. The only baby-sitter I'll trust with Becky is out of town for two days. I know because tomorrow afternoon there's a wedding shower I was supposed to go to, and I tried to get the woman to sit. How about Friday? There's a British film opening that should be good."

"It's a date. But look—why don't you go ahead and do what you were planning to do tomorrow and let me baby-sit."

Janet gave me a mildly stunned look over which a cartoon dialogue bubble saying, "Who? *You?*" would have been perfect. But, of course, she was too polite to let that look linger. In its place came the friendly brush-off look.

"That's really nice of you, Dave, but I really couldn't ask that of you in your condition."

"You're not asking. I'm offering."

"I couldn't really—"

"Janet, I know how to baby-sit. I'll make up some sardine sandwiches and read her *The Brothers Karamazov,* and we'll just be fine."

"I don't—"

"I'm kidding. We'll watch "Sesame Street" together, and I'll help her learn her alphabet."

"Becky hasn't—"

"It's another joke. Look, Janet, do you trust me with your niece or not?"

"I—" Janet broke off and laughed. "I guess it would be pretty stupid to say no after what you did for her."

"Then it's all settled. Becky may not count tomorrow as one of the more memorable days of her life, but at least she won't starve to death. Not if she likes sardine sandwiches, anyway."

▽

16

IN THE DREAM the machinery exploded in slow but deadly motion, hunks of metal hurling through the metal screen, everything around us shaking as in some enormous earthquake. Something knocked me to the ground, dazing me, and it was a moment before I could look for Amy. I saw that she was across the landing, near the far stairs, a huge fissure beginning to open in the ground beneath her. She cried out for me to help her, but I must have been hurt, it was so hard for me to move now.

As I struggled to get up, my body began to grow dark, began to give off that awful stench. By the time I'd gotten to my feet, I had become large and clumsy, so that I stumbled as I tried to walk. I struggled toward Amy, but as I got to her and reached out my hand, her eyes filled with terror, and she started screaming, "No, please, don't!"

I woke with a start, still half submerged in the dream, confused by the change in its ending, confused by my impression that I could still hear screaming. Then I realized it was Becky I was hearing. I pushed myself off the couch, where I must have dozed off after Becky had gone to her room for a nap. I stumbled before I remembered my bad leg, then grabbed my cane and limped toward her bedroom.

Becky was thrashing around under the covers, her face wild with fright, screaming, "No, Mama, no." I wasn't quite sure how I should wake her—I was afraid that shaking her might just accentuate her fear, that my being too close might startle her when she woke. I tried calling her name, telling her that it was all right, that she was just dreaming. When that didn't take effect, I reached out a hand and patted the side of her shoulder.

She came awake—or at least half-awake—saw me, seemed afraid of me, sat up, and pulled away, pressing her back against the headboard of her bed. "Who are . . . ?" she began, then seemed to recognize me, which diminished her fear a bit but obviously gave her no comfort.

"Where's Janet?" she demanded in a near hysterical voice, her head swinging in different directions in apparent search. "I want Janet."

"She's not here, Becky, remember? She went to a wedding shower."

"Call her—please!"

I glanced at my watch. "I'll call her and leave a message, but she won't get it for another forty-five minutes. She's somewhere shopping."

"I can't wait." The words came out violently in a half scream, half sob. "Something awful's happening. Call Dr. Blake. *Please*."

"All right, I will."

"Now!" she screamed. "Please!"

"Okay, okay."

I hobbled my way to the kitchen, where I knew Blake's number was posted next to the wall phone. I got his answering service and was told that the doctor was at the hospital with a patient and that they would get the message to him as quickly as possible. I also called the number of the shower and left a message for Janet. Then I hurried back to Becky's bedroom, feeling all keyed up, not sure how I was going to handle this.

Becky was pacing back and forth next to her bed, her face twisted up with fearful crying. She was pulling at her hair as she paced, and she seemed to be shivering just a little.

"Is he coming?" she asked in a teary voice.

"Yes, Becky, as soon as he can."

"He's not coming right now?"

"It won't be all that long. They're getting a message—"

"I can't wait," she cried, bursting into tears. "I feel awful, I'm so scared, oh, God. . . ."

Her fright was building into hysteria. She looked so frantic, and her pacing was picking up speed, and she was yanking at her hair as if she might really hurt herself. If this went on much longer, I'd have to call an ambulance.

"Becky, listen to me," I said. "I know you're scared. But you're just making yourself more scared. If you'll stop pacing for a minute, sit, and talk to me, you'll feel better. I know you will."

My words had no effect. The pacing and the hair pulling and the hysterical look continued as before.

"Becky, I know what you're going through. I've gone through it myself. It feels awful, but nothing bad is happening to you, except that you're feeling afraid. If you'll tell yourself that and try to relax a little, you can handle the fear. I know, really I do."

"You don't know!" sobbed Becky.

"Don't you remember the hospital—how scared I got?"

"That wasn't the same. You were sick."

"There were other times. A few years ago my wife and baby died. . . ."

"They did?" she asked in a quivery voice.

Becky's pacing had slowed a beat, and her hands had frozen for a moment in the process of pulling her hair. If I wasn't any good at reassuring, maybe at least I could distract her.

"Yes, they did," I said.

"How?"

"The baby died of a disease that only little babies get. And my wife got so sad from missing her that she just sort of gave up. Losing them made me so sad. Night after night I went through what you're going through now. But I made it, kiddo, and so will you."

"What did you do?"

That she was talking was a victory, but a very small one.

Becky still looked awful. Her face was twisted into a grimace that was like a frozen sob. Her hands were no longer yanking at her hair, but they had stopped in a tense pulling position with the hair taut. She wasn't exactly pacing, but her feet were fidgeting as if she were about to. She was like a time bomb that had been delayed but not defused.

"At first I just got scared—the way you are. I was sure I was going to die or go crazy or some other awful thing. Then I started talking to someone the way you talk to Dr. Blake, and he explained to me how the fears weren't real—they were just part of being afraid. And that was fine except that when the fear came again it was so strong, it was like I couldn't help believing the fear rather than him. Or maybe I believed him, but even if I knew I wasn't going to die or go crazy, feeling afraid felt so bad that I would do anything to make the feeling stop—like running home to hide, or calling the doctor, or taking a pill, or whatever it took."

Becky was still suspended in that half hysteria, and all I could think to do was to keep talking.

"Then—I don't know—I just got tired of being scared. I told myself I wasn't going to run anymore. I heard you telling Janet one time, after you'd had a bad dream, about how hard it was to not give in, and it is, and sometimes I couldn't do it. I used to get anxiety attacks the worst in restaurants—I would just get so scared—I'd start sweating, and I'd feel dizzy, and it would seem like something horrible was about to happen—and sometimes I couldn't help it, I just had to race out of the restaurant right in the middle of eating. But I kept trying, and sometimes I made it through, and then it got a little easier the next time, and little by little I got less and less afraid. You can do it too, Becky. I know you can. You've just got to stand there and fight."

I watched, not knowing which way it was going to go, having just about run out of things to say. Slowly Becky's feet stopped fidgeting, and her hands dropped from her hair, and her face lost its contortions. As she stood there in her jeans, sweatshirt, and socks, her body started shivering—

big shivers, as if she were standing barefooted on a sheet of ice.

"You know," I said, "these things are easier if you get a hug."

After a moment Becky made an outward gesture with her arms, a movement inhibited by her own trembling. I led her over to the edge of the bed, sat her down with me, leaned her against me, and put my arms around her. I could feel her shivering against me, could hear her teeth chattering. I had gone through these anxiety spasms from time to time myself—violent energy surging up beyond the ability of the nervous system to work it off.

"It's all right, Becky, it's all right," I kept saying. "Just hang in there—it'll be over in a little bit."

I kept holding her, and patting her back, and saying soothing things, and gradually her shivering diminished. Then she began to cry, working off the last of that energy in tears. She felt like such a small, thin, fragile thing against me, the bones in her back so prominent against my fingers. I had the irrational thought that I could hurt her by holding her too tightly, and I loosened my hold a bit.

"Better?" I asked when the tears had stopped and Becky was still.

She nodded. Just then the phone rang.

"I'd better get it, Becky. It might be Janet or Dr. Blake. I'll be right back."

Janet's bedroom was just a few feet away from Becky's, and I took the call in there. It was Blake.

"Strickland? What's wrong with Becky?"

"She woke up screaming from her nap and started acting hysterical. Janet's not here, and Becky insisted I call you. Since then, though, I've managed to get her calmed down."

"I'm in a mess here at the hospital with an emergency case. I'm not going to be able to get there for at least an hour. I could call in a psychiatric emergency team if you think the situation is serious enough."

"No. I think she'll be okay. I could bring her to your office later if you'd like. I was practicing with the car this morning, and I found I have enough leg control now to drive."

"Thanks, but I have to head in your direction anyway when I'm done. I think it'll be easier for Becky if she just stays there."

After I'd hung up the phone, I went back into Becky's bedroom. She was sitting on the edge of her bed, hugging herself, her eyes closed. She looked tired and miserable, but not frightened, and her body was still. I sat down next to her and put one arm around her.

"How you doin'?" I asked.

She gave a small shrug.

"That was Dr. Blake. He's got an emergency case at the hospital, but he'll be along in an hour or so. I told him I thought you'd be okay till then."

Becky just sat there, not agreeing, but not disagreeing either.

"Did you have that dream again?" I asked.

"Yes." The word came out in a soft, dry sob. "It's awful."

"Do you want to tell me about it?"

Becky shook her head.

"I have an awful dream I keep having," I said. "It's about my sister. She was a real unhappy little girl, and she got hurt real bad when she was young. In the dream I keep trying to save her, but I can't. I had a dream like that about my wife for a while after she died."

"At least they don't try to kill you when you try to help them."

"That's what your mother does?"

"I'm just trying to help her, you know. She looks really hurt—her head's all beat up, and there's blood on her face, and her neck's all twisted around. I try to wake her up, and she does wake up, but then she gives me this horrible look, like she really hates me, and then she comes after me to kill me."

"That sounds really scary, Becky. In the dream, where's your mother when you find her?"

"I don't know. A room. A bedroom. In some kind of house."

"Your house?"

"I guess."

"It's not a house you remember?"

Becky shook her head.

"How does the dream start?" I asked.

"I'm in my bed, I guess. There's this awful noise, and everything starts shaking, and I can't make it stop, and I'm afraid my mom's going to get hurt—and I climb out of my crib and run into her room, but I'm too late, she's already hurt."

"She's lying on the floor?"

"Uh-huh. I get down next to her on the floor, and I try to shake her so she'll wake up, and then her eyes open, and I start feeling real happy—you know?—except then she looks at me like she hates me, and she says she's going to kill me, her baby, and I say, 'No, Mama, please,' but she won't listen, and she starts to get up—it's horrible!"

Becky shivered once and pressed her head against my shoulder. I gave her a one-armed hug and waited. After a few moments, I felt her relax.

"What happens then, Becky?"

"I try to run away, but I can't—all the buildings and things keep getting bigger and bigger, and I keep trying to run faster, but it's like I'm not going anywhere."

"You said buildings—where are you when you're running?"

"I don't know. It's like some city or something, and it's too big—everything has gotten big except for me. I can hear my mother running behind me, getting closer, and I'm so scared. I run into this church, and I think maybe I'm safe, but then I see my mother's there and she looks all horrible—there's blood all over her and she's got this big knife—and I try to run, but I trip over this little kid, and he's lying on the floor all covered with blood, and I can tell he's dead, and then there's another, and another, and I know my mother's killed them all and now she's going to kill me. There's someone else there in the church—some man—and I ask him to help me, but he doesn't, I don't know why, and then I feel my mother grab me, and I start screaming, and then I wake up."

Though Becky had told her dream with a rushed urgency, the emotion in her voice had been gradually lessening, as if the words had somehow taken on a life of their own. Now she yawned. The anxiety seemed to have run its course, and whatever limited sedatives her body could offer were now kicking in.

"This man in the church, Becky—do you know him?"

She shook her head. "I don't see him really."

"Are you sure it's a man?"

Becky shook her head. Another yawn came out.

"Sleepy, huh?" I asked.

"Uh-huh."

"That's good."

I pulled her close to me again for one last hug before putting her back in bed. Again it occurred to me how fragile she was. But this time the intrusive thought didn't pass quietly through my mind—it set off all the alarms. Suddenly, irrationally, my mind went into full-blown panic, full of the fear that I was going to hurt this girl. A voice in the back of my head was crying, *Run, Becky, run*.

I don't believe my body tensed or trembled, but only because I summoned every bit of willpower I had to hold still, to keep any of my fear from showing itself to Becky. I gave her a quick pat on the back to reassure her in case she had sensed anything at all, then stood and hid behind a brisk friendliness. The foremost thing in my mind was to get the hell out of that room.

"Go ahead and get back into bed, Becky. I'll go . . . fix us some hot chocolate."

I turned and left without waiting for the girl's response. I rushed toward the kitchen, my body trembling, my head full of voices that sounded like a crowd in total panic. I swung the kitchen door shut behind me and leaned against one of the counters. Both my hands were fists, and I ground them against the tiles.

"Goddamn it, stop," I told myself in a fierce whisper. "This is all bullshit. You know it is. Stop it!"

Cursing myself didn't help. I tried comforting myself, but what had worked with Becky didn't work with me. I'd never felt anything like this before—this engulfing fear that I might hurt a child. Maybe what was happening was more than anxious fantasy. Maybe my mind was really breaking down. My therapist had always been adamant in reassuring me about my sanity, but how could I take that seriously after what Blake had said the other day: that no matter what optimism you voice to the patient, you never really know what's going to happen. God, I'd been basing my confidence on statements even the therapists didn't believe. Anyway, even if my therapist had been right before, maybe I'd suffered some sort of brain damage in the accident and that had altered the whole equation.

I felt a tremendous surge of panic, a sense of safe boundaries giving way all around me. I realized I had to stop that kind of thinking or it would just lead to disasters and self-fulfilling prophecies. *Fight,* I told myself. *Stick to the old techniques: They've gotten you through so far, and they will again.*

I knew I had to go back into Becky's room—just as once I'd had to go back into restaurants—just as later I'd have to go back out onto crowded streets. I quickly heated some milk, got out the cocoa powder, and made up two cups of hot chocolate. I put the cups on a small tray and took them back to Becky's room.

Becky had fallen asleep in a partial sitting position, her head slumped back and to the side against propped-up pillows. I realized as I saw her that I was relieved to find her asleep, in spite of my good intentions: I wouldn't have to test myself after all. I started to leave, but I noticed an adult-sized rocking chair there in the room; it occurred to me that I could give myself an easy, preliminary test—and maybe reassure myself a bit—by sitting in the chair and watching Becky for a while. It would also be a chance, perhaps, to observe my own reactions, to try to get some fix on what the fear of hurting her was all about. I set the tray down on top of a nearby bookcase, took one of the cups, and sat in the rocker. I leaned back, sipping chocolate, watching Becky.

She was sleeping peacefully now, with no hint of nightmare in her face, no hint of pain except for a slight redness around her eyes. Her face had the softness of deep relaxation, and her mouth held a slight smile. There was no sullenness, only sweetness. The masklike quality I had seen so often in her face was gone. She seemed much younger somehow, and I had the feeling that I was seeing traces of a much smaller and happier child. I wondered in passing whether there is any sense in which our youngest selves are preserved intact in us—or whether, like ancient stone houses, they've been dismantled to build new dwellings, whether, like old cars, they've been sold for parts. I thought of the end of Amy's life, when everything had turned so bad for her, and wondered whether even then the small child I had loved and played with might have existed in Amy somewhere—perhaps still playing in its own memory world.

Thinking of Amy, I felt myself grow sad. I remembered her as she had been at about age five, with that crippled leg of hers that some incompetent doctor had set wrong and others had never been able to make right. I would have been about six when she was five. I remembered how seeing Amy with that leg had saddened me so, and frightened me—and later on embarrassed me. I had tried to fight those feelings for her sake, but gradually the feelings had won, pulling me away from her. Thinking of that now, I felt a faint wave of self-disgust. If only I'd stayed closer to her, loving and trying to protect her, perhaps I could have made the difference.

I looked at Becky, thinking how vulnerable each child is, how endangered. I felt a little nauseated as I imagined how startled and scared she would be if I were to reach out now and slap her hard across the face. I felt myself start, realizing that the thought made no sense unless it meant I wanted to hurt her—but I didn't want to, I would never hurt her, I would kill myself first. Suddenly I was filled with cold terror and violent self-loathing. I could feel my body trembling. *Stay,* I told myself, *fight it*—but I could not. I stood up, reached for my cane, and limped out of the room on my knotted-up leg, the cup rattling in my hand.

I was sitting on the couch, my head in my hands, feeling hung over and shaky from the violent bout of feelings. I heard Becky's door open, and I looked up. Dr. Blake took a step out of the room, leaned back in to catch something Janet was saying, called good-bye to Becky, then came out into the living room. I stood up and forced a smile, but felt transparent: I imagined that the terrible things inside me were on display for him, slithering before his eyes like snakes in a glass cage.

"Are you all right?" he asked, his face concerned. "You don't look so good."

"I guess baby-sitting is harder than I thought it would be," I said, trying to force a light tone into my voice.

Blake laughed. "I've always found that to be true myself." He cocked his head at me, smiling. "I want to know what's going on here, Mr. Strickland. I come here to talk to my patient about her problems, and all she wants to talk about is *your* problems. Are you using a new therapy technique I should know about?"

I tried to return his smile. "Just the old so-you-think-that-you've-got-problems technique. Or maybe we're-all-in-the-same-boat. I don't know—I was just rattling on, trying to reassure her, or distract her, or whatever."

"Whatever you did, it worked. By the way, I think you just made yourself a new friend."

"I'm glad," I said, but what I felt were reverberations of fear.

Blake looked at me for a moment. He was still smiling, but his eyes had turned serious. Again I had the feeling that his eyes could penetrate me, could see those violent thoughts I'd had toward Becky.

"How are you really doing?" he asked. "From what Becky said, and from some things that Janet added, I take it you're having a tough time of it."

"Yeah, I'm not doing that great. I seem to be on edge most of the time, and sometimes I get really terrified."

"That's not unusual after an experience like the one you've been through. If you decide you'd like to see someone around here—for medication or just to talk—I'd be happy to give you some names."

"I appreciate that. But I've got a therapist in Santa Cruz I like. I think I'll call him."

"Can't hurt." He gave me a smile of encouragement. "I know you'll do fine."

Foolishly—even though a short while back I'd told myself how little such reassurance was worth—I felt better.

"Well, I'd better be going," said Blake.

I wanted to let him go, then escape to my room, where I'd be safe from the fear of hurting Becky. But there was something I knew I should do, and I forced myself to do it.

"I'll walk you out," I said softly. "I need to ask you some questions about Becky."

I took my cane, squeezed out between the coffee table and couch, and at Blake's silent invitation, limped in front of him toward the door. Because my nerves were still shaky, and my body tight, I had more trouble walking than usual; a couple of times I seemed on the verge of losing my balance. As I struggled along, the thought occurred to me that Blake might think I was drunk. I told myself this thought was absurd—Blake knew about my injury, knew I had just been through an ordeal with Becky—but some other part of my mind, speaking with the calm reason of an urbane paranoiac, kept taking exception.

Just because you're crippled doesn't mean you're not drunk, reasoned the voice. *I'm sure many cripples drink to help them live with their condition. Also, you didn't tell Blake how terrified you got when you were with Becky—you couldn't, of course, he'd have to lock you up, or at least kick you out. But because you didn't tell him, how is he to understand your red eyes, the flush in your face, your mussed hair? He must think you're drunk. What else could he think?*

Though I tried to ignore the voice, I found myself making a special effort to walk steadily as I descended the front porch steps. But the effort at control tightened me up all the more, and, as the voice correctly noted, made things worse. At the bottom of the steps I gratefully took a seat on the two-foot-high cement block that served as a base for the outside lamp; the voice immediately suggested that sitting had been a mistake, that my sitting would be taken as evidence that I couldn't stand. Other voices joined in the dispute, presenting their arguments and counterarguments, producing one of those obsessive debates that made me want to reach inside my skull and scoop out globs of gray matter just to make it stop.

"I'm sure Janet must have told you about Becky's reaction to Tiny," I said. "I assume she discussed her suspicions as well."

I realized that I was enunciating my words carefully, as if to prove my sobriety. I silently cursed myself for my own stupidity.

"Janet said she thinks Becky recognized Tiny either from the beach or from the evening Ann Schrader was killed," said Blake. "She says the police are reopening their investigation."

"That last part may be optimistic," I said, forcing myself to speak normally. "One policeman will reluctantly—maybe casually—recheck an alibi he's sure is solid. I'm not certain we're going to get much from that direction."

The voices in my head were quieting down, as they usually did when I was engaged in conversation. But my mind was never fully engaged, at least not when I was feeling anxious, as I was now. I felt as if I were in the lighted second-floor sitting room of an otherwise darkened old house, chatting with a very proper guest, trying to pretend that nothing was wrong, all the while monitoring what seemed to be the sounds of violent people breaking in downstairs.

"What's your opinion about Tiny now?" asked Blake.

"I'm not sure. Sergeant Deffinger suggested that maybe the reason why Becky knew Tiny was that some kid had pointed him out to her. It seems Tiny's actually been back in town for several months. Deffinger's idea is that maybe Janet got Becky so worked up about Tiny that Becky panicked when she saw him up close. I'd like to have more information about that before forming a conclusion."

Blake was leaning against the front fender of his Mercedes, facing me, his arms folded across an expensive-looking brown sport coat woven with threads of rust and black. He shifted his loafered feet on the slippery gravel.

"I just asked Becky about that," he said. "Deffinger's been calling me trying to get an interview with Becky. I've been telling him it's too early, but I did promise that I'd ask Becky a few questions—which I did today. My provisional judgment is that Becky did not consciously know who Tiny was when the three of you ran into him the other day. I'm going to tell Deffinger that. But, as I say, that's only a provisional judgment. We'll know better when Becky's able to be questioned further."

"In that case, I'm leaning toward Janet's view. Except that I don't believe Becky recognized Tiny from the beach. I think that if her reaction has any real significance, it has to do with her mother's death. Have you gotten any indication from treating Becky that she might have seen someone the night her mother died?"

"No," said Blake. "But you've got to remember Becky has no conscious memories of that night. It's possible that her dreams contain memories, but those memories are all coded and distorted."

"Is there anything at all in the coded dream material that points toward Becky having seen the killer? Becky described her dream to me earlier, and I didn't see anything. What about you?"

"I'd have to say no again, though there was one element of the dream that did give me pause."

"The man in the church?"

"Yes," he said.

"Maybe I should have said 'person.' Becky used the word 'man' in describing the dream, but when I asked her about that, she wasn't sure."

"Becky's always used the word 'man' when reporting the dream to me. Most therapists consider the report of the dream to be as revealing as the dream itself. In any case, I have wondered about the figure in the church. However, I don't think there's nearly enough in the dream right now to justify thinking he is, or represents, the killer. The figure could represent a dozen other things. Maybe if the dream expands, we'll be able to tell better."

"Do you think that could happen? That the dream might grow to include more details?"

"It's certainly possible. They often do. Particularly if the events portrayed in the dream are coming closer to consciousness."

Blake shifted position on the fender, small stones crunching as he moved his feet. He glanced down at his folded arms, turning his left wrist slightly, taking a surreptitious look at his watch. I said:

"Janet told me you interpret the dream as representing a conflict between Becky's desire to have her mother come back to life, and Becky's fear that she'd be punished if that happened—the fear coming from Becky's feeling that her anger was responsible for her mother's death."

"It's a bit more complicated than that, but, yes, that's basically it. If that seems a little odd to you, remember that these dreams are coming from the wishes, perceptions, and fears of a young child who saw the world in a magical sort of way. They don't have to make rational sense."

"If your interpretation is correct, though, doesn't that

mean that Becky couldn't have seen her mother's killer? I mean, how could she possibly feel responsible and yet know that someone else was responsible?"

Blake thought about it. His right forearm hinged upward like a crane from his folded arms; his thumb and forefinger began pinching at the dark beard as if it were some sort of debris that had to be removed. After a few pinches, Blake said:

"My interpretation *could* mean that Becky didn't see her mother's killer, but it doesn't have to. I can think of at least two possible ways in which her own guilt and a memory of the killer could coexist in her mind. One: that she saw the man who killed her mother, but didn't understand that he, rather than she, was the killer. Or two: that her guilt registered in one part of her mind, and the recognition of the murder in another. The unconscious doesn't work by rational principles. It can believe contradictory things."

"The first possibility wouldn't fit with Tiny," I said. "If Becky didn't know him to be the killer, why would she be frightened by him?"

"Then you need to consider the second possibility. But remember, it's only a possibility. Other than Becky's reaction to Tiny—which is suggestive, but by no means definitive—there's absolutely no evidence that Becky saw her mother's killer."

Blake pushed himself away from the fender of the Mercedes and stood, straightening his coat. I said:

"Just one more thing. As dramatic as Becky's reaction to Tiny was, there are still two factors that make it difficult to believe that Tiny could be involved in this. One, of course, is that alibi. The other thing is, why on earth would Tiny ever go after Becky? What possible threat could she have posed for him? What could have set him off?"

"That, I'm afraid, is your area, not mine," said Blake.

"I'm not so sure. The only thing I can think of that might have gotten him nervous is the work you're doing with Becky. But how would he know about that?"

Blake shrugged. "It would have been easy for him to find out I was working with Becky. All he had to do was follow her. Or he could have heard talk. A lot of people around town know she's been having problems lately. She's had some very difficult moments at school. And everyone knows about her mother. What knowing that Becky was seeing me would mean to him, I wouldn't know. He certainly couldn't have found out what we were discussing." Blake looked at his watch again. "I'm sorry, but I really have to go."

We said good-bye, and Blake drove off. I leaned back against the lamppost, closing my eyes. I began to take slow, deep breaths, trying to soothe the dark, jittery fearfulness within me. Just as I was feeling the onset of calm, I was distracted by the grating sound of tires on gravel. I opened my eyes and saw the silver Mercedes coming back. As Blake got out of the car, I could see that there was excitement in his face.

"I thought of something while I was driving," he said as he walked around the car toward me. "I'm not sure it's relevant, but I thought I'd better tell you just in case."

"What?"

"A few weeks ago someone broke into our offices, poured gasoline over a drawerful of my files, and set the files on fire. One of the files belonged to a troubled young man who had been forced into counseling by the court and had recently been terminated. I was convinced at the time he was the one who had started the fire. And it probably was him. But I thought you ought to know: One of the files that got destroyed was Becky's."

"When was this?"

"A few weeks ago. I don't remember exactly. You could check the police report. Or call Louise, my secretary. She's the one who filled out all the insurance forms."

"Did it happen before the attack on Becky?"

"Let's see . . . I remember it was after Christmas—oh, yes, it was late January. It would have been a couple of weeks before Becky was attacked."

I realized in passing that I was on my feet, and I couldn't remember the act of standing. I adjusted the position of my cane to give myself better balance.

"You say it was a break-in?"

"Yes," said Blake. "Not that it would have been much of a trick. Our offices are in a one-story house we own in an area that got rezoned from residential to commercial. The house is pretty old. Whoever it was pried open a window at the back. The whole thing would have been pretty simple. We don't have any kind of alarm. The small backyard is packed with bushes and trees. Once a person got back there he wouldn't be noticed by anyone."

"Was anything taken?"

"No."

"Anything else destroyed?"

"No."

"Did the police investigate?"

Blake laughed. "They asked us a few questions and made out a report for insurance purposes, and that was that. I imagine they got a good laugh out of the whole thing—shrinks who coddle crazy people getting theirs, that sort of thing." He hesitated. "Maybe that's not quite true. I'm sure if I'd mentioned the boy they would have been happy to go after him. But I didn't want to get him into any more trouble than he was in already. Certainly not without any real evidence."

"You're saying maybe it wasn't him? Maybe it was someone after Becky's file?"

"Possibly. But now that I'm thinking about it, it doesn't really make much sense. Why burn files? Why not just read the one he wanted and then leave?"

"Maybe he spotted something in one of the files that he thought pointed to him—maybe some small item he figured you hadn't deciphered and wouldn't remember. That's just one possibility; I'm sure there are others. As for burning the files, of course that would make it almost impossible to know which one he was after. By the way, do you know for sure that Becky's file was still there among the burned ones?"

Blake thought for a moment. "No, I guess I'm not sure. Some of the files were just ashes."

"Let's suppose for a moment that Tiny did kill Ann Schrader, knew Becky was in therapy, and read her file. Was there anything in that file that might have gotten him excited? Anything about Ann Schrader's murder?"

"There were notes on the dream material and on possible interpretations. I'm afraid that the notes would have included some written speculation as to whether Becky had seen her mother's killer."

"I assume you're trying to get Becky to remember that night?"

"Yes."

"Would that be said in the notes?"

"Indirectly. But pretty obviously."

"So if the killer did read that file, it would be apparent that Becky was a threat."

"I suppose so."

"If Tiny did get hold of that file, it would help explain a lot. But it's a big if. And even if it's true, we're a long way from proving it."

▽

17

"I'M SCARED, MICHAEL. I'm really scared."

"I can see that, David. I'm sorry you're having such a bad time."

Dr. Michael Walachek, the Santa Cruz psychologist I'd seen after my wife's suicide, was a gentle hulk of a man, with unkempt dark hair and a doughy, thick-featured face that looked as if it had been molded by an art major who needed more practice. He was wearing jeans, an old saggy sport jacket, and a heavy white cotton turtleneck sweater; around his neck was a string of love beads he always wore, even on those few occasions when he was forced to wear a tie. His office was scruffy, funky, and disorganized, with papers and books sitting in piles on the floor, on a chair, and on a counter that also held some unwashed coffee cups and a small coffee machine. His walls were hung with posters from an old Monet exhibit in Los Angeles, from a Monterey Jazz Festival, and from some symphony in San Francisco. On his desk were two pathetic-looking plants that always seemed to need water and contrasted oddly with his Save the Planet coffee cup.

Michael—for so he insisted on being called by his patients—was sitting in his orthopedic desk chair, which he had swung away from his desk toward me. One of Michael's long legs, its ankle resting on the knee of the other leg, jutted out like a monstrous chicken wing. Occasionally he'd reach over and take a sip of the coffee that he'd offered and I'd refused. I was too wired up to want coffee, and anyway I found Michael's coffee almost undrinkable: Milk disappeared into it like light into a black hole. I was sitting in a large recliner meant to relax patients, but I was in no mood to recline, being anything but relaxed. I was perched on the front part of the recliner seat, my feet on the floor, my forearms resting on my thighs, my hands clenched together.

"Goddamn it, Michael: I get so sick at the thought I might have hurt that girl. I don't understand what's happening to me. What the hell is going on?"

"We'll find out, David," said Michael soothingly. "Tell me again what happened. Try to take it more slowly."

I went over it all for him again, in as much detail as I could remember. When I'd finished, Michael said:

"When you look back now over the whole episode, do you feel there was any time when Becky was actually in danger from you? Do you think there was ever a real chance you might have hurt her?"

Michael's voice and facial expression were casual, but his eyes were not. He seemed to be studying me. I had the sudden feeling I was on trial here. In fact, I was. I knew the laws that would require him to report immediately any client he believed might be a danger to another person. My first thought was to cover up. But I realized there was no point. If the worst was happening, I wouldn't be able to hide it indefinitely.

"I don't really know, Michael. What I *think* is, no, she wasn't in danger, as long as I stayed sane. The moment after the thought came, a voice in me said, I would kill myself first. Before I would hurt her, I mean. It's true, too. If I could, I'd kill myself before I'd hurt a child. What frightened me was the thought that I might go crazy and not know what I was doing—that I might go out of control."

"But you not only protected Becky from your aggressive impulses, you also protected her from any sign that you were afraid or upset. That seems like a lot of control to me."

"I had to leave the goddamn room."

"That was a kind of control," he said. "At any time did you feel that you might not be able to leave?"

"No. If you put it that way, I felt like I had the opposite problem—to keep myself from running out of there."

"So if you ever felt like that again, you could handle it the same way—by leaving the room."

"If I ever feel like that again, I'm going to handle it by getting the hell out of the house for good."

"That's one approach."

I felt annoyance form on my features. "Every time you say 'That's one approach,' what you mean is, it's the wrong approach."

"No, that's not what I mean. Only you can decide what you should do. But if you did feel safe enough to stay where you are, you'd have a better chance to learn something from the experience."

"That's the same damn thing you said to me about not running away from the panic attacks I used to have in restaurants. I kept trying to stick out the fear, and eventually I beat it—not to mention finally getting something to eat. But I never did *learn* anything in the sense you mean. I can make some guesses about what was going on, but I never did get anything like a catharsis, or a revelation, or great insight, or even a couple of crucial memories."

Michael shrugged. "You beat the fear. Wasn't that the most important thing?"

"Yes."

"I'd think the past would give you real confidence about doing that again. And who knows? If you keep digging down inside all that anxiety, you might just get your insight."

"If I get one, it damn well better not be one of those fortune-cookie insights like 'I'm terrific just the way I am.' I don't need to go through all this shit for some pop-psych cliché."

Michael laughed. I didn't.

"Look, Michael, what the fuck is going on? You tell me I'm suffering from some kind of posttraumatic stress. Okay. I can understand why I might be feeling anxious or depressed. But what the hell does this stuff with Becky—or that dream of Amy—have to do with posttraumatic stress?"

Michael was silent for a moment, considering the question. Idly one of his hands started fingering the love beads around his neck. As I watched him, it occurred to me in passing that I never had known what love beads were for.

"It's not so much the stress itself, as its side effects," he said. "Sometimes enough stress will break down the boundaries we've built up inside us, destroy the safe places we've made for ourselves. The memories and feelings we've tried to hide or avoid over the years surge up and overwhelm us. I think that's what's happening to you. Some of that also happened after your wife's death."

"But this feeling that I might hurt Becky—what the hell is that?"

"If you're asking me what it means specifically, I don't know. You're going to have to find that out for yourself. But I can give you a couple of general possibilities you can be thinking about. One, of course, is buried anger. We both know that there's a lot of anger deep down inside you; we discussed it during your first course of therapy. A person stores up enough anger, it's got to leak out somewhere—if not in action, then in thoughts and feelings."

"So maybe I think a nasty thought, or I snap at someone, or I throw something across the room. How come I'm not doing that instead of having anxiety attacks?"

"It all depends on how deep the anger is buried, and why, and how much childish mythology goes with it, and how much of your life has been built on avoiding it."

"But why toward Becky?"

"What do you think?"

"I don't know—maybe because she seems so vulnerable."

"That's a possibility."

"Or maybe it has something to do with the fact that she reminds me of Amy."

"I think that would definitely be worth looking at."

"But I don't see how that could fit with my dream," I said. "In the dream I'm not trying to hurt Amy, I'm trying to save her."

"From what?"

"From whatever it is that's after us."

"And what's that?"

"I don't . . . oh. You're saying that what we're running from could represent me?"

"Some part of you, anyway. While you were feeling frightened that you might hurt Becky, were you aware of being angry at her or of wanting to hurt her?"

"No—neither one. That's what was so strange. The thought was so . . . kind of hypothetical. Yet I still went into panic."

"So it was a very indirect sense of danger. Imagine a hint of that experience in a child who's less self-aware than you are, and imagine that sense further distorted in a dream. You wouldn't be so far from your nightmare."

"So you think that's what the nightmare is about?"

"I think that's one thing it *could* be about," said Michael. "There are others. Maybe you're trying to save your sister from your parents. Or from some troubles you see coming for her. It could also be tied to some very specific memory. And it could be more than one of those things."

"You said that there were a couple of possibilities related to my fear of hurting Becky. One was anger. What was the other?"

"The other is that the things children see their parents do become possibilities for them. If the acts were frightening, the possibilities become frightening. For instance, if a parent has been violent, the child becomes afraid of being violent. And it isn't just a kind of abstract fear. We internalize our parents; in part we become them, and their impulses."

"So I could be trying to save Amy from me, or them, or them in me."

"Those are just thoughts—ideas to run through your mind as you're exploring your dream. What's important, what will help you, are not the general ideas, but your own specific experiences."

"And how exactly do I 'explore' my dream?"

"You think about the dream, you try to feel the way you felt in the dream, you think about the details and images, and you see what any or all of that might suggest to you. And you leave yourself open to any memories that might get evoked."

"I'll try, but I'm not any good at that memory stuff. Look, you helped me a lot last time, and I'm grateful. But what I got from our working together was reassurance, some good company through bad times, and some tricks for dealing with anxiety and depression. It was really important, but that was it. Like I said a few minutes ago, I don't think I learned anything about the past I didn't already know, uncovered anything that was buried. I've got no reason to think I'll do any better this time."

"There's no guarantee. But here's one suggestion that might help. Last time I had the feeling that when you tried to put yourself back into the past, you always remained on the level of the angry adult lashing out on behalf of yourself as the child. If you really want to get back there, try to let yourself become the child."

"What do you mean?"

"Let yourself become more vulnerable; try to feel things as the child felt them. When you try to do that, it helps if you take someone down there with you, an ally, someone who can make the child feel less alone. And less afraid."

"Like who?"

Michael shrugged. "There are lots of possibilities. Some of my clients take Jesus . . ."

"Terrific."

". . . or a figure from some other religion, or a fantasy figure, or some adult you knew and trusted as a child. It can be anyone or anything that makes the child in you feel safe."

"Jesus," I muttered, still mesmerized by the thought. "What a farce that would be."

I was sitting in the darkness, on a chair in the center of my room, eyes closed, giving myself over to that desolate world inside my chest and head. I could feel rage and tears in me, but though I could feel them enough to be made miserable, I couldn't feel them enough to make them mine. I sensed something in me that wanted to sob and scream and smash things, wanted to rip at the world with its hands and teeth. But whatever that thing was, it was locked away, and I hadn't come close to finding the key that would let it loose. I had pretended to be that thing from time to time, in the midnight solitude of my home, pounding on the floor with my fists and cursing through clenched teeth, or screaming into towels or pillows that would muffle the noise. Sometimes, afterward, I would feel as if I had emptied myself of pain. But in a day, maybe two, I would again feel that same misery sitting in my gut. It was as if I had only belched when I needed to vomit, and all the sickness was still there.

Feeling that sickness now, I tried to force my mind back into the past, searching early memory images. But what images I got were so dim as to be almost useless, like the negatives of photographs taken of ghosts. I strained after those images, trying to focus them in my mind's eye, but they wouldn't come clear. I tried to sink down into that vague desolation, to find within it specific feelings with specific memories, but I could not. I played at sadness and anger, hoping the act would evoke the reality, but all I could squeeze out were a few halfhearted tears. I called up images from the dream and tried to impel myself into them, but the images remained as dim and distant as memories of old movies.

After a time I began to feel exhausted, and I leaned back, letting my mind go blank. I may have dozed—a brief dreamless doze; when I opened my eyes I was thinking of Amy. The memories were of her before her accident. Before the fall she'd been such a cute little thing—with short, curly hair, an impish face, and a bubbly, comical manner. With the bossiness of an older brother, I'd tell her to watch this and be careful of that, but she never seemed to object, would instead look up at me with her good-natured affection, and pretty soon I'd find myself laughing and hugging her. But there was much more to my watching over her than simple bossiness: Underneath I always feared for her, sensing dark things in wait for her just beyond the horizon. The fear wasn't so much premonition as knowledge: Even at age five I knew how it was when the heart has shrunk and the future is already spoiled.

I'd always felt a lot of rage in me on Amy's behalf. No doubt there was self-delusion in this; no doubt some of the mourning I felt for her was at bottom mourning for myself. But there was true rage on her behalf. I could understand why my mother and father might have mistreated me, but not why they had neglected her, someone that cute, that innocent. While they'd fought me, and fought over me, they'd mostly ignored Amy, doing the minimum but never engaging her, never encouraging her, never demanding of her, never fighting her, never bothering about her. After her accident, when she'd needed their help so badly, they'd seemed more confused and put out than caring. Without their love and their help, Amy had gradually locked herself up inside a self that had never been stocked with provisions for survival. Later on, as her life had become a series of failures and missed opportunities, my parents had watched her from a distance, tsk-tsking and wondering aloud what could possibly be wrong with her.

As I thought about Amy, there in the dark room, I suddenly felt my chest melt into a sadness so pure it startled me. Tears came, this time easily, gushing up from some powerful tributary that had been tapped this night. In my mind's eye I could see the small boy in me sobbing for his sister, for all that she had lost, and all that he had lost as well. I could see him go to her to comfort her—for she was crying now too. I saw them huddle together, he with his arms around her, pretending to a strength he knew he did not have, hoping the pretense would somehow get them through.

Don't be afraid, said a voice. *I'm here.*

In my mind's eye I could see the children turn toward him eagerly, then run to his arms. It was an anachronism, this scene, because there had been no Jesus for them in those early years. He had only come much later, and then not to comfort: He had come with the angry moralism of a bitter young mother grown old in her despair. It was only later, when I was locked away in the prison of my faith, when my submission was total, that Jesus had showed me his gentleness. Yet I suppose that in those nights when I clung to him, part of the clinging was done by these two children in me, so perhaps their imagined reaction was not false after all.

I wasn't surprised that he had come tonight. No doubt the talk with Michael had something to do with it, but this visitor came unbidden into my mind often enough. Gods, like old habits, die hard.

When I had believed, what I'd experienced most often in those moments when I'd felt I was communing with him had been a powerful sense of presence and a gentle voice speaking from the back of my mind. Sometimes he would appear in one of his standard Sunday school forms—with a white robe, brownish-blond shoulder-length hair, a handsome oval face, trim beard, sad eyes. Thus he came now to the children.

As usual the rational part of me greeted him with skepticism and cynicism, mixed with a kind of abstract affection. But it was quite different down within the deeper reaches of the soul where the world is magical and myths survive and where talking with the living and the dead and the purely imaginary is all the same. There some sad and frightened part of me reached out to him in longing, while some embittered part of me wanted to lash out and hurt him: For in that magical world, the Lord's imaginary crimes had fully as much reality as his imaginary love.

"Go away," I said, but there wasn't much force in it. I was distracted by the sight of the children pressing themselves against him.

"Let me stay," he said.

His voice was always soft and sad, with an undercurrent of what sounded like infinite exhaustion.

"No."

"Why?" he asked.

"Because you're not real."

"Suppose I'm not." It was a point he always refused to concede me. "For what you must do now, it doesn't matter."

I was silent, still watching the children.

"Please," he said. "The children need me. And you—you need me too. You loved me once. It would help you to love me again. If only in make-believe."

I could feel the children's longing, feel it as my own. If only there were someone who could truly keep all children safe, protecting their hearts from desolation and their bodies from the horrors of the world. But suddenly I felt bitterness seeping up into my throat like bile.

"I don't want to play let's pretend with you," I said. "I don't want you to be my imaginary friend. Damn it, you should have been there for real. With Amy through those years when her heart was slowly dying inside her. With Becky that night she sat alone by her mother's body until finally her mind couldn't take it anymore. None of your Sunday school bromides count for anything against their pain. 'Suffer little children to come unto me.' What a farce."

No matter how I ranted at him, it was always the same. He stood there placid and pitying, as beautiful, as majestic, as inhuman as a stained-glass window.

After a time, he said, "You are going to help Becky, aren't you," and I couldn't tell from the inflection whether it was intended as a question or a command.

"Christ," I said with disgust, "someone has to."

▽

18

"HOW WAS THE shower?" I asked. "With everything that happened the other day, I never got a chance to ask."

I was sitting at the kitchen table, eating a roll and drinking coffee, while Janet, in a white terry-cloth bathrobe, worked at the sink. Janet was cleaning up the remains of the breakfast that Becky had eaten much earlier, before either of us had gotten up.

"It was fun," said Janet. "It was a bridal shower for the daughter of a woman I teach with. She and her husband are planning a wedding for two hundred people. At one point they had to decide whether or not to pay two thousand dollars to have hors d'oeuvres before dinner. Her husband thought that was a ridiculous waste of money. So he told the kids that they could have either hors d'oeuvres at the wedding, or mixed nuts and two tickets to Europe."

"Tough choice."

"Yeah, wasn't it. This was a travel shower—things to take on the trip, money for museum tickets and meals. They had the place all decorated with travel posters and had a buffet of different European dishes. It was a lot of fun."

Janet finished up at the sink. She dried her hands, poured herself a cup of coffee, and sat down at the table with me.

"Hey, I won a prize," she said, obviously delighted. "A basket with red wine, pasta, spaghetti sauce, and dried mushrooms. I hardly ever win anything. It was nice."

"How'd you win it?"

"In a game. My friend's husband got a couple of VCRs

and checked out some travel tapes and made a tape of short clips of different cities. He showed us the clips, and we had to guess. I won."

"Good for you. I take it you've traveled a lot."

"Not really. I did spend a summer in Florence during college, and we traveled around Europe some. That helped. More of it's from reading, though. I daydream about traveling. It's one of my escapes."

Janet was still sitting there in that plain terry-cloth robe, still sleepy-eyed, having done little more for her appearance since waking up, I judged, than brush her hair a bit; yet I found myself thinking how pretty she looked. In part it was her hair: Unwaved and uncurled, it lay close to her head in a way that flattered and softened her face. Remnants of drowsiness softened her face even more, giving it a vaguely sensual quality that I hadn't seen in it before. The top of her robe was open slightly, showing the lacy, high-scooped neck of her nightgown. There was nothing immodest about it, and the nightgown seemed quite ordinary, yet the sight somehow struck me as sexy. I kept thinking how soft her skin seemed. I realized that this was not a direction in which I wanted my thoughts to go.

"Have you traveled much?" asked Janet.

"I bummed around Europe for a few weeks with a few friends after college. The trip was mostly beer and wine and unsuccessful attempts to seduce ladies of many lands. Later my wife and I talked a lot about going back. She was an art history major and would have given me a real education there. We never made it."

"Do you think you'll go back some day?"

"I hope so."

"Where would you most like to go?"

"Oh . . . I guess . . . southern France . . . or northern Italy. I really liked—"

My voice froze as Becky entered the kitchen. Janet didn't seem to find my reaction odd, taking it, I suppose, as that automatic interruption for children that so many women find so natural. Becky came around between us, carrying a textbook that she put on the table. I felt myself draw back, monitoring myself, feeling a fear of fear, and waiting for the fear itself.

"You guys," said Becky, "I don't get this stuff. We're supposed to write about this myth we're reading, and there's something that doesn't make any sense."

"Are you still doing the Greek myths?" asked Janet.

"Uh-huh. The one we're doing now is about this woman who lets all these bad things out of a box."

"Pandora," I said.

"Uh-huh." Becky turned to Janet. "What I don't get is—"

"Hon," said Janet, interrupting her, "why don't you let Dave help with that. I've got a couple of things on the stove."

I had noticed Janet's eyes moving back and forth from Becky to me, had seen the small smile that in retrospect seemed gently calculating. As a literature teacher, she was bound to know a lot more about Greek myths than I ever would, and from Janet's behavior in the past, I knew it wasn't like her to put off Becky for anything short of an emergency. I assumed she was trying to include me, to help Becky and me become friends. Ordinarily I would have been grateful, but after what had happened the other day, being at close quarters with Becky was the last thing I wanted.

Becky made no objection, in fact slid over to me easily and naturally, like a child shifting from one parent to the other. Every nerve ending in me seemed to be on anxious alert, waiting for the panic to come. You can always leave, I told myself. Yet I didn't want to give myself away to these two.

"Let me see if I remember the myth," I said, in what seemed to me a steady voice. "The gods gave Pandora a box with a bunch of evils in it and told her not to open it. I can't remember why they gave her the box. Was it a test, like Adam and Eve?"

Part of me, sitting somewhere at the center of my mind, forced itself to focus on Becky and what she was saying, while at the same time willing my voice to be steady and my body to be still. The outskirts of my mind were humming with a low-grade panic that could suddenly surge like electricity, making me want to jump out of my seat. From a sentry out on the edges came a constant flow of excited reports—"I think it's all right—Oh, God, here it comes—No, I guess it's okay—Oh-oh—easy, easy . . ."

Becky was saying, "The gods were mad at people because Promithus . . ."

"Prometheus."

". . . tricked 'em into taking the bones and fat for offerings so that people could have the meat."

"Good for him," I said. "If it hadn't been for Prometheus, all we'd have to eat today would be vegetables and tofu."

"Dave," said Janet from the sink, "we like vegetables and tofu."

Suddenly I knew I was going to be all right for now, that the real panic wasn't coming today. Maybe last night's crying had relieved some of the pressure. There was a giddy sort of nervousness in me, but I knew from experience that it was safe, that it was okay to ride it. I could feel myself smile.

"So, anyway," I said, "if I remember correctly, back in those days nobody was liberated yet, and they thought all women were nosy and didn't have any willpower . . ."

"Careful," said Janet.

". . . so they gave Pandora the box full of evils and purely by coincidence it turned out that that particular female individual just happened to be nosy and didn't have any willpower, and she opened the box, and all the evils were loosed on the world, and that's why we're so miserable today."

"According to certain male myths," said Janet.

Becky was smiling, her eyes moving back and forth from Janet to me, apparently enjoying our little exchange.

"Oh, I forgot about hope," I said. "Pandora slams the lid shut just in time to keep hope in the box. We suffer, but we have hope. Also peanut butter. She slammed the lid down in time to keep the peanut butter in there too."

"Yeah, right," said Becky, giggling, giving me a jab with her elbow.

It was good to see Becky smile. I felt a sudden surge of affection for her, this little thing with so much pain in her life, felt a sudden longing to see her free of her terrible troubles, to see her safe and happy. And I felt another kind of longing, that someday there could be more moments like this one in my life, moments that dark moods didn't spoil.

"That's the part I don't get," said Becky.

"About the peanut butter?"

"No. About the hope. If hope was inside the box, how could she have hope?"

"Because . . . uh . . . the box represents what she has."

"Yeah, but when the bad things were in the box, she didn't have bad things. She only had bad things when they got out of the box."

"Hmm . . . ," I said, glancing toward Janet.

"You got me," said Janet.

"We've got a literary critic here," I said. "That's a great point, kiddo. Mention that in your paper. Your teacher will be impressed."

Becky beamed. I looked down at her textbook.

"I don't know about this study question, though," I said. " 'Discuss why you think women have been the cause of so many of the world's problems'?"

"Let me see that," said Janet.

She grabbed the textbook, skimmed the page, then looked up at me with exasperation.

"A little joke," I said mildly. "Maybe not a great joke . . ."

"Maybe a really bad joke," said Janet.

"How come women get blamed for everything?" asked Becky.

"Good question," I said.

"Becky," said Janet archly. "I think it's time we had a serious talk about Men."

I pushed back my chair. "Perhaps this is something you'd prefer to discuss by yourselves."

I stood up, grabbed my cane, and addressed Becky.

"Whatever she tells you, Beck, I want you to remember one thing: In spite of occasional murder and mayhem, and a few world wars, we're basically sensitive, misunderstood guys."

I left the room followed by a string of half-humorous, half-not, carefully-edited-for-children epithets, and the sound of Becky laughing in the background.

I was limping through the downtown section of Ocean Point. I was there to try to pass a test that had apparently been canceled for today—because of rain. I had determined to face my anxiety on the streets, but there was no anxiety, not beyond the low-voltage kind that seemed to be with me almost every waking moment these days. There were also no crowds. It had rained earlier and was still misting, discouraging strollers. What people there were on the streets seemed too distracted to be observers, even to a paranoid temperament.

Since there wasn't to be a test, I decided to focus on errands and exercise. I went into a small hardware store to get picture hooks for Janet and into a stationery store to get notebook paper for Becky. Then I headed toward the bookstore to do some browsing.

I was almost to the bookstore when I heard a car pull up to the curb and a gruff voice call my name. I turned. The car was an old red Corvette. The passenger door was open, and the driver was leaning across the empty passenger seat. The face at the open door was Tiny's. I felt myself start.

"Strickland. I want to talk."

There was no sign of a weapon in the man's hand, no sign of threat in his voice. Yet I could feel myself trembling. I was conscious of how fragile I was, how incapable physically. But what was worse was the way the physical weakness seemed to seep inward, infecting my mind and my will. God, I hated this self that my accident had stuck me with. I kept feeling as if I were in the middle of one of those science-fiction stories about mind transfer or brain transplant. It was as if I had woken up one morning in the wrong body—maybe that of an alcoholic—a body wasted and nerves shot.

"Come on, Strickland. If I wanted to hurt you, I sure as hell wouldn't come after you like this. I just want to talk. Maybe we can help each other."

I hesitated a moment longer, then limped to the curb and got into the car. Tiny was wearing jeans and a thick plain navy sweater that looked like something a fisherman would wear. His dark hair had been slicked down, accentuating a few tight curls that jutted out like black fishhooks from the back of his head. His stubble had darkened since the other day; his silver earring was now gold. His thick chest and arms, as well as his large gut, seemed huge to me, though the impression, I sensed, came in part from my own feeling of frailty.

"How 'bout I park down by the water," said Tiny. "Plenty of people there too if you're worried."

"Okay."

We drove in silence down a San Francisco–steep street. The pavement was wet and slick; above it hung wisps of mist, like puddles in the air. I found myself feeling as small and fragile as a child next to Tiny, and I couldn't shake the illusion, no matter what mental tricks I tried. I hated that feeling.

At the bottom of the hill we turned left along the water and pulled into a diagonal parking space. I looked out my window toward Monterey Bay and the coast.

Up toward Santa Cruz I could see that dark, downward rushing of cloud that indicates rain in the distance; perhaps it was our rain, moved north. Everything in the world seemed to be gray or graying, as if rain and mist were slowly draining the world of color. Ocean and sky swirled together, their energy compressed and useless. It was like a painting done by a god trying to express his despair.

"How do you know who I am?" I asked when Tiny had cut the engine.

"I asked around. Got your name and checked up on you. People I talked to say you're straight enough. I figured maybe it was worth trying to talk."

"Before we talk," I said, "I want to tell you one thing: If I ever find out you did this to me, you're going to pay."

I didn't try to dramatize it. I was too feeble to play tough guy. I just said it quietly and matter-of-factly.

Tiny didn't look particularly impressed. He smiled.

"Strickland, you don't look like you could give an old lady problems, the shape you're in."

"I won't be in this shape a few months from now."

"I'm a lot bigger than you are. And a lot meaner."

"You won't even see me coming. Why should you get a chance? I didn't."

Tiny looked at me for a moment, the smile fading from his face. He didn't look nervous, just thoughtful. Then he let out a breath.

"This is all bullshit, Strickland. I'm not the one did this to you. That's what I wanted to tell you. I want you off my back. You and those cops. I got a few months left before I get off parole. I got a nice business deal lined up. I don't want anything screwing that up."

"I sure wouldn't want to screw up your business."

"Don't moralize with me," said Tiny. "I sell happiness, that's all. They don't want it, they can just pass me by. I won't give them any trouble."

"You save the trouble for your customers."

"Only if they don't pay. They buy, they gotta pay. That's just business."

"So killing Ann Schrader was just business?"

"I didn't kill the woman, Strickland. Why would I want to kill her?"

"Because she owed you money."

"How am I gonna collect the money if she's dead?"

"Maybe you don't. Maybe it's just to discourage other customers with the same idea."

Tiny started to say something, then didn't. He looked at

me for a few moments, the tips of his thick fingers scratching at his dark stubble.

"Look, man," he said. "I didn't come here to argue. I don't expect you to believe me. I'm gonna tell you some things. You check 'em out. Maybe they help you figure out who killed the woman. Maybe they just show you I didn't. I figure you'll report what I say to the cops. That's okay. But the cops ever come down on me for any of it, I'm going to deny everything, and it'll just be my word against yours."

"I'm not making any deal with you."

"I'm not asking you to make a deal, for Christ sake. I'm just asking you to check out what I say."

"Okay."

"I didn't kill the Schrader woman, Strickland. And I didn't try to hurt the kid. Why the hell would I want to hurt the kid?"

"Did Ann Schrader owe you money?"

Tiny hesitated.

"You want to tell me stuff, or not?" I asked.

Tiny nodded. "Okay. Yeah, she owed me money."

"How much?"

"Almost two grand."

"Bullshit. She had no property and no support money. She had a child to take care of. And she had borrowed what little she could. Why in hell would you let her go on a string for two grand?"

Tiny shrugged. "She was gettin' money from somewhere."

"Where?"

"I don't know."

"So you're telling me everything was just great between you two?"

"No," said Tiny. "It took work to get money out of her. Far as I could tell, it wasn't like she had money coming in regular. It was more like she had a source she could tap when I got her nervous enough."

"Janet Kendall said you were threatening her sister just before she died. That your usual way of getting her nervous?"

"Yeah."

"Bullshit."

"What do you mean?"

"It wasn't business as usual. Ann Schrader was really scared. Something special was going on."

Tiny just looked at me, a tooth nibbling at his right lower lip.

"If you're going to tell me, tell me," I said. "Otherwise I got things to do. Like proving you killed Ann Schrader."

"Okay, okay," said Tiny. "You're right. It was something different. About a month before she died, the Schrader woman went into rehab. She told me the money had dried up. She was feeling really shitty without her stuff—I figured that's why she went into rehab in the first place. She told me she could get more money on condition she stay straight for a few weeks. I figured it was her father givin' her the money, and it made sense he might cut her off till she got straight. So I gave her a month. Except a couple of weeks later I find out she's buying stuff from one of my competitors. I mean, it's obvious the bitch is holding out on me. I figured I better go scare the shit out of her and set her straight. So I go over to her place, make with my best bad-guy routine, and slap her around a little bit."

"With her daughter there?"

"Hell, I didn't know the kid was there. She was usually off in school. Schrader didn't tell me she was home. Didn't know it until I hear the kid bawling in back of me. Then I laid off the mother."

"So the girl saw you hit her mother?"

"Yeah. But like I said, I didn't even know she was there. I gotta say, though, it really shook the broad up. Really got through to her."

"What did Ann say to you?"

"Said she could get more money. Said she could pay me in two days. We set up an appointment, and I left. I figured there was no problem. Like I said, seeing her daughter seeing us like that really shook her up. I figured she'd come through all right. Only the day I'm supposed to collect the money, I find out she's dead."

"And it wasn't you?"

"Hell, no, I didn't do it. Like I told you, she was gonna pay. I heard whoever did her tossed the place. I figured he got what was coming to me."

"Let's suppose for laughs that you didn't do it. You got any ideas who did?"

"Nope. I poked around a little. Figured if I could find out who, I'd have some leverage to pry my money loose. But I didn't turn up nothing."

"Any ideas where she was getting her money?"

"I knew Corky—her old man—didn't have shit and wouldn't've given it to her if he did. I knew her sister didn't have that kind of money. Like I told you, I figured maybe her father. You should be able to find out about that. If it wasn't him, try that boyfriend of hers. What the hell, Strickland, what could be better for an addict than fucking a rich druggist?"

"There was a rumor she was dating a guy she called Angel. Any ideas who that could be?"

Tiny laughed.

"I don't meet too many angels in my line of work. The only angels I know are in church."

"What do you think?" said Deffinger after I'd gone over Tiny's story with him.

The sergeant was leaning back in his swivel chair, legs crossed, staring at me from across the desk. In his lap he cradled a half-finished cup of coffee. His maroon tie was pulled down, the sleeves of his blue dress shirt rolled up. The inevitable corduroy sport jacket—this one worn and beige—hung from a peg on the wall behind him. His *Criminal Investigations* textbook lay open to the side of his desk. In a few years this sort of setting would be office hours, the what-do-you-think? directed toward some student struggling with some point of criminal procedure.

"I don't know," I said. "It would make sense of a lot of things—the solid alibi, Becky's reaction, the bruises. On the other hand, it could be just a story. Suppose he hits Ann

Schrader and a day later kills her: Admitting to the first helps him explain that run-in with Becky without putting him in serious jeopardy. I don't think we should ease up on Tiny. But I think we ought to recheck the old suspects. Especially the pharmacist."

"I agree."

"Where did Triplett say he was the night Ann Schrader was killed?"

"Home, I think." Deffinger tilted forward and placed the coffee cup on his desk. He opened a folder and flipped through it. "Yeah—said he was home alone doing some reading. Says he went to bed early."

"You must have looked into their relationship. What did you find out?"

"They knew each other in high school, where he was a couple of years ahead of her. They even dated a few times before she got interested in someone else. He went off to UC Santa Cruz for undergraduate, then UC San Francisco for pharmacy school. She stayed here, got married, and had her child. By the time Triplett came back and opened his pharmacy—with financial help from his father—Ann Schrader's husband had split, and she and Triplett started making friends. People we talked to about Triplett generally had nice things to say about him—nice guy, was in love with the Schrader woman, wanted something serious with her, didn't like her taking drugs. She seemed to like him well enough, and they were intimate, but she wasn't interested in anything exclusive—maybe was taking advantage of him in the sense of leading him on, using him for a friend in need, that sort of thing."

"How long had he been dating her before she died?"

"On and off for six months."

"So he obviously couldn't be Angel."

"No, but of course he could have killed her over Angel—or killed her over something else altogether."

"Like money, maybe. You get any indication he might have been giving her money?"

"No. But I'm not sure anyone asked."

"Would you be willing to ask him? Maybe look into his financial records for that period?"

"I'll talk to him. We'll see about the rest."

"Where was he living at the time of the killing?"

Deffinger flipped a couple of pages of the file. "He was in an apartment complex. We interviewed the neighbors. No one noticed him or his car going or coming on the night of the killing. Of course, that doesn't have to mean anything. Just a minute . . . something odd here. One of the people interviewed talks about his car as a Mustang, someone else as a Thunderbird. It's probably nothing, but I'd better clear that up."

"So he really has no alibi."

"No, none to speak of."

"You told me before that he might have played with drugs in graduate school, but now was supposed to be off them. How firm is all of that?"

"The graduate school stuff is just rumors—things one or two people had heard from other people who were students at UCSF when he was. As to the other, we interviewed what friends he had—he seemed to be kind of a loner—and they were all firm that he would have nothing to do with drugs. We never found anyone who contradicted that."

"There certainly wouldn't be any problem explaining how Triplett could know Becky was seeing Blake: Even if Janet didn't tell him—which she probably did—Becky's prescriptions get filled at his pharmacy. By the way, after I called you the other day, did you get a chance to check for a report on the break-in in Blake's offices?"

"Yeah. A report was filed. It supports the description of the break-in he gave you the other day. It wasn't that much of a report. Like he told you, it was pretty routine."

"I just wanted to be sure that he was telling the truth. What other people would be worth looking at again?"

"I'll go back over the list of users and losers Ann Schrader was hanging out with and talk to whichever ones we can find. I suppose I should do a little more thinking about Mrs. Kendall and Dr. Blake, though we went over them pretty thoroughly last time. I don't know, Strickland. I wonder if we could just be going around in circles. What if it was someone we never thought to look at?"

▽

19

WE WERE DRIVING the Monterey–Salinas highway through the Laguna Hills. I was in the front passenger seat of Janet's Honda, my head turned toward her, watching her drive. A few days ago I'd mentioned to Janet how flattering her hair looked brushed down; she'd worn it that way on our Friday night date and was wearing it that way again today for the Blakes' reception. She had on a tight gray wool skirt, a mohair sweater in a forest green that did nice things for her skin and eyes, some gold jewelry, and light makeup. She had been telling me some funny stories about Becky, and she was smiling, her eyes sparkling. She looked very attractive.

"So Mom and Dad took us up to Flagstaff to visit some friends of theirs—the Kyles—for a couple of days. The Kyles had a little ranch where they raised some animals—sheep, goats, chickens—different kinds. When we arrived the Kyles took us on a tour and let Becky pet and feed the animals. Becky was about seven or eight at the time. That evening we had lamb for dinner. Someone let slip a remark about the lamb being one of theirs, and Becky went pale. She got all upset and started to worry about a couple of animals she really liked—a rabbit, I think, and a little goat. The Kyles were very nice and explained to Becky that she didn't have to worry—that those particular animals had names, and they made it a rule never to kill animals they had given names to. The next morning Becky got up before everyone else and went out and named every animal on the ranch."

"Cute," I said, watching Janet smile.

Something had changed in Janet's and my relationship ever since that day we'd made it clear that neither of us was interested in anything intimate. It had taken much of the pressure off, particularly where Janet was concerned. Since then she'd become more relaxed and less guarded; I'd responded in kind. On our Friday night date we'd gone out for dinner, intending to go to a movie. But instead of the movie, we'd ended up talking for three hours over dinner at a small seafood place in Carmel, then continued talking on a beach walk and during a nightcap at a quiet cocktail lounge. We'd talked of many more sad things than happy ones, but it had felt good to share them, and it had been anything but a sad evening.

I was getting to like Janet a lot, and looking at her now, I found myself thinking things I shouldn't have been thinking. I'd have to keep reminding myself that I was waiting for Charlie. But I knew that without any certainty of Charlie's returning, those reminders might not always sound so compelling.

Janet turned right and took a winding road up into the hills, ascending past homes that became more and more impressive, with increasingly spectacular views of Monterey and the Bay in the distance. At the crest of the hill, she took another right onto a narrow road that descended into a canyon. The area was thick with coastal scrub oak—small, gnarled trees packed together like underbrush. One house at a time would come into close view, then disappear. At some points it was impossible to get more than a glimpse of the surrounding hills.

After a time the road dead-ended at an open metal gate in a large stone wall. As we passed through the gate, I heard myself make a small sound of surprise. The Blakes had their own private canyon—their house backed by a half bowl of hills, with no other houses visible. The house itself was beautiful, a wood-shingled ranch house, which though obviously new and plush, fit beautifully with the setting.

Just to the left as we entered the gate were stables and a corral; behind them was a broad, sandy path—what I took to be a riding trail—snaking its way up one hill. To the right was a huge oak tree and to the side of it a broad, graveled area full of cars. Since there was no room left, Janet U-turned and parked along the road.

"Talk about a fantasy house," I said as we were walking through the gate.

"You really like it?"

"I love it. What about you?"

"It's sensational," said Janet. "But if I really had my choice, I think I'd take one of the those huge houses up above with the great views."

"Yeah, those are beautiful. I don't know why this one seems so special to me. Yes, I do too. It's those cowboy shows I used to watch as a kid. The isolation, the sense of land, the ranch house, the corral, the trail into the hills. This is the homestead."

"The multimillion-dollar homestead."

"Those are the best kind. Ask Gene Autry."

We went up the front walkway, passing between two large makeshift signs that read Thanks Everyone and Ocean Point For Drug-Free Youth. At the door we were greeted by an attractive young woman named Susan, whom Janet knew; in the course of the introductions I was told that Susan "helped Mrs. Blake with some things" and gathered that she was a sort of part-time secretary. We hadn't been inside the house for more than a couple of minutes when an elegant-looking woman detached herself from a nearby group and came our way, greeting Janet with a kind of dignified effusiveness. Since Janet called her Cynthia, I gathered it was Mrs. Blake. After a moment the woman turned to me, and Janet introduced us.

"It's so nice to meet you, Mr. Strickland," said Mrs. Blake, her voice warm. She shook my hand with a small, firm handshake. "My husband's told me good things about you."

She looked me in the eye as she spoke. If she was taking

in the wig and the scars, as she had to be, she was too polite and too much in control to betray any reaction.

"It's nice to meet you too," I said. "I like your husband. And I love your house. I hope I'm not gate-crashing."

"No. We're delighted to have you after what you did for Becky. And any friend of Janet's is welcome here."

I liked Mrs. Blake. She brought to mind women I had met from time to time who were usually wives of top executives. Whatever clawing, sniping, or one-upmanship they ever had to do, it's all behind them now; in their relaxed middle age, their husbands are company president or some such thing, they have more money than they could ever spend, and their social status is secure. The women have that poised air and tailored elegance that leaves no doubt as to their status, but in their role as semiprofessional hostess, often to underlings, their manner is so solicitous and so friendly that you almost believe they mean it, and maybe they do; but if they don't, the performance is so good that you are grateful for it, the same way you'd be grateful for the smile of a waiter in an elegant French restaurant that you know is way over your head.

Blake, as a relatively young psychiatrist, couldn't have come close to achieving anything that would warrant *noblesse oblige,* and would have had a hard time carrying it off in any case. That Cynthia Blake could indicated to me that she must have come from money. That she conveyed such presence perhaps had to do with her being, I guessed, seven to ten years older than her late-thirties husband.

As Mrs. Blake and Janet started talking about something related to the house, I glanced toward the large glass doors opening onto the back of the house. In the foreground to the left was a free-form pool edged with stone that ended in a large diving rock. All around the pool was an area landscaped with boulders and gravel and ground cover and flowers and plants. Out beyond all that was a large, open grassy area where the party was taking place.

Half-consciously I'd followed the two women a few feet off

the hallway into the living room where Cynthia Blake had pulled back a sheet of plastic to show Janet some fabric covering a couch. The living room was a jumble of covered furniture and stacked boxes and loose odds and ends; I remembered Janet telling me that the Blakes weren't quite moved into this new house yet. I noticed some framed photographs of cars leaning against a large carton near the couch. They all turned out to be photos of Blake with different sports cars. I stopped at one of him in front of a Testarossa. Nice.

"I can assure you we won't be hanging those in the living room," said Mrs. Blake in a humorous tone as she noticed me examining the photographs.

I stood up, feeling suddenly awkward.

"I'm sorry," I said. "I shouldn't be touching things."

"Nonsense. As you can see, those are photographs of my husband and his cars. Quite frankly"—here Mrs. Blake lowered her voice in mock conspiratorial fashion—"if you could manage to lose those for me I would be quite grateful." She smiled. "If it were up to Barry, I'm sure they'd be hanging prominently in the living room. In our other house, he insisted they be hung in the hall where everyone could see them. Not in this house, though. I'm putting my foot down. They go in his study." She shook her head, a fond look on her face. "My husband certainly loves his cars. I've never been able to see what all the fuss is about. I guess it's one of those male things."

"I gather from something he told me that you were the one who started him on his car habit," I said.

"He told you that?" said Mrs. Blake, looking a little embarrassed, but also pleased. "I suppose I am partially responsible." She pointed to a photograph of her husband with an Alfa Romeo. "I gave him that one. The Spider. A horrible name. But a handsome car."

"I remember that car," said Janet. "It was adorable."

"It was," said Mrs. Blake. "But, dear, please don't let my husband hear you call one of his sports cars 'adorable.' Or 'cute.' You'd be likely to wound him deeply. I believe he prefers adjectives like 'sleek' and 'dynamic.' "

"I'll be careful," said Janet, laughing. "I was just remembering that John Triplett had a little red sports car back then too. He and Dr. Blake had a little game going. They were always driving around town with the tops down, showing off their cars. When they'd meet in town they'd make a big joke of exchanging fake insults and pretending to challenge each other to race. It was a riot."

"I remember now," said Mrs. Blake.

"Becky loved that. She was always on the lookout for those cars. One day her mother and Becky and I were standing at a corner when both the cars pulled up. Becky waved madly, and when they saw how enthralled she was, each ended up giving her a little ride. It was the high point of the year."

"Nice memory," said Mrs. Blake gently, noticing as I did that Janet's gaze had turned vague, then sad. After a moment, Mrs. Blake said, "Mr. Strickland, would you mind excusing Janet for a few minutes? I have some girl things I'd like to discuss with her."

I gave my token assent, added a few pleasantries, then wandered outside.

Beyond the landscaped pool area was a broad grassy area, perhaps thirty yards wide and fifty yards deep, separated from the base of the hills by thirty yards of scrub brush. There were about fifty or sixty guests wandering around on the grass. There were tables of hors d'oeuvres, soft drinks, and desserts, as well as an espresso bar. A young man and woman, both in formal wear, were playing something light and classical on guitar and flute.

I was heading for the food when I saw Triplett looking my way eagerly. Obviously the eagerness wasn't for me: His eyes searched the area all around me. Finally he walked toward me with a mildly suspicious look, as if suspecting I had hidden Janet somewhere. I half expected him to search me.

"She'll be along in a minute," I said. "She and Mrs. Blake are conferring about something."

Triplett seemed embarrassed that I'd read him so easily, apparently unaware of how transparent he'd been.

"I . . . was just . . . ," he said, awkwardly, then abandoned the fabrication. "How are you?"

"I'm doing okay. Thank you."

Triplett was wearing a pair of black pleated dress cords and a sweater with a large cross-hatch diamond pattern of rust and green and beige that suggested a subdued stained-glass window. His longish brown hair had been trimmed and carefully combed; his granny glasses had been replaced by lightly tinted glasses in regular frames. He was a good-looking guy—oval face, fine features, bright blue eyes. There was a passivity about him that I thought detracted from his looks, but I could imagine it appealing to a woman with a mothering urge. I found myself suddenly resenting his interest in Janet. It was ridiculous, of course: Janet had already told me she wasn't attracted to Triplett, and more to the point, I had no intentions toward Janet. Still, the resentment lingered.

"As long as I've got you here," I said, "I'd appreciate it if I could ask you a few questions about Ann."

"Ann?" he asked, with such a blank look that for an instant I had the absurd impression that I'd have to remind him who she was. "Why?" he added after a moment.

"Because it might help me understand some things that are going on now, including the attack on Becky."

"Do you think they're connected?"

"They could be."

"Has Janet hired you as a detective?" asked Triplett.

"No. I'm just advising her as a friend."

His lips compressed, giving subtle signs of annoyance. He shook his head.

"I'm sorry," he said. "I don't like to talk about Ann. It's just too painful."

"I understand," I said sympathetically. "You don't really know me. When Janet comes outside, I'll ask her to ask you, and the three of us can discuss it together. Would that make you feel more comfortable?"

I was trying to box him in, figuring he wouldn't want to discuss Ann in front of Janet, but wouldn't want to turn down a request from Janet either. He looked at me for a moment, hesitant, then gave a small sigh of concession.

"I don't want to subject Janet to that," he said. "All right. Let's do this as quickly as possible."

"For starters, how long had you known Ann?"

"I dated her my senior year of high school—she was a sophomore. That was in the late seventies. It was just a few dates, actually, at the beginning of the school year. After high school I went away to college, then pharmacy school, and only ran into Ann occasionally during the few summers I was home. Ann had gotten married right after high school, and she and her husband tended to hang around with his surfer friends—not a group I had anything to do with. I came back to Ocean Point in 1987 and opened the pharmacy. Ann started coming into the pharmacy regularly, and we'd talk. I knew she was having troubles in her marriage, and I could see that she was unhappy, but she didn't confide in me then. Once she knew her marriage was over, she did want to talk about it, and our conversations often turned into long coffee dates. After a time we started seeing each other seriously."

"Were you dating each other exclusively?"

Triplett stiffened, looking at me sharply through the reddish tint of his glasses.

"I'm not an idiot, Mr. Strickland," he said. "I assume you're not either. I think you already know the answer to that question. Which means you asked it to upset me. I don't know why."

"I wasn't trying to upset you," I said, not quite truthfully. "I phrased it badly. What I should have said was that I'd heard that Ann was also seeing other men and was that true. It could be important."

Triplett seemed appeased. His body lost the rigidity of indignation. He said, "Yes, it was true. She was involved with other men. She never pretended otherwise, though she didn't throw it up to me. It wouldn't have done any good for me to demand that she stop. I knew she'd break off with me if I forced the issue. I was very much in love with her. I was willing to take her on those terms. I kept telling myself it was the drugs that made her that way, that one day she'd get off them and see that I was the one who really loved her, who could take care of her. I suppose that was just a pathetic fantasy."

Triplett's gaze saddened and turned inward. I suspected that his fantasy of Ann still had a hold on him, even now, six years after her death. I said:

"Janet tells me that Ann had given up drugs shortly before she died."

Triplett blinked at me for a moment. Once he'd managed to focus on what I'd said, he glanced around to make sure there were still no listeners.

"That's what Janet believes," he said. "I haven't wanted to tell her differently. It isn't true. Ann was smoking crack again before she died. I was really disappointed, and I told her so. She threatened never to see me again if I kept criticizing her. I shut up, but I think that was the first time I really considered the possibility that I'd have to give her up. What would have happened eventually is impossible to say, but I remember having the impression she was going to have to hit bottom hard before she'd really try to quit—assuming that hitting bottom didn't kill her first. I didn't want to watch her fall. I'd already seen one fall too many."

"What do you mean?"

Triplett hesitated, then said, "It was in pharmacy school. Some of us were playing around with something we shouldn't have been—shouldn't morally, I mean, there was nothing illegal about it—that was the apparent beauty of it. For most of us it was just fun. But there was one guy who couldn't handle it and couldn't let go. One day he had a psychotic episode and jumped out the window twenty stories up. I saw the way his body looked, lying on the asphalt where he'd landed. I've been strongly antidrugs since then. That's part of the reason I'm involved in this."

Triplett made a vague gesture that seemed to encompass the whole party. I said:

"I assume the police must have asked you about that guy, Angel—the one Ann was supposed to have taken up with just before she died."

"Yes. They did."

"Do you have any idea who he might have been?"

"No. I thought about it hard then, and I've thought about it from time to time since. I have no idea."

"There's some indication that Ann was getting a substantial amount of money from someone, money that helped pay for her drugs. Any idea if that was true or where the money would have come from?"

It might have been my imagination, but I thought I saw the pharmacist's eyes falter.

"No," he said.

"Didn't it strike you as peculiar that she could afford a drug habit on a salesperson's salary?"

"Yes . . . no . . . I don't know. She never told me how much she was spending. Maybe I didn't want to know what she might be doing to get that money. I told myself that perhaps she had a big allowance from her father. It could be true. Apparently he's pretty well off."

"The money wasn't from her father. Janet checked. Her father was sending her small amounts from time to time, but nothing like what Ann would have needed to sustain her drug habit."

"Then I'm afraid I can't help you."

Triplett looked away suddenly and waved. I saw Janet heading in our direction. Before she could get close, she was waylaid by a group of women who looked as if they were ready for an extended conversation. Triplett got up.

"I think I'll go say hello," he said. "Are you coming?"

"No, you go ahead," I said. "I'll do some wandering."

Triplett hurried off toward Janet, and I headed for the food. On my way I noticed Blake break off from one of the groups, and I veered to intercept him. We made about thirty seconds of small talk about the party before I told him I had a quick question.

"I'd like to know what Ann Schrader said to you about the person she called Angel. Deffinger gave me a report, but I'd like to hear it from you."

Blake gave me a tired smile. "Quick question, huh?"

"It could be important."

"All right, then. But let's go over there."

As I followed Blake away from the house and the guests, my eyes scanned the small canyon. I couldn't get over the thought of real hills in the backyard, especially hills that looked as if they had just come out of an old Gene Autry movie. I had an image of Gene riding up one of those slopes on Champion, singing "Old Faithful Pal of Mine," the song that had brought tears to my eyes when I was five years old. My heroes have always been cowboys. I knew that if I owned this place I'd have to get a horse. Hell, I might even start taking up the guitar again. I laughed at the thought. Cowboy Dave.

"Strickland?"

I saw that Blake had stopped just ahead and was looking at me oddly.

"Oh . . . sorry," I said as I came up next to him. "I guess I was daydreaming. Go ahead. What did Ann say about Angel?"

"The name came up during our last session," said Blake. "I hadn't seen Ann for a couple of weeks. I'd been concerned when she'd canceled the prior week, but I called her and she assured me she was attending her CA meetings."

"How long had you been seeing her?"

"A few weeks."

"How'd you happen to start seeing her?"

"Back in 1987 I was on staff at the hospital while I was trying to build up a private practice. I was assigned to Ann when she came in. She was badly depressed, and her thinking was pretty confused. I knew how little support she could expect to get with no money and minimal insurance—maybe a few sessions with a counselor who'd have little if any training in drug counseling. CA is marvelous, of course, but I felt Ann needed a transition. So I agreed to see her for a few sessions. I don't want to make my action seem totally altruistic. It's true she wasn't an attractive client from an insurance standpoint: Her policy, which she had through her job, paid for five sessions of counseling at less than half my normal rate. But I was just trying to open my practice, and I wasn't exactly loaded down with clients. I thought making a connection with her provider might generate other such clients to help me through the initial period. So I agreed to those five sessions. Actually I ended up agreeing to two more since I felt she needed more monitoring before I trusted her completely to CA.

"The last time I saw her was two days before she died. That was to be our last session, and I don't think she was very happy about that. Drug addicts are very dependent personalities, and as any therapist would expect, she had become dependent on me. Drug addicts are also people who want and expect immediate gratification. It didn't matter that I had been seeing her in part as charity work. She was angry that I wasn't willing to keep seeing her for free.

"The reason I'm telling you this is that I'm not completely sure this Angel wasn't just an invention of Ann's—maybe in a juvenile attempt to make me jealous, maybe as a way to pretend she was going to be just fine. With that said, what happened in the last session was this: Ann came into the session pouty and irritable. After some prodding, she admitted to being angry that I was breaking off treatment. We talked about that for a while, but didn't seem to get anywhere. Then she started telling me about this special man she'd started seeing, and how gentle and kind and good he was, and how different he was from other men she'd known, and how happy he was making her. She referred to him twice as Angel. The first time she said 'my Angel,' which I assumed was merely a term of endearment. But the second time she said 'Angel is something or other,' and that's when I took it to be a name or nickname. While she was telling me this, she seemed really up; she also had a kind of teasing manner about her. That's what I remembered and reconstructed from my notes. That's what I told the police."

"I'm sure the police asked you if you got any hints about race or age or employment or any other specifics."

"They did, and no, I didn't."

"Did Ann say definitely that she had just met this man?"

"No."

"Did you get the impression that she had just met him?"

"Yes. But I've wondered from time to time if I could have been wrong." Blake closed his eyes. "It's odd. I can see and hear that session as if it were yesterday—I suppose because Ann's death forced me to go back over it for the police. There was one point in the session, while she was talking about this Angel, when she drifted off into a kind of reverie and got a look of wonder on her face. I suppose that would be some evidence that she wasn't just making this guy up—that look would have been hard to fake. Anyway, she said, 'He's so good. And he loves me. Who would have expected it?' At the time my take on the last line was, who would have expected that I would ever find such a good man? But it has occurred to me since that you could read that line in a couple of other ways. It could have meant, who would have expected that he was so good? Or who would have expected that that particular person would love me? Under either of the last two readings, she could have been referring to someone she already knew."

"Is there anything else you can tell me—no matter how wild, or speculative—that might possibly have any bearing on the identity of that man?"

Blake looked pained.

"I'm sorry, Mr. Strickland," he said. "I thought about that a lot back then. I still think about it some. I'd give anything to have something that would help you and the police catch Ann's killer. But, I'm sorry, I just don't."

▽

20

IN THE DREAM my body began to grow dark, began to give off that awful stench. By the time I'd gotten to my feet, I'd become large and clumsy, so that I stumbled as I tried to walk. I struggled toward Amy, but when I finally got to her and reached out my hand, she became terrified and started screaming, "No, please, don't." I felt my hand touch her, and suddenly she fell away into emptiness, calling my name. I closed my eyes and covered my ears and began to scream.

I woke trembling in the darkness, more frightened than I'd ever been after that dream. "I didn—, I didn—," I kept muttering, but the words wouldn't come out right. I felt so disoriented: The dream—it was all wrong.

I got out of bed and began limping back and forth across the room. I'd had that dream for years, and it had never changed—why now? In the dream I was always trying to save Amy—that was the whole point. Why would she look at me now as if I frightened her? I'd never been able to get to her—that had been the point too. Why now, all of a sudden, did my hand touch her just as she fell?

I had a vivid image of Amy as she would have been after her accident, with that odd little walk that her bad leg had caused her, the walk that had brought such teasing from the other kids. I felt so sad for her, and in my imagination I reached my hand out to touch her face. Suddenly the hand moved contrary to my intent, as if it had taken on some malevolent life of its own, slapping Amy hard across the face. She looked at me with such a startled, hurt look. I felt sick—I would never do that—and I reached out my hand again to reassure and apologize, but suddenly it was as if I had been thrown back into the dream, and Amy was screaming, and my hand was touching her, and she was falling.

"Goddamn it, Michael," I said frantically. "I think I might be the one who crippled her."

"Okay, slow down a little. Let's talk about it."

"All this time I've been making myself out to be the damn hero, trying to save my sister, and I think it's all a lie. At the end of the dream now she's terrified of me, and I can feel my hand touch her just before she falls. I think maybe I pushed her. And what I told you about imagining my hand hitting Amy—that's just what I was afraid of with Becky. Maybe the reason I'm afraid I'll hurt Becky is that I know I hurt Amy. And this sadness I have in me, it feels like such a weight, like maybe it's some awful guilt."

Michael was sitting in his desk chair, an old olive-colored sport jacket hung over the chair back; the collar of his blue dress shirt was open, and his tie, painted with a red-and-black children's drawing, was pulled down so that the knot rested just beneath his love beads. I had wanted to see Michael early that morning, but he'd been in L.A. for a conference all day; when his secretary had reached him, he had agreed to see me on this special evening appointment. He looked tired, and I knew he had given up a free evening, and I was grateful. I'd been nervous as hell all day, sometimes having full-blown panic attacks in which my mind seemed to be exploding with violent images and senseless memory fragments. It would have been awful to go through a whole night of that before talking to Michael.

"David," he said, "I don't know whether you hurt your sister or not. But I want you to know there are other possible reasons for that dream. It could be fantasy—representing something far less dramatic that you're feeling guilty about. It—"

"I don't think that what's going on with me is just fantasy. It feels like something more."

"Okay. Let's focus on the dream—see if we can make a start on really figuring it out." Michael stretched his long legs and leaned back in his desk chair. He quickly ran the closed fingers of both hands across his eyes. "Tell me the dream again."

"When it begins, Amy and I are running out the door of our apartment, running away from something that's behind us. I'm terrified of it, but I don't have any sense of what it is. Maybe you were right before when you suggested that it might stand for my anger. Anyway, we start down the steps, and it's like Amy becomes weighted down, and it's hard to move her. I yank at her, and yell that we've got to go farther, but it's hardly doing any good. What I'm trying to do is get us across the basement landing and down the far stairs that lead to the passageway to the garage; I'm convinced that if I can just get us down those stairs, we'll be safe. That doesn't make any sense really: Why couldn't whatever is following us catch us in the passageway? Maybe I'm trying to save her from the fall. Maybe the idea is that if I could have gotten her past those stairs, the fall wouldn't have happened. But, of course, it always does."

"That makes sense."

"I don't know what the machinery represents. As we're going down the stairs, the machinery is starting to explode, and the idea is that if he doesn't get us, the machinery will. Maybe it's just—"

"Wait a minute. What did you mean by 'he'?"

"What do you mean?"

"You just said, 'If he doesn't get us, the machinery will.' Who's 'he'?"

"I didn't say 'he.' "

"That's what I thought I heard."

"Well, you heard wrong," I said, suddenly irritated. "Do you mind if I continue?"

"Go ahead."

"We get to the bottom of the stairs, and the machinery explodes, and I get knocked on my ass, and I can't get to Amy on time, and she falls, and that's it."

"What's that? The *Reader's Digest* condensed version?"

"Yeah, for our simpler readers."

"What are you angry about?"

"I don't know. I just got really pissed off when you interrupted me."

"I'm sorry, then."

"No, I'm sorry. It didn't make any sense to get angry." I took a deep breath. "Anyway, I was starting to say that maybe the exploding machinery represents my anger, too. Maybe that's just my dream telling me that something terrible is going to happen, and there's no way to avoid it."

"Maybe."

"What I don't get is that part about my body changing. After the explosion, when I get up after being knocked down, my body gets big and clumsy, and there's this awful smell on me. I've never known what that's about. Maybe it's like I'm changing into a monster or something. Didn't they get created by explosions sometimes in those old horror movies?"

"Tell me about your sister's accident. You've told me before about her being crippled. I forget if you told me exactly how it happened."

"She fell down some basement stairs. I always figured that was the reason for the dream—that I was trying to save her from what ruined her life."

"The actual stairs your sister fell down—were they the same ones you're dreaming about?"

"I don't know. I suppose so. The basement stairs in the dream are real. They were just across the hall from our apartment, and they went down to a landing where there were other stairs leading to a passageway to the garage. And there was all that machinery behind the wire mesh. I remember it made a kind of frightening noise."

"How old were your sister and you at the time she was hurt?"

"She was four. I was five."

"Do you remember her being hurt?"

"No. I never thought I was there. But maybe I was. Maybe that's what the dream's about. Maybe I keep trying to save her from myself but it's too late, because I've already hurt her somehow. I'm sure I didn't mean to hurt her—maybe I bumped into her by accident. Or if I did mean—"

Suddenly I felt as if I couldn't breathe. My heart started beating wildly, as if it were some creature trapped in my chest, trying hopelessly to break free. I put a hand to my chest.

"Are you all right?" asked Michael.

I put my other hand up in a wait-a-minute gesture. I was getting my breath back, but my heart was still going too fast. I sat there waiting as it gradually slowed.

"I was just . . . going to say . . . I hope I . . . God, I feel awful."

My heart was fluttering again, and I had the feeling that if I tried to speak it was going to come exploding out of my mouth.

"Maybe we should stop," said Michael. "Do you want to lie down?"

I shook my head. "It's . . . just . . . same old crap," I muttered.

I waited until the flutter diminished. I felt myself getting breath now, but my chest still felt so heavy, as if my lungs were made of lead. I had to work to force the words out.

"I hope . . . didn't mean . . . to hurt her," I said. I took a long, labored breath. "I just hope it was . . . an accident. I'm going to feel . . . like shit . . . either way . . . but I hope I didn't mean to hurt her."

"You were only five, David. Even if you did mean to hurt her, you wouldn't really have been aware of what might happen."

"Doesn't matter. If I hurt her, I hurt her."

Michael studied me for a moment. He reached over for his coffee cup and lifted it to his lips. As I watched him drink, I could read the single word "Save" on his coffee cup. My mind was suddenly flooded with phrases from my early Christian years—"Jesus Saves," "saved by the blood," "Whosoever believeth in Him shall be saved." A long time ago I had gone to my knees with a load of guilt too great for a lonely twelve-year-old to bear, and he had taken it away. There was no going back, even had I wanted to. There was no one else who could lift this awful guilt from me.

"We might have to talk a lot about that," said Michael as he put down his coffee cup. "But first let's see if there's any need. If what you believe is true, it should be reflected symbolically in the dream. Let's see if there's an interpretation that fits. We've talked about the thing pursuing you as your own anger. What about the struggle you have trying to keep your sister moving?"

"Maybe it's . . . that I can't get away from myself. Or that I can't save her from what's already happened."

"You think the explosion also represents your anger?"

"Yes. It's as if I'm running from my anger and also toward my anger—in other words, I just can't get away from it."

"The explosion knocks you down, and you have trouble getting up to help your sister. What's that about?"

"Maybe that's saying that my anger is stronger than I am—stronger than the part of me that wants to help her and keep her safe."

"What about the body changes you mentioned?"

"I don't know. Like I said, maybe I'm changing into something awful—the person that's going to hurt her."

"After being knocked down?"

"Maybe the angry part of myself knocked me down."

"And the part that got knocked down changed into a monster?"

"That doesn't sound right, does it. Maybe . . . it means . . . that the anger has taken me over after the other part of me is beaten."

"That's possible," said Michael. "Describe the changes to me again."

"They're not all that clear. My body grows larger. I feel all clumsy. That's why it's so hard for me to get to Amy to help her."

"Why would the monstrous part of you want to help her?"

"I don't know," I said. "Let me think a minute." I ran that

part of the dream through my head again. "The way we've been talking about the dream, it's kind of a combination of admission and cover-up. Maybe that's going on here. Part of me is admitting that I was that angry thing, and part of me is still trying to deny it. But the denial is losing its power. That's why I'm now starting to dream that my hand touched her just before she fell."

"Let's go back over the first part of the dream." He took a quick glance at his watch. "I'm going to have to call a halt to this pretty soon, but we'll do what we can."

"All right." I took a deep breath. "The dream starts when we're running out of the apartment."

"Do you see the inside of the apartment at all in the dream?"

"No."

"Do you have any sense of something having happened in there?"

"No."

"We've already talked about the vague sense of some dark thing behind you. What about the smell?"

"I only get that later, when we're on the stairs and whatever it is is getting close."

"Do you identify the smell in the dream? Does it have any particular characteristics?"

"No."

"Tell me more about the struggle to get Amy moving."

"Well, when Amy and I are first running out of the apartment, it's clear to me that she can't run as fast as I can, that I'm going to have to help her. I know part of me would like to leave her and run away, but in the dream there's the sense that I would never do that, that I have to try to save us both. I pull her along with me, but once we're on the stairs, she keeps slowing down and getting harder to pull. It's not as if she's resisting me. It's more like she's got weights tied to her. I'm really getting frantic, and I'm yanking on her, and I'm yelling, 'It's Father, Amy, please run,' but she doesn't move any faster, and I'm—"

"Wait a second. What do you say to her in the dream?"

" 'It's farther, Amy, please run.' Why?"

"That's not what you said a moment ago. You said, "It's Father, Amy, please run.' "

"No, I didn't," I said emphatically, suddenly feeling angry again.

"That's what I heard you say."

"Then you need to get your hearing checked. How the hell am I going to tell you the dream if you keep nitpicking and playing word games with me. I said 'farther.' That's what I say in the dream, that's what I always say—and you know that. If I swallowed the *r*, which I don't think I did, it doesn't mean anything. I've got gripes against my father, sure, but he had nothing to do with this, nothing to do with hurting Amy. I don't think he was even there with us."

"So you *were* there when your sister got hurt."

"No . . . I don't know. You're getting me all confused."

"Well, think about it. We'll talk about it more next time. You have an appointment scheduled for tomorrow. Do you want to keep that one too?"

"I don't know," I said, my tone peevish.

"No problem canceling if you tell me now."

"I'll come," I said grudgingly. No matter how annoyed I felt, I knew I needed him.

"Between now and then, think about those slips. And about why you're getting so angry."

"I'm not getting angry. You're just pissing me off."

" 'It's Father, Amy, please run.' "

"Shut up, will you. That's bullshit."

It was so difficult to keep myself from driving too fast—I was so nervous I could barely sit still. I was angry, and I wanted to put my fist through something, or do something violent to myself. In the back of my mind I kept getting flashes of that dream, the exploding machinery, the stumbling toward Amy, the touching her, the falling away, and my screaming, only now the darkness into which she fell gave way to cement stairs, and her body hit with sickening thuds, each thud reverberating in my body as if I were the one falling. I was crying and saying, "I'm sorry, Amy, I'm sorry," but I knew it was no use—this was something terrible that could never be forgiven, that I could never forgive myself for.

The images kept coming, new ones now, and it felt as if my head were going to burst, and I was telling myself to hold on, seeing the lights of Monterey just ahead to my right. The images were awful—we're in that old apartment, my father's drunk, and I'm so frightened, frightened for myself and my sister, and I don't want her to make trouble, she doesn't know what he's like, but she won't shut up, and suddenly he's slapping her hard, and the scene keeps replaying itself in my mind, like a revolving door, the same image again and again, slapping her, slapping her, slapping her. . . .

It was a relief that Janet and Becky were in bed, that there was no one I had to pretend to, because tonight I didn't see how I could. I was sure I'd feel better there in my room, and I slumped down in the easy chair, waiting for a sense of relief, but instead it was as if I had let down my guard, and there was a sudden awful sense of depths opening up, of a terrible panic bursting upward from the center of me. My mind was churning, and I got myself down to the floor, curling up in a ball, as if by doing so I could somehow protect myself from these feelings, but it didn't do any good, the panic was just getting worse. Something was spitting off images in my head like some projector gone crazy, and something in me was telling me to face it, but I didn't want to face it, this was awful, I felt like my mind was coming apart. I tried to shut down my mind, to stop the rushing of these terrible images and feelings. But still they came.

It's night. Mother is gone—gone to visit her sister for a few days—and it's just the three of us in the apartment, Father and Amy and I. Father's in an awful mood—he must have had a bad day, and he hates having to take care of us. He tried to forbid Mother to go, but she wouldn't give in, and they fought this morning before she left, and he's angry about that too. I could tell he'd been drinking when he came home—I could smell it on him—and now he's been drinking all evening. He wants us to get ready for bed, and he's telling Amy something, and she's saying that it's not the way we do it, and I can see him getting angrier, and I'm trying to shut her up and get her to go along with him, but she's cranky herself and doesn't seem to sense the danger. She talks back to him one time too many, and he reaches out and slaps her across the face—something he's never done to her before. She looks at him, shocked, and then she starts screaming, and he tells her to shut up, and she goes on screaming, and he slaps her again, hard, and I'm so scared, but I know I have to do something, and suddenly I run hard into one of his legs and he stumbles, falling against a straight chair, which tips and sends him sprawling with an awful clatter. Amy is standing there stunned, but I have seen the look in his eyes and I know what's coming. I take a step to run, but I can't leave Amy with him like that, and I grab her arm and yank her with me as I hear him struggling to his feet. It takes me a panicky moment to unlock the front door, and then we're outside and starting down the basement steps, Amy struggling with the steps, almost falling once, as I try to pull her with me. I try to get her to move fast, but we're not moving fast enough, and I can hear him behind us, tripping and cursing, but getting closer, and I know it's all hopeless even as my terror drives me on, hearing the awful clanging of the machinery and the licking of the flames on the wall like some prophecy of doom. My fear is urging me to drop Amy's hand and run away, but I can't—I can't leave my sister behind. We're on the landing, and I'm pulling her toward the far stairs, and suddenly a hand grabs my shoulder and spins me around, and a fist knocks me hard to the ground, and looking up from the cement floor I see his livid alcoholic eyes burning in the firelight, and he waits, seeming to dare me to get up. I know I should get up to distract him from Amy, who's standing near the far stairs, but my father's eyes are so angry, and I'm afraid he's really going to hurt me, and so I hesitate, pretending to be more dazed than I am. He turns away and stumbles toward Amy, slapping at her, and suddenly she's falling backward, and I lunge up, far too late, and I hear her body make those sickening sounds as she falls, my little sister whom I should have given my life to protect, and I feel sick for her hurt, and sick at my cowardice, and suddenly he's grabbing at me, and shaking me, and spitting his whispery words at me, that it was an accident, and if I ever tell anyone he hit her he'll do the same to me, and I am terrified of him, but also so sick at myself, that maybe, just maybe, I'm happy to forget.

▽

21

"YOU HAD QUITE a night," said Michael.

It had been an awful night, and I couldn't seem to get out of it. I felt suspended between light and darkness, present and past. I was looking at Michael, his office—everything outside me—as if from the mouth of a cave: The world seemed bathed in glare, too intense and a little unreal. The cavelike darkness around me was filled with the shapes of the basement landing, everything motionless as in some ghastly tableau, a photo of dark forms barely illuminated by firelight. Within that darkness my body felt immobile, weighted down with misery. It seemed like one of those punishments from Dante's *Inferno*: The boy whose sin was to lie still is never to move again.

"Now you know," said Michael.

"Yes," I said. "Now I know."

"You must be feeling relieved."

I just blinked at him, not understanding.

"Because you weren't the one who hurt your sister," he said.

"I should have tried to protect her."

"You did try to protect her, David."

I shook my head hard. The pain that flared through my head felt as if the back of my eyeballs had just caught fire. I'd had a terrible headache all morning, and I couldn't afford any sudden movements. I pressed a hand against the top of my head, as if to keep it from coming off. I said:

"I let him get to Amy because I was afraid. I should have

gotten up, but I was too much of a coward. Because of that my sister was crippled."

"Come on, David," said Michael. "You were five years old. You were scared to death. No one would seriously blame you."

"I blame me."

Michael uncrossed his legs and tilted his chair forward, planting his feet, leaning toward me. His face showed both compassion and exasperation.

"Suppose you had a son who'd acted just as you had and was eating himself up with guilt," he said. "Would you tell him to keep after himself, that he deserved all the punishment he got? Maybe kick him a few times yourself to help him along?"

"Of course not."

"What would you do?"

"I'd do everything I could to comfort him and take away his pain."

"Why can't you do the same for yourself?"

"Because I can't. I won't."

I let my eyes drift away from Michael toward the wall behind him where the Monet poster hung. The painting was of a midday, midsummer scene, a tall garden dominated by sunflowers. The painting was beautiful, but I found it excruciating to look at. My nervous system was worn so raw that every sensation was a form of pain. My eyes were creating a world in which colors blazed, much as in the painting, only now the intensity of the painting was doubled by my act of seeing it. In its fierceness of color—the way the yellows seemed to singe my eyes—the painting took on a malevolent aspect. A hundred sunflowers, taller than men and crowded together like a mob, seemed to strain their faces upward toward the sun in a hysteria of worship. Among them was a small girl, and I had the sense that she was about to be devoured.

I looked down and put a hand over my eyes to block out the burning colors. Then I slowly closed the hand, letting my thumb and index finger drag across my closed eyes in mild massage.

"There was some question I wanted to ask you," I said. "I can't seem to remember what it was."

"It'll come to you."

I let my hand drop from my face. I glanced over my shoulder at the small sink Michael used for his coffee things.

"Do you mind if I splash some water on my face?" I asked. "I'm still sort of out of it. It might wake me up a little."

"Go ahead."

"Do you have any aspirin?"

"I think so."

Michael searched through the bottom desk drawer and came up with a small, yellow-labeled bottle containing three aspirin. I looked at the pills as greedily as a child staring at the last helping of dessert.

"Take them all if you like," said Michael. "I'll bring more tomorrow."

"Thank you."

I went to the sink and turned on the tap. The water was pleasantly cold and I drank two cupfuls as I swallowed the three aspirin. I began splashing water over my face; it felt so good that I dipped my head and held it under the tap. Gradually I could feel the coolness moving throughout my body as if the water had permeated my bloodstream. After drying my face and head with paper toweling, I fixed myself a cup of Michael's thick coffee, diluting it with some water, then loading it with creamer and sugar. It wasn't good, but it was drinkable and sweet, and I figured some of the weirdness I'd been feeling had come from lack of sugar. I took a couple of swallows, then carried the cup back to my chair.

"Better?" asked Michael.

"Yes," I said.

In fact, I did feel better. It was as if someone had switched off the floodlight that had bathed the world in glare; I could look around comfortably now, without always wanting to blink. And I seemed to be out of the cave for the moment, the darkness having receded behind me.

"I remembered the question I wanted to ask you," I said. "About the dream. I figure the changes in my body have to do with my father: He was huge compared to me, he was clumsy because he was drunk, and he smelled of alcohol. I'm not sure why I change into him in the first place, but I was thinking maybe it has to do with my feeling responsible. I change into him after I've been knocked down and can't get up—which is my cover-up in the dream for being too scared to get up. Because I lie there and let him get at Amy, I'm as guilty as he is—I'm just like him. Does that make sense?"

"From the child's perspective, yes."

"But why do I become like him in the dream and still try to pretend that I'm trying to save Amy? That seems inconsistent."

"Dreams mostly are inconsistent," said Michael. "They come from a contradictory jumble of all the different people you've been and the different feelings you've had. Part of you is two, part four, part ten, part forty. Part of you is trying to remember, part to forget; part to hurt, part to save; part to forgive, part to blame. Different parts of you believe different things. No one in you is either in charge, or even fully aware, of these different elements. They're all battling inside you, and the dream is their unstable compromise. As to why you're dreaming about this at all, your forced decision not to remember built up a psychic pressure that has to be released. Since the memory has to come out in some version or other, all the different interest groups inside you are trying to get in on editing the story."

"What about the interpretation where I'm running from my own anger in the dream? Do we throw that out? Or can it also be true?"

"It could also be true. Suppose you'd been repressing a lot of anger prior to your sister's fall—which I'd guess you would have been in that household. In that case you'd have been trying to protect others from your anger, particularly your little sister. Then she gets badly hurt. That primitive part of you that thinks magically rather than logically is going to be convinced that your anger crippled your sister, even as a more rational part knows it was your father."

"That sounds a lot like what Becky's therapist said about her dream. I want to talk to you about her dream, Michael—go over it with you like we did my dream. Maybe you can help me try to figure it out."

Michael gave me a skeptical look. I knew at once what it meant.

"I'm not trying to dodge my issues," I said. "Even if I am, so what? I'm going to have to live my life knowing I failed Amy. Nothing's going to change that. I don't want to fail Becky too." When Michael didn't respond right away, I said, "Please. It's really important to me. I've got to try to help her."

Michael studied me for a moment. His mouth and cheeks moved in thought, bunching up, distorting. It was as if whoever had sculpted that nondescript face had decided to start over.

"Okay," said Michael after a moment. "I'll let you off the hook for now. I'm glad you want to help the girl. I hope you can. Go ahead; tell me the dream."

I described Becky's dream, from the shaking of the house to that moment in church when her mother is about to stab her. In the course of the narrative, I got an idea.

"Look," I said, "I don't know if there's anything to this, but we've just been talking about how I'm both my father and myself in my dream. Do you suppose it's possible that in Becky's dream she might represent both the killer and herself? I mean, knowing who killed her mother, but also feeling responsible, and associating herself with the killer."

"It's possible."

"If that's what's happening, the girl in the dream should have some characteristics of the killer. Especially, I'd think, as she's running away. If she's . . . oh, hell, that brings me right back to Tiny. If everything else gets big, that makes Becky small—tiny. So are the children in the church. Every time I begin to think it's not Tiny, something else points to him."

"Then keep investigating him. But don't let the dream go at that. Try to look at it more carefully. Look for more confirmation of Tiny. But also look for other possibilities."

"How do I go about that?"

"The most important thing is to go over the dream again with Becky. Maybe she'll remember more details. Maybe she'll come up with associations that help. Do your own associations. Look for puns, wordplays, that sort of thing. Check the dream against what you know about reality. Real details can be selected for their symbolic value, but made-up ones are an even better bet."

"You mentioned wordplays. You mean like with names?"

"Yes. Can you give me the names of any other suspects?"

"Sure . . . there's . . . Blake—Becky's therapist."

"If you were going to free-associate with the name, what would you come up with?"

"Black . . . also lake . . ."

"All right. Now ask yourself whether there's a lake in the dream . . . or whether the color black plays a prominent role."

"I don't think there's any water. It is night, but I don't know if black fits in otherwise."

"I'm just throwing out examples. You mentioned that the girl's room is shaking. Shake would be another soundalike."

I laughed.

"What?" asked Michael.

"Nothing. I was just thinking of shake and Blake."

"Okay. But don't just laugh it off. You should start by brainstorming—free-associating with your critical faculties on hold; write down any idea you get, no matter how ridiculous it might seem. Once the ideas are out, then look at them critically. You got another name?"

"John Triplett. My God—the children in the church."

"How many were there?"

"I don't know, Michael, but I'm going to find out."

* * *

I drove past the cemetery. I found myself remembering the small figure sitting by the grave in the twilight, my sense of foreboding as she disappeared into the trees, and my pursuit of those two ambiguous figures. I tried to stop remembering short of the rocks, but I failed. I felt my body start and shudder at the memory of the fall.

After a few blocks, I noticed a police car pull out of a driveway some distance ahead. Moments later I stepped on the gas, realizing whose house it was. I came skidding into the gravel drive and saw Deffinger standing by the driver's door of a dark, green sedan. My skidding must have startled him, because he jerked around toward me and started to reach inside his coat. Then he recognized me and relaxed.

"What happened?" I asked as I got out of the car. I'd forgotten to grab my cane, and I had to make my way around the car using the car body for support. "Are they all right?"

"Yes," said Deffinger. "They're all right. Just upset. As for what happened, someone left this."

Deffinger reached up and took a large plastic pouch off the roof of his car. He handed the pouch to me, indicating that I should hold it with an open hand. Inside the pouch was a five-inch plastic doll of a young girl. The head of the doll had been snapped to the side so that the head lay on her shoulder, still partially attached. A larger doll—perhaps seven or eight inches tall—had its hand on the broken neck of the smaller doll. The larger doll was a Christmas angel. On the angel's face, in black felt-tip pen, someone had drawn a frown in the shape of a quarter moon, with jagged teeth, such as one might see on a malevolent pumpkin. It made the angel look grotesque and insane.

I looked up at Deffinger.

"It seems someone left these dolls on the front steps. Ms. Kendall and her niece found the dolls when they came home."

"Was there a note?"

"No. Just what you see there, minus the pouch." Deffinger took the pouch from my hand, glanced at it, then placed it back on the roof of his car. "We talked to a few of the neighbors. None of them remember any cars coming or going from the house. I'll send the dolls to the lab and see if they come up with anything. Meanwhile, I'll ask the patrols in this area to keep a special eye on the house."

"Thank you," I said.

Deffinger nodded. "I don't know if this is some kind of sick joke or if it's for real, but if I were you I wouldn't leave those two alone for the next few days, especially the girl."

"I won't."

"By the way, something kind of interesting turned up on Triplett. Remember I said there seemed to be some confusion about what kind of car he had. It turns out that five and a half months before Ann Schrader was killed, Triplett's 1987 Mustang convertible was reported stolen and then found burned. The insurance paid him close to twelve thousand dollars. Seems he turned around and bought a 1981 Thunderbird for a little over three."

"Quite a comedown."

"Yeah. Except in the ready-cash department. That little exchange put close to nine thousand dollars in his pocket."

"A pretty good deal for a man who desperately needs cash—say, to pay his girlfriend's drug bills."

"Yeah."

"Did you talk to him?"

"Yes. He seemed pretty nervous. Whether it had anything to do with Ann Schrader, there's something going on there. We'll talk to him again."

When Deffinger had gone, I went into the house. I found Janet and Becky together on the couch, half sitting, half lying, their eyes drooping in a half doze. A dining room chair had been set in the middle of the living room, probably for Deffinger. I moved the chair closer to the couch and sat down. Janet's right hand was resting on the armrest of the couch. I put my hand on hers and gave it a slight squeeze.

"How're you doing?" I asked quietly.

"We were pretty upset," said Janet. "Now we're mostly worn out."

"I'm sorry this happened," I said.

"Thank you."

Becky was resting against Janet's left side. I noticed that Becky's eyes were open. She gave me a small smile. Letting go of Janet's hand, I reached over and tousled Becky's hair.

"Hey, kiddo."

"Hey."

"Look," I said, turning back to Janet, "I'm sure this whole thing is just somebody's sick joke. But we can't afford to take any chances. I don't want either of you to be alone in this house or anywhere else for the next couple of days. I can be with you most of the time, but tomorrow there are some people I need to talk to. Do you have some friends you could visit tomorrow afternoon? Maybe go shopping with?"

Janet looked down at Becky, running her fingertips through the girl's hair. "Becky has an appointment with Dr. Blake tomorrow morning, but I think we can figure out something fun to do after that, can't we, Becky? Maybe buy you a couple of things?"

Becky's head nodded against Janet's shoulder.

"If I could, I'd like to buy you each a present," I said. "Some kind of pick-me-up gift."

"Don't worry about me," said Janet. "Maybe for Becky, though."

"That sweater," said Becky, disengaging herself from Janet and sitting up.

"Becky, it's too expensive," said Janet. "It's fifty dollars."

"Perfect," I said. "Just what I was planning to spend."

"Dave—"

"No, really, please," I said. "I'd like to."

"*Please,*" said Becky.

"Oh, all right," said Janet.

"Can we get it now?"

"No, Becky."

"Call, then. Ask them to hold it."

"They're closed. I'll call first thing in the morning." Janet gave Becky a nudge. "What do you say?"

"Thank you," said Becky, giving me a big grin.

"You're welcome."

Janet shook her head, looking at Becky with amused bewilderment. "Is there anything a new sweater wouldn't cure."

I said, "I think it would be a good idea if we all slept in the same room tonight. Maybe we put a couple of mattresses on the floor in here. You two take one, and I'll take the other. Or one of us can use the couch."

"I think I'd feel a lot safer that way," said Janet.

"In fact," I said, "what we could do to perk ourselves up would be to rent a funny video or two, maybe get a pizza, pop some popcorn, and have ourselves a slumber party."

"Sounds like fun," said Janet.

"Yeah," said Becky enthusiastically.

"Good," I said. "But before we do that, though, I need you to do something for me, Becky. I'm sorry, but I need to go over that dream of yours again. It could be important."

Becky gave me an uphappy look. "Do I have to?"

"He's getting you the sweater," said Janet in a singsongy voice.

"I'll tell you what," I said. "Go over your dream with me again, and we'll also fix sundaes tonight—any kind of sundaes you want."

"Hot fudge," said Becky.

"Nuts?" I asked.

"And whipped cream," she said.

"You got a deal," I said. "Good girl."

I reached out and patted her hand. I realized suddenly, and gratefully, that there were no fears as I did so.

"Go ahead, Becky," I said. "Start at the beginning. I'll ask questions as you go along."

Becky gave a big sigh and sat back against Janet. Becky said:

"Like I said, I wake up in my room and everything's

shaking, and I'm afraid my mom's going to get hurt, and I get up and go running into her room."

"Do you see anybody else in the house?"

"No."

"Is there noise while the room is shaking?"

"There's this big rumbling noise, kind of like with those big earthquakes you see on TV."

"Do you hear any voices—anyone speaking?"

"No."

"So you go into your mother's room. . . ."

"Yeah, and she's lying on the floor, and there's blood on her head, and her neck is all twisted and broken—kind of like on that doll. Her body's all crumpled up, and her dress is kind of up on her legs. I start shaking her, trying to wake her up, and I keep thinking, it's wrong, he did it all wrong. Then I—"

"Wait a minute. That's something you didn't mention before. You're thinking, 'It's wrong, he did it all wrong'?"

"Yes."

"Who's 'he'? Who are you talking about?"

"I don't know."

"What did he do wrong?"

"I don't know. I'm not really thinking of anything particular. The words are just kind of going through my head."

"Then what?"

"I start shaking my mom, trying to get her to wake up, and she opens her eyes, and I'm all happy that she's all right. Only when she sees me, she looks real angry like she hates me, and she says she's going to kill me, her baby, and I say, 'No, Mama,' but she gets up and comes after me, and I try to run away."

"Does she say why she wants to kill you?"

"No."

"In the dream do you have any sense of why?"

"No."

"So then you run away. . . ."

"And I'm running in this city, and everything's so big, and

it keeps getting bigger, and I look behind me, and Mama's there and she's getting bigger too, and I try to run real fast, but it's hard to get anywhere because everything's so big and I'm so small."

"What do you see in the city?"

"I don't know. Just buildings."

"People?"

"No. I don't think so. If there are people, I don't see them."

"Does your body change in any other way while you're running away?"

"No. I don't think so."

"Is there any kind of water in your dream? A pond . . . a lake?"

"No. First I'm home, then I'm running through this city, then I go into the church."

"In the dream do you have a special reason for going into the church?"

"No. It's not like I decide to go in or anything. I just go there. I don't know, maybe I think I'll be safe there. When I'm in the church I try to find a place to hide or someone to help me. I fall over something, and when I get up I see it's a little kid, and then I see that he's all covered with blood, and I know he's dead. I get up and try to run again, but there's another kid, and another, and they're all bloody and dead, and then I see my mother with a knife, and I know she's killed them, just like she wants to kill me. There's someone in the church, and I ask him to help me, but he won't help, and then I see that my mother's almost there, and I know I'm going to die."

"And that's when you wake up?"

"Yes."

"Every time?"

"Yes. Unless Janet hears me dreaming and wakes me up."

"Have you seen the person in the church yet?"

"No."

"Do you have any idea who he is?"

"No."

"Do you know why he won't help?"

"No."

"These kids. Do you recognize them?"

"No."

"Are they boys or girls?"

"I don't know. They're too small."

"Infants?"

"Yes."

"Do you know how many there are?"

"Three."

"Always?"

"Yes."

"You're sure of that?"

"Yes."

"Think about the church: Is there anything else you can remember about it?"

"I don't know. It's got those seats that churches have."

"Pews."

"Yes. The church is real bright, and there are colors on the walls, maybe those windows that churches have."

"Do you talk to your mother during the dream?"

"Yes. I keep begging her not to hurt me, but it doesn't do any good. She hates me, and she wants to kill me. I don't know why. I don't know how to make her stop."

"You'll find a way, Becky," I said. "I know you will."

And I had to find a way to stop whoever was after her. I just had to.

▽

22

I PULLED THE Ford to a stop in front of the one-story house in which Blake's psychiatric group had its offices. I turned to Becky.

"Here you are, kiddo. Your aunt and her friends will be along to pick you up after your appointment. If they're a few minutes late, make sure you stay inside, okay?"

Becky nodded. She was wearing jeans, a purple sweater, and a pair of purple, pink and white running shoes. She seemed in pretty good spirits this morning—a little tired, but then that could have been last night's videos as much as yesterday afternoon's scare.

"Can we have another party tonight?" she asked.

"Sure. You enjoyed that, huh?"

"Uh-huh. If I tell you my dream again, can we have more sundaes?"

"Good grief. You're really trying to cash in on that dream. Next thing I know, you'll be selling it to *People* magazine."

Becky laughed.

"You don't have to tell me the dream again," I said. "Not unless you think of something new. And, yes, we can have more sundaes."

"All right!"

"You'd better go. Okay if I give you a hug?"

Becky leaned toward me with a little self-consciousness but no apparent reluctance. I gave her a big hug, patting her back as we pulled apart.

"Have fun today," I said.

"I will. Bye, Dave."

"Bye, Beck."

I watched as Becky went up the walkway and into the building. "Keep her safe," I whispered, to no one in particular. "Keep her safe."

As I entered the dark church, my eyes took in the pews, the altar, the large crucifix, and the stained-glass windows. I half closed my eyes and tried to half see, half imagine, the church as Becky had dreamed it, with the dead children, the mother with the knife, and the mysterious somebody who wouldn't help. After a time I began to walk the interior circumference of the church, starting with the side aisle to my left. The stained-glass windows there comprised a narrative of events leading up to the birth of Jesus. The windows were beautifully colored, the colors intense in today's bright sunlight. The figures were done in a purposely primitive style, perhaps derived from some South American Indian tradition. The images were crude and powerful, full of feeling.

The first window showed the Annunciation—the angel telling Mary that she would bear the son of God. The angel was otherworldly, majestic, and a touch barbaric; the expression on Mary's face showed consternation as well as wonder. The other windows along that aisle showed three grotesquely beautiful Magi pointing to the star, the Magi consulting with a seductively villainous Herod, and the Magi and shepherds adoring the Christ Child who slept, even then, with sadness in his face, as if already dreaming of Golgotha.

I walked past the altar to the other side of the church where the same series of windows continued. The first showed the Flight into Egypt: Joseph and Mary fleeing in panic with the baby, as a stern angel ordered them onward, out of Herod's reach. The second window showed Herod's soldiers skewering babies with spears and swords in the hope that among them would be Jesus, the prophesied king of whom Herod was afraid. This window stood out from the others in its intensity of feeling, the faces of the soldiers and the babies being stylized caricatures of brutality and pain.

I stood there for a long time, absorbed by the drama of the window, wondering if these five dead or dying infants could have been the babies of Becky's dream.

There was a rustle of clothing next to me. I turned. It was Father Matthew.

"The Slaughter of the Innocents," he said softly.

"The ones God didn't warn."

"Yes."

"How long has this window been here, Father?"

"Let me see . . . '86? . . . no, early 1987. We had a fund-raising campaign to redecorate the church. There were other things done later, but the windows were completed in 1987."

"Before Ann Schrader died."

"Yes," he said, giving me a quizzical look. "Ann was killed in late 1987. What does that have to do with this window?"

"It may figure in a dream that Becky's having, a dream of her mother's death."

"I feel so sorry for that poor girl," he said, his face pained.

I was struck again by those eyes of his, with their ruined, haunted quality.

"Father, I know you can't violate any confidences, but I'd appreciate it if you'd tell me anything you can about Ann Schrader. I think Becky's life is in danger, and her mother's murder is the key. The more I can learn about Ann, the better."

"There's no confidentiality problem," said the priest. "I never heard her confession. She never came to me for formal counseling. We just talked. What do you want to know?"

"What was she like, especially toward the end?"

"She was . . . unhappy . . . angry. She felt she was out of control: Part of her desperately wanted to regain control, and part of her could have cared less. She was searching for something, but she was also flippant, sarcastic, and cynical, and so cut herself off from the things that might have served as answers. She was intelligent but not introspective or very self-aware. She tended to be impulsive and overly energetic."

"Did she strike you as a decent person?"

He considered the question.

"There was some decency in her—toward her daughter, toward her sister. But I don't think she had a deep set of values. She tended to be self-involved and swayed easily. And there was darkness in her. With the drugs, I think, she was giving herself up to that."

"I understand that you were friends of sorts in high school."

"Friends of sorts." Father Matthew seemed to mull over the phrase. He nodded. "Friends of a very odd sort. An awkward, God-haunted boy who's already separated from the world, and a wild, popular party girl who couldn't have been more a part of it."

"Janet told me you helped her with homework."

"That's how it started. With a math puzzle she couldn't solve. Then a literature paper she was having trouble with. But it went beyond the homework. I think she was intrigued by me, as one is intrigued by another life-form, because it's so different. Also, she'd been a Catholic once when she was quite young, and though she had turned her back on the Church, it's impossible to ever escape completely. The sense of darkness, of mystery, of otherness stays with you."

"Did you talk about such things with her? I mean, theological things."

"Not in high school. Not the deep things. She would tease me with such conundrums as whether God could make a rock so big he couldn't lift it." He shook his head, smiling slightly. "Stupid things, but not easy things, the kind of things young minds can make such a fuss over. She would ask me about my choice to be a priest. And she would tell me her troubles, knowing that I would never betray her secrets, that I would take her, in spite of all her pettiness, with absolute seriousness."

"Do you feel you were real friends? Or were you more like curiosities to each other?"

"I suppose I was a curiosity to her. To me she was much

more than that. But then, I was very much in love with her."

My surprise must have been apparent. Glancing at my face, Father Matthew smiled again. But the smile was tired.

"Oh, yes, I was in love with her—even as I was telling her how the joys of this world and the pleasures of the flesh were as nothing compared to eternity. I believe that if she'd loved me back, I might have given up becoming a priest. But there was no chance of that. I found out she was God's way of testing me, of letting me taste a bitterness more profound than any I have tasted since."

He glanced off toward the large crucifix at the front of the church, his expression dark and pained.

"Did you tell her you loved her?" I asked.

"No," he said, "but she knew. In part I was a game she was playing. She won, and she knew she'd won."

"You left for seminary after high school?"

"Yes."

"Did you see Ann much during those years?"

"I never saw her at all. I assumed that I would be sent far away and never see her again. But Father Paul—the pastor here—had taken a liking to me when I was an altar boy, and he asked for me to be assigned here. When Ann learned that I had come back, she came to say hello. It was a very awkward meeting—at least, for me. She looked happy then, and more beautiful than I had ever seen her. After that she rarely came around to see me—not until her life started falling apart."

"Why do you think she came here?"

Father Matthew shook his head. "I honestly don't know. Sometimes it seemed she was coming for solace. Sometimes because she was searching for answers. Sometimes just to make fun of me and all of this. She was erratic toward the end—she had wild swings of mood. I don't know what was really in her heart. Only God knows that."

"Did she bring Becky with her often?"

"Not often. But sometimes."

"Do you have any memory at all of the sorts of things you would have talked about in front of Becky?"

"When Ann was being serious, we'd often talk about forgiveness—whether a loving God would be kinder and more forgiving than the Church makes him out to be. Or maybe, if she was really down, whether it is possible for a person to go so far that forgiveness is no longer possible."

"Did Becky seem to be listening to any of that?"

"It's hard to know. I do remember one episode with Becky. Ann and I were looking up at the crucifix, and I was talking about the sacrifice of Jesus and how he would save us if we'd pray to him. I didn't know Becky was paying any attention. But then she said, 'If Jesus is dead, how can he hear us?' I tried to explain about the resurrection, but she just kept staring at that beautiful dead face, looking perplexed. I don't think she understood. Sometimes I don't think I do either."

Father Matthew stared hard at the crucifix as if he were trying to discern signs of life. As he watched Jesus, I watched him, wondering if this priest could be our dark and fallen angel.

I was crossing the street toward the pharmacy when I saw Triplett emerge, turn, and thread his way through the lunch-time crowd stretched along the sidewalk. I took a diagonal to intercept Triplett farther up the street. The pharmacist was wearing dark blue slacks and a lavender sweater; the color of the sweater made him easy to track.

I caught up with him at a crosswalk where he'd obeyed the blinking Don't Walk sign.

"Triplett," I said, touching his shoulder. "I need to talk to you."

The pharmacist glanced at me with annoyance and pulled his shoulder away from my hand.

"I'm busy, Strickland. I've got lunch to eat and errands to do. You bullied me into talking with you the other day. Not today."

The pedestrian sign changed to Walk. With a brusque "excuse me," Triplett stepped off the curb and started across the street. I limped after him, almost stumbling as the tip of my cane caught on some patched pavement. I wasn't going to be able to keep up with him like this. I decided the only way to stop him was to shock him.

"Triplett," I called after him. "Are you trying to kill Becky?"

He whirled around and took a step back toward me, his face a violent mix of emotions. He seemed shocked, angry, and embarrassed all at once. His eyes shifted back and forth from me to the curious crowd that parted and slowed as it moved around us.

"What the hell did you say?" he demanded.

"I asked you if you're the one trying to kill Becky."

"You ass," he said. "What kind of stunt are you trying to pull? Come over here."

Triplett reached out and grabbed my arm, half dragging me, half supporting me, as he moved us away from the crowd toward a line of cars parked a little farther down the street. Apparently this hippie pharmacist wasn't as mild as I had taken him to be.

Triplett stopped us on the street side of the parked cars. He pushed his face into mine. "Are you crazy, Strickland, following me around and yelling stuff like that at me? I ought to knock you down, except that you're hurt and what you're saying is so insane. I care deeply about Janet and Becky—much more than you do. I wouldn't do anything to hurt them."

Triplett glared at me. I glared back. I said:

"If you really care about them, why don't you stop being such an ass and help me. I think someone is going to try to kill Becky again. If it's not you, then help me stop whoever it is. What the hell good is your caring about Becky if you'd rather play games than keep her alive?"

All the anger drained out of Triplett's face. He let go of my arm and took a step back, bumping into a yellow Camaro. He looked at me for a moment, his tongue playing along his lower lip.

"I don't know if I know anything that would help you," he said finally, in a subdued voice.

"Why don't you let me decide that."

He still looked hesitant. When he spoke, his voice was close to a whisper. "Suppose that telling what I do know could get me in trouble?"

"That depends whether you think it's important enough to let Becky die for." I watched Triplett shift uncomfortably. "It won't necessarily be that tough a choice," I said. "If you had nothing to do with killing Ann Schrader or trying to kill Becky, I don't give a damn what it is. I can promise you that I'll say nothing to the police unless it's absolutely essential to convict a murderer. Even then, if it's something that can't be verified, it would be just my word against yours."

Triplett slowly let out a breath so deep, it was as if he'd been holding it in for a long, long time.

"Okay," he said. "Where can we talk?"

We walked back to my car. Along the way we picked up a couple of turkey sandwiches and coffees at a delicatessen on the main street. I drove down to the water, parking in almost the same spot where Tiny had taken me the other day. We were parked on a diagonal, just above a paved path that ran between the street and the Bay. Because the weather was good, there were streams of bicyclists, skateboarders, roller skaters, joggers, and strollers moving beneath us. We ate for a few minutes in silence. Then I said:

"I need to know if you were giving Ann money."

"Yes."

"Was there any connection between the money you were giving her and the theft of your car?"

Triplett didn't answer for almost a minute. He stared off toward the water, working something over in his head; whether it was truth or lies, I didn't know. He put a last piece of sandwich in his mouth and chewed it down. He made a fist around the waxed-paper sandwich wrapper, crunching it so forcefully and noisily that he might have been a human trash compactor.

"Ann was after me for money," he said finally. "I told her I didn't have any. The money my father had given me was all tied up in the business, and I was already borrowed up to my eyeballs. I had this '87 Mustang convertible that I'd splurged on, mostly using a ten-thousand-dollar inheritance I'd gotten from my grandfather. Ann was after me to sell the car. I told her I'd try, but I kept stalling. I loved that car. One day I got up to go to work, and the car wasn't there. I reported it stolen to the police. A few hours later the police called to tell me the car had been found on a deserted stretch of beach, gutted by fire. When I told Ann what had happened, her first response was, 'Now you have the money.' I could tell from the way she said it that she'd taken the car."

"Nice lady."

"No. Not nice at all. I don't know if she ever had been. If she had, drugs and disappointment had changed her. But she was . . . so beautiful. And there was something wild in her . . . like some magnificent and dangerous animal you might come across in the wild. You're frightened and awed and excited all at once, and seeing it makes you wish you were somehow different. And when she played up to you—when she wanted something—she was pure fantasy."

"How much money did you give her?"

"Close to seven thousand dollars—not all at once, but in installments over about four months."

"You had to know that she was spending the money on drugs."

"Yes."

I took the last sip of my coffee, studying Triplett over the top of the cup.

"It doesn't add up," I said. "Your not-nice girlfriend, who's drug-addicted and who sleeps around, burns your car and demands the money so she can buy more drugs—and you, the antidrug crusader, give it to her? I don't care what kind of love or need or obsession you had for her, that doesn't make any sense."

Triplett's lips formed a small smile. But there was no humor in it.

"I guess it doesn't. I'd hate to admit how close to that I

did come—the kind of power she had over me. She could suddenly toss back her head and brush the hair from her eyes with her fingers and give you this teasing smile, and it made you feel as if all the screws she'd put to you had all been a big joke, even though they hadn't been. But, no, I wasn't quite that bereft of my senses. The fact is, she was blackmailing me."

"For what?"

"One night, when she was staying over at my place, she'd run out of coke and couldn't get any more. Her usual suppliers didn't seem to be around that night, and her so-called friends claimed they couldn't help. She was really down, and crying, and talking about killing herself, and it got me scared, and I did a stupid thing. I got her some amphetamines from the pharmacy. A few days later my sweetheart returned the favor by threatening to turn me in for giving her prescription drugs unless I paid her money. She might not have been able to make out her case to the police, but the licensing board wouldn't have needed so much convincing. I told her I didn't have any money, but then she burned the car, and in the end there wasn't much I could do."

"Couldn't you have played her blackmail off against the car she'd burned? You had something on her too."

"Maybe. If I'd been gutsy enough. In fact, I took a stab at it, and she just laughed at me—told me she'd swear I burned the car. Normally, I suppose, you have the other person's sense of self-preservation to count on. But not with Ann. Toward the end I had a sense she didn't give a damn anymore. She wanted her drugs, but beyond that, if she couldn't have them, she'd just as soon self-destruct. So I gave her the money."

"So you were paying up until the day she died?"

Triplett shook his head.

"After four months of paying, I could see that it was going to go on and on, and that I'd never get out from under, and anyway by that time she wasn't trying to sugarcoat the pill anymore. I got to the point where I didn't really give a damn either. She could see that, I think, and that's why she let me go so easily. She had a real rough time of it there for a few weeks when the money ran out, and I thought she might turn me in just for spite. Then all of a sudden she had money and was back on drugs again. I remember wondering if she'd found someone else to blackmail."

"Did you have anything particular to base that on?"

"No—not beyond my own experience with her. And the fact that I couldn't figure out how else she could be getting the money."

"If she was blackmailing someone else, do you have any idea who it might have been?"

"No. I'd been pretty much dumped out of her life by that point. I didn't know much about what she was doing."

"Back when you were in her life—when she was seeing other men—did you have any idea who any of those men were?"

"No. She didn't discuss the other men with me. And I didn't want to know anything about them."

"You never got any hints? She never made any slips?"

"Not really. Well, one thing maybe. I remember coming home one time and overhearing her talking on the phone. It was obvious that she was talking to a man from the throaty, flirtatious tone in her voice. I heard her laugh and say, 'Oh, so you don't just use them on the bad guys, then.' The first thought that came into my mind was that she was joking with some cop about handcuffs. I don't know if that was right."

"Did you ask her about the conversation?"

"No. Like I told you, we avoided talking about other men."

"When did this conversation take place?"

"I don't know. Maybe . . . two . . . three months before she died."

I turned away from Triplett and looked out toward the sun-speckled water, thinking it over.

"A cop," I muttered. "Jesus. Wouldn't that be a mess."

▽

23

THE MOMENT I drove up to the house, Janet came rushing out to meet me, wearing a burgundy-colored wool dress, long earrings, and no shoes. As she got closer, I could see that she was upset.

"Dave, I'm so glad you're here," she said.

"What's wrong?" I asked, reaching out and touching her shoulder.

"I got a call from him—from that Angel person."

"When?"

"This morning. I was so frightened."

"Where's Becky?"

"She's at the Blakes' house. The call came while Becky was at her appointment. I phoned Dr. Blake to tell him about it and to make sure that Becky was all right. He offered to have Cynthia take Becky back to their place. They're going to keep her tonight to give us a chance to decide what to do."

"Does anyone else know she's there?"

"No."

"You haven't told anyone at all? Those friends who were here with you this morning? It's important for me to know."

Janet shook her head. "No. My friends and I talked about the phone call. They knew I was calling Dr. Blake. But I didn't mention anything about Becky staying overnight. In fact, I didn't know it then. It was only decided later when I talked with Cynthia."

"Good."

I glanced down at Janet's bare feet. It had been a beautiful day, but it was February, and getting toward evening, and there was a nip in the air.

"Why don't we get you in the house," I suggested. "Just as easy to talk in there."

We walked to the house in silence. Once inside, as we stood together on the heavy brown carpet, I said:

"This whole thing is starting to make me very nervous. The possibilities are coming from too many different directions. Becky will be all right at the Blakes' tonight. But I think tomorrow I'd like to take you both up to my place in the mountains for a couple of days. I'll make some calls, find some friends in my area you'd be safe with. Then I'll come back here and try to figure this thing out."

Janet gave me a look of confusion. "I don't . . . I mean . . . are you sure that's really necessary?"

"I'm not sure of anything," I said. "But I think we should go. We can't afford to make a mistake with Becky's life."

"No," she said. "Of course not."

At Janet's suggestion, we moved to the couch. Janet sat on one end, her body turned toward me, her feet tucked up under her for warmth. I said:

"Tell me about the call. What did he say? Was it a he?"

"I think so. The voice seemed awfully low."

"What did he say?"

"He said, 'The Angel of Death is upon you.' "

"Anything else?"

"No. That was all."

"Did the voice sound at all familiar?"

"No. I could barely make out the words. It was all muffled."

"Did you call the police?"

"Yes. The man I talked to said he'd alert the patrols. He said Sergeant Deffinger was transporting a prisoner down to San Diego and wouldn't be back until noon tomorrow. The man said he'd let Deffinger know as soon as he got in."

"I'd like to leave in the morning," I said. "After breakfast, why don't I go pick up Becky at the Blakes' while you pack up whatever you two will need. Make it for a week or so, just in case. As soon as I've got Becky and you're packed, we'll take off."

"I'd better call and tell the Blakes," said Janet, sliding her feet out from under her and letting them slip to the floor. "I was going to call anyway to talk to Becky."

"Please don't tell the Blakes we're leaving town. You can tell them later, after we get where we're going."

"*Dave.* The Blakes would never tell anyone."

"They might if the police asked them. And I don't want the police to know either."

"I don't understand this. You're making me frightened."

"I don't mean to. But this is serious stuff, Janet. People let things slip. Maybe I'm overreacting, but I don't want to take any chances. I'm just doing this to keep both of you safe."

Janet's face softened. She reached over and touched her fingers to my arm.

"I know you are, Dave. Thank you."

After Janet had made her phone call and had changed into slacks and a sweater, she offered to make us spaghetti, using the ingredients she'd won at the shower. I hobbled around the kitchen helping her—setting the table, opening the Chianti, washing the lettuce. My leg had improved to the point where I could get around the house without my cane, though I still needed the cane when I had to walk some distance or when I was tired or tense. There was still some spasticity in the leg and not all the muscles were working yet. Also, the leg was very weak, as was my whole right side.

We sat down to eat with all the bonhomie of two death-row prisoners sharing a last meal. But gradually the food and the Chianti brought on a feeling of relaxation, insulating us for a moment from whatever might be out there or up ahead. There was comfortable talk, interspersed with comfortable silences. At one point Janet's face took on a look of reverie.

After watching her for a few moments, I asked her what she was thinking.

"I was just trying to imagine a time when all this would be over," she said. "When Becky would be well and out of danger. When the two of us would start living again."

"Could you?"

"I don't know. I get images, but they seem unreal. It's hard to believe in them."

After a moment, she said, "I guess it must have been that way for Ann. She kept daydreaming about something better, even as her life got worse and worse. It's so sad she had to die just when her life was finally turning around."

Janet took another sip of wine. After a moment a small smile formed on her face.

"I was just remembering a little game she used to play with Becky. She'd say, 'Hon, go over to the window and tell me if there's any money growing on that tree yet.' Becky would go over to the window and look out and say, quite solemnly, 'No, Mama, not yet.' And Ann would say, 'Darn, I know it's a money tree—the man who sold it to me told me so. Maybe we need to water it a little more.' Looking back, I suppose it seems a little mean of Ann, but at the time it seemed kind of cute. Becky was so serious about it.

"Sometimes Ann would say to Becky, 'Sweetie, come over here and tell me if my head's on straight.' When Becky came over, Ann would kind of tilt her head to one side, and Becky would look it over and say, 'No, Mama, your head's not on straight.' And Ann would say, 'Well, don't worry, my shrink will fix it.'

"And sometimes Ann would come in and say, 'Becky, is there any fuzz on me?' I guess it was awful when I look back on it—Ann had probably just come back from buying her crack. But Becky was so cute about it—she'd look all over her mother's clothing and maybe pick a piece of lint off the back of Ann's slacks. And Ann might say, 'Hey, you got him. And he was right on my tail, too.' "

Janet laughed at the memory. I let her enjoy her laugh. Then I said:

"Do you know if your sister was ever dating a police officer?"

"Let me think . . . no . . . at least I don't remember her ever saying anything about it." Janet gave me a sharp look. "Does that question have anything to do with why you don't want me to tell the police where we're going?"

"Maybe."

"Are you saying that some policeman was involved in Ann's death?"

"I don't know. But it's possible."

"That policeman who gave Tiny his alibi?"

"Could be."

As I spoke, a name flashed into my mind. Douche's last name. Bigelow. I got an image of a frightened little girl running through a nightmare city, not being able to get anywhere because everything kept getting bigger.

I woke, hearing a soft, whimpering sound. I propped myself up on one elbow and peered into the darkness of the living room. As my eyes began to adjust, I could make out Janet's outline across the room. She was sitting up on the other mattress, her quilt wrapped around her.

"Janet," I said, "what's wrong?"

"Noth-ing. I'm . . . sorry . . . I w-woke you."

"What's the matter? It sounds like your teeth are chattering."

"Th-they are. Had a b-bad dream. G-got scared. Can't g-get warm."

"For heaven's sake, bring your quilt and come over here. I'll rub your back."

"Th-thanks."

Something that looked like a quilt with a head rose up and came toward me. As it melted down onto the bed next to me, I could just make out the details of Janet's face. I noticed that her feet were exposed, so I slipped a section of my quilt out from under her and used it to cover her feet. I had her turn away from me, and I started vigorously massaging her back and arms through the heavy material.

"F-feels g-good."

"Don't try to talk until your teeth stop chattering. Try to relax."

I massaged Janet's back and arms for a while longer, then did her feet through my quilt, then returned to her back again. I could feel the shivering diminishing under my hands. Finally she said:

"Thank you. That's much better."

"Tell me what happened."

"I had this awful dream about Becky. Someone was carrying her away, and she was calling to me, and I couldn't get to her. I woke up all frightened, and I started feeling cold, and I couldn't get myself warm."

"You're okay now?"

"I'm still a little chilly. But I'm much better."

"Look, keep yourself wrapped in the quilt and lie down under my quilt, but on top of the blanket. That way the blanket will be our . . . what do they call that board they used to put between unmarried couples back in Puritan times? You know, when they'd lie in bed visiting because there was no heat in the house."

"Bundle boards, I think."

"The blanket will be our bundle board."

"Okay."

When we had Janet arranged under the covers on her side facing away from me, I rubbed her back again—or tried to through the two quilts. After a little while, I asked her how she was feeling.

"I finally feel warm. I'm still feeling a little scared, though. Would you mind talking to me?"

"I don't mind. What do you want to talk about?"

"You do the talking. Talk about anything. Tell me about your house."

"You don't want to get me started on that."

"Tell me. Please."

"Okay."

I started talking about my house, and, as always when I talked about it, I was really talking about the land and the view. The house was modest—a small ranch house with lots of glass—but it was set on a lot near the top of one of the Santa Cruz mountains, with a view down the mountain to the ocean and as far away as Monterey. I told Janet about how the entire view might disappear in the morning in the heavy fog and then slowly reveal itself during the morning, as the billowy clouds with their twists and swirls slowly receded down the slope. I told her about the spectacular orange-and-red sunsets and the crystal night views up on that mountain, far above the San Jose smog.

I was just starting to talk about the small corral with the geese and the pygmy goats when I realized that Janet was sound asleep, maybe had been for a while. I laughed at myself, remembering how it had been with Katie when she was tired and upset, or when she was worried and couldn't sleep, and I'd try to help by reassuring her and the advice might get a little elaborate, and before I'd ever get close to finishing, Katie would be sound asleep. I'd thought she'd wanted information when all she'd really wanted was a soothing voice.

Oh, well, I thought, if I can bore them to sleep, at least I'm performing a valuable service.

I yawned, wondering if I had managed to bore myself. I put my head down and fell asleep.

I had a dream of Katie as she'd been early on, when we'd started going together. I won't push you to go to bed with me, I told her, if you won't be so nervous about my touching you. And we both laughed because we knew in the dream what was going to happen.

I woke with my arm around Katie, my body against hers, only, of course, as I realized after a moment, it wasn't Katie. As I tried to orient myself, I realized that I had an erection.

The quilt that Janet had wrapped around herself seemed to be gone, though there was still the blanket between us. I hoped she couldn't feel what was going on, if she was even awake, which I doubted. I slid my pelvis back away from her. Then I started to remove my arm, only to feel her hand take hold of mine.

"You don't have to move," she whispered.

She turned onto her back, turning her face toward me. She said:

"I didn't know if you could . . . you know . . ."

I laughed, a little self-conscious.

"Yeah, that was one of the first things I checked. Sorry, I was having a dream. I guess we needed a bigger bundle board."

"Can I get under there with you?" she asked.

"You sure you want to?"

"Yes."

"Then, yes."

She slipped out of bed, then crawled in under the sheet and blanket that I lifted up for her. She turned onto her right side, facing me. I could just make out her face in the dim light from outside. I put my hand out and touched her hair.

"You want to take a moment to reconsider?" I asked.

"No."

"I'm a wreck."

"That's okay. I seem to be partial to wrecks."

"I'm not sure how well I'll be able to move."

"We'll manage."

We kissed, and I ran my hand slowly along the soft cotton of her pajama top, over her breasts and down over her stomach. I slipped the hand under her top, and moved the hand upward again, then around to her back and down toward her hips. Her hands began to move over my skin. Perhaps it was deprivation, or the pain and fear I'd been through, but it was as if I had taken some drug that had intensified tenfold the feel of her flesh under my hands and the feel of my body under her fingers. What I felt was not so much pleasure as urgency, longing, need; at times the feeling was almost excruciating, and I'd feel my eyes watering up. We lay still as we made love, channeling the tension into slow touching and gentle writhing. She came before I ever entered her, straddling my thigh, and when I did enter her, it was over in a moment, my heart seeming to explode out of me with the rush of excitement, so that I found myself weeping against her as she stroked my hair.

Eventually we pulled back just a little, still touching in a kind of memory of wonder.

"That was *very* nice," I whispered. "You feel wonderful."

"You too. You were so gentle, and you touched me so nicely, I almost couldn't stand it."

"Thanks for letting me cry," I said. "I've had all this pain in me. It felt good to get some of it out."

"It's all right. It was lovely. I was crying along with you, and it felt good to me too."

Gradually our touches and whispers slowed as we grew sleepy there in each other's arms. Just as I was starting to drift off to sleep, I heard Janet giggle.

"What?" I asked.

"Nothing."

"Come on—what is it?"

She giggled again. "I was just thinking how it was better for you to light up one Kendall than to curse the darkness."

"That's awful," I said, starting to laugh with her. "That's really awful. . . ."

▽

24

A THICK EARLY-MORNING fog hung just above the car like the ceiling of a cave, tendrils of white trailing downward like ghostly stalactites. In the rearview mirror, the ceiling of fog kept collapsing like a cave-in behind me, blocking my view. Frustrated by my inability to see what was back there, I killed my lights, took two quick turns onto residential streets, pulled to the curb, and waited. Only two cars appeared in the next ten minutes, and both of those had emerged from the carports of nearby houses. Apparently I wasn't being followed, but as an extra precaution, I took different side streets back to the main road. Then I headed for the Blakes' house.

Feeling more at ease now as I drove, I gave myself up to memories of this morning. I'd woken well before Janet, but hadn't moved from her sleepy embrace, relishing the feel of her against me. When she had woken, there'd been none of the awkwardness I'd half expected there to be between us; instead she'd been happy and soft and affectionate. Later we'd gone to the kitchen to fix pancakes, playing house like a couple of newlyweds for whom it was all a new game, joking a lot and managing to bump into each other much more often than was necessary.

With all that, I felt as if I had a full morning behind me; yet it was only ten to seven. Perhaps a little early to be disturbing the Blakes, but I doubted they'd be sleeping in under the circumstances. If Becky hadn't had a chance to eat, we could get her something on the road. I wanted to get us out of town as quickly as possible.

The fog thinned as I approached the Blakes' house, yielding vague gray glimpses of a large Victorian: This was the house they would soon vacate for the Laguna Hills ranch.

Cynthia Blake opened the door. I was relieved to see that although she wore a robe, her hair was fixed and her makeup was on: Obviously she hadn't just bolted up out of a sound sleep.

"Morning," I said.

She squinted at me as if I were somewhere out there in the fog rather than standing just in front of her. Only as she spoke did I realize that what her expression signaled was mild confusion.

"Didn't my husband get hold of you, Mr. Strickland?"

"No. Is something wrong?"

"No. Not now. But last night Barry thought he heard someone outside. I guess he stayed up most of the night, keeping watch. And a little while ago he thought he saw someone out back. He decided he'd better get Becky away from here, so he drove her out to the ranch. They left a little while ago. He said he'd call Janet's and let you know. I don't think he expected you this early."

"I didn't expect me this early either."

"Barry said he'd wait for you at the ranch. Do you remember how to get there?"

"Only vaguely."

"I'll write down the directions. And get you Becky's jacket. They left so quickly she forgot it."

I waited in the hallway, dividing my time between looking out the window into the fog and glancing at old photographs sitting on the hall table. Several were from what I guessed to be Mrs. Blake's early childhood, judging from the style of clothing and the fact that the same young girl was prominent in every photo. There was a picture of a high school–age Blake with some of his buddies, inscribed, "To Bebe, from the gang," and what looked to be a high school graduation picture.

Once I had the directions and the jacket, I left, driving

through Ocean Point and Monterey toward Route 1. From time to time I'd study the rearview mirror to make sure I wasn't being followed. Otherwise I occupied my mind by thinking over Becky's dream.

I thought I understood now the role the church played in the dream. It was natural that the child, having been taken there by a mother seeking solace, might think of the church as a place of escape. At the same time, the window portraying the Slaughter of the Innocents must have come to represent for Becky's guilty mind the punishment it feared. The man who wouldn't help was, I believed, the Jesus of Becky's conversation with Father Matthew, the Jesus hanging dead on the cross, unable to hear.

What I didn't know was if, and to what degree, the church episode in the dream might also have been selected for what it conveyed about Ann Schrader's murder. In some ways Father Matthew was the perfect candidate for the Angel who had seemed so good and kind and different from other men, who had evoked from Ann the wonder expressed by, "Who would have expected it?" And, after all, Father Matthew had admitted loving her.

A little bliss, then blackmail. The priest wouldn't have had much money of his own, but Ann could have suggested the church treasury—maybe that building fund he'd mentioned. If Becky had seen the priest standing over her mother's body, couldn't he have become associated in her mind with the violence of the stained-glass windows, with the dead Jesus who didn't help?

I took the Route 1 on-ramp going north, then soon after took the exit for Highway 68. Here, away from the ocean, the ground fog had completely disappeared, giving way to a cold, gray sky.

There was still Tiny. The possibilities with him had become more real and more complex. Tiny and Bigelow: Those were two names that would fit well with the middle part of the dream, when the city becomes big, and Becky small. Before I had wondered, along with Janet, whether Tiny might have paid Bigelow—Douche—for an alibi. But what if it had been the other way around? What if Bigelow had been the blackmail victim and had gone to Tiny for help? The thought that Tiny and Bigelow might have conspired in Ann's murder provoked my curiosity, but what provoked my fear was the possibility that they had been aided by another cop who obviously liked Bigelow, a cop with a last name and nickname that would fit only too well with that of somebody who didn't hear or help. Deffinger. Deff.

I glanced in the rearview mirror, seeing nothing but empty road behind me. I was grateful Deffinger would be out of town until noon, when Janet and Becky and I would be long gone. Just as I returned my full attention to the road ahead of me, I caught a glimpse of the Laguna Seca golf course off to the left. I slowed, then took a right turn some distance ahead. The road climbed steeply into the hills.

There was also Triplett to consider. The pharmacist's story had sounded convincing enough, but with slight modifications it would constitute one long motive for murder. What if Ann Schrader hadn't let him off the hook so easily, maybe threatened to turn him in just for spite? In fact, wouldn't that have been more in character for her?

There were five babies perpetually dying in that stained-glass window, but only three dead in Becky's dream. Didn't the fact that she was so definite about the number three make it likely the number had some significance? There was no way to see five children in the dream. Four, maybe, with Becky, but not five.

Four, maybe, with Becky.

Four infants.

Four babies.

4 babies.

4 B B.

I felt suddenly cold. At the same time I told myself this was nonsense, an accident of ideas. My thoughts began to scatter, searching out reasons the murderer could not be Blake. I struggled to pull the thoughts back. Don't go after the negative, I told myself. Focus on the dream: See if anything else fits.

4 B B was the license plate Blake had had ever since his wife had given him the Alfa Romeo Spider. Becky had known the car—she'd been fascinated by it—she'd had a ride in it. She had to have noticed the plate; she was in kindergarten—the number and letters wouldn't have been a problem for her. BB sounded like "baby"; it's an association that could have stuck. Maybe she'd even heard her mother call him "baby" one time. Or "Bebe," the nickname I'd just seen in the photograph.

Assume the dream is a reversal in which Becky is, in part, a stand-in for the killer. The wish/fear is that the mother kill the killer, rather than the other way around. So the mother kills Bebe. She kills babies. She kills, counting Becky, four babies—4 BB. Was it still too tenuous? Did baby fit anywhere else in the dream? Yes . . . wait a minute. Becky had said, "My mother gives me this horrible look, and says she's going to kill me, her baby"—or something like that.

Was there anything else? Becky goes into her mother's room and finds her mother crumpled up on the floor; and she thinks, "He did it all wrong." Did what wrong? The mother's dress is pulled up. Her head's bleeding. Her neck is all . . . twisted. Neck . . . twisted. What was that story Janet had related? Ann says to Becky, "Hon, is my head on straight?" and Becky says, "No, Mama, it's not on straight," and Ann says, "Don't worry, my shrink will fix it." The man Becky saw that night was supposed to fix her mother's head, not leave it all crooked—because the man was her mother's shrink. In fact, couldn't that be what Becky/the killer was really doing when the town seemed to grow bigger—shrinking?

Christ, it *was* Blake.

I barely saw the next turn in time, took it too fast, almost lost control of the car as it skidded down the narrow, potted, gravel-strewn road that dipped into the canyon. I had to go slow, much too slow, as I drove along the winding lane—any speed at all was likely to send me sliding off into some thicket of scrub oak.

I tried to focus all my attention on the driving, but my mind wouldn't cooperate, kept working through the details of the crime. Ann must have had something on Blake—maybe there'd been a sexual relationship between them—that made him a good blackmail substitute for Triplett. Only instead of paying, he'd killed her—though perhaps by accident, during a quarrel. Afterward he'd diverted the investigation with lies and fake clinical notes: "Angel" must have been an invention, and they'd all been chasing a phantom. The break-in too must have been a fake, or maybe a real event fictionalized after the fact, in order to defuse a question that might have blown up in Blake's face: the question of how anyone else outside the family could have known enough to be threatened by Becky's dreams. Why Blake had ever treated the girl and how he could be doing this to her now—those were matters that still didn't make any sense.

Blake's ranch was just ahead now; I could see his Mercedes in the driveway. As I drove through the gate, my eyes scanned the yard and house for glimpses of Becky or Blake and got none. I was out of the car, stumbling toward the house, when I heard what sounded like a muffled human cry. I stopped and swung my head about, trying to locate the source of the cry. Then I had it: I glimpsed the two of them on foot at the top of the riding trail, Blake dragging Becky, one of his hands pressed against her face. The moment after I saw them, they disappeared over the ridge.

The riding trail was a sandy track that snaked its way back and forth along the slope of the hill to give the horses an easier climb. I tried to shorten my ascent by going straight up the hill, climbing from one tier of trail to the next, half walking, half crawling, struggling through bushes that caught at my clothes and tore at my hands.

I had no plan. There was no question of surprise: Blake knew I was there. There was no question of pretense: He'd already made his move against Becky and would know that her cry had alerted me. There was no time for anything clever; my only thought was to get to them while Becky was still alive.

I was tired and limping badly by the time I reached the top of the hill. I pushed myself on, following the sandy trail as it wound its way through a grove of trees. Beyond the trees I came to a meadow. The meadow, lined with trees to the left and right, was open ahead, extending to the far edge of the hill where it yielded vistas of hills and sky. The meadow was empty. I walked out into it, eyes scanning the trees, trying to guess where Blake and Becky had gone. Then I heard a rustle of underbrush and turned.

Blake stepped out from the tree line, a knife blade held to Becky's throat. For a moment I just blinked at them, still not quite believing what I saw—this bear of a man, whom I'd taken for Gentle Ben, threatening the life of the young girl he'd spent years trying to save. I looked at the knife blade, then up into Becky's terrified eyes. I felt sick.

"Do what I tell you," said Blake. "If I cut her throat, she'll die, no matter what you do."

"Okay," I said. "Don't hurt her. I'll do anything you say."

Blake ordered me to toss my cane to the ground. Then, keeping a safe distance, he directed me through a series of maneuvers—lifting up my sweater and shirt, rolling up my pant legs, emptying out my pockets, all designed to show him I didn't have a weapon.

When he was satisfied, he waved me back and maneuvered himself and Becky over to where my cane lay. There was a moment there, as Blake reached his knife hand down to pick up the cane, when Becky might have had a chance to make a break. But it would have been a long shot, and anyway, she looked frozen with fear.

As Blake straightened up, Becky cried out, "Dave, I'm scared."

"I know, hon, I know."

I felt panic for Becky surge up inside me, felt a fierce urge to do something desperate. I fought back the urge, muscles clenching all through my body as if the fight were physical. With fifteen yards between us, Blake holding that knife on Becky, and me trapped in this crippled body, making a move now would be fatally stupid. I had to make myself wait for my best chance. No matter how desperate it might turn out to be, it couldn't be worse than this.

"He killed my mother," said Becky, the words bursting out of her like a sob.

"Your mother was a bitch," said Blake, spitting the words out. He looked at me. "I helped Ann as a charity case, and she paid me back by playing with me, then threatening to ruin me if I didn't give her money. I kept telling her the money was Cynthia's—I couldn't pay anything close to what she wanted. I went to see Ann that night when my wife was in one of her sleeping-pill slumbers. I tried reasoning with her, but she just laughed at me. I hit her, and she fell. It was an accident. It wasn't my fault."

"If it was an accident, why don't you turn yourself in? They wouldn't be all that hard on you. Certainly not hard enough to risk killing us for."

"Don't be stupid, Strickland. Even in the best case, I lose my career, my reputation, my wife—everything I've worked for. Anyway, they'd say I let Ann die, even though it turned out that calling for help wouldn't have made any difference. You know, for a second there, I actually did think about calling. But then I thought about that slut watching my ruin, and there was no way that was going to happen."

Blake was trembling slightly, as if with remembered fury. After a moment, he said, "Let's go, Strickland," gesturing with the knife blade toward the unwooded edge of the hill. When I hesitated for a second, he brought the knife blade back to Becky's throat and barked out, "Now!"

I turned and began to move in the direction he'd indicated. As I limped along, I kept glancing back over my shoulder to keep track of Becky and Blake; they were walking about fifteen yards behind me. Blake had the cane as well as the knife now; he was holding the cane with his left hand, the same hand he was using to grip the back of Becky's sweater.

As I got to within forty yards of the edge of the hill, I suddenly realized that what I'd assumed to be a gentle downward slope was in fact a cliff, its edges jagged from what I guessed had been a rock slide. Directly ahead was a small peninsula of land jutting out over the cliff. I had a sudden premonition that the peninsula was our destination, that Becky and I were to be herded onto it and over the edge.

I felt a shock of vertigo; my heart began to pound, my mind race. My right leg seized up, muscles cramping, toes curling under the foot. It became hard to walk, and I grabbed a handful of slacks at the front of my thigh to yank the leg along. Goddamn it, I thought, cursing the leg and myself. Don't you dare freeze up on me. Don't you dare.

I had to think. If Blake wanted us over the cliff—a way of getting rid of us that might help him concoct a halfway plausible story—he'd have to get close to me as I got close to the cliff; I certainly wasn't going to jump off. What would he do? I had the feeling that this was all extemporaneous, that he'd planned an easy-to-manage accident for Becky and now had to deal with a totally unexpected complication. What were his options? He could herd us both onto the peninsula, then come after us swinging the cane. Or better: get me out onto the peninsula, push Becky off near the base, and then come out after me. It wouldn't take much of a blow to topple me with my crippled leg.

So I couldn't risk letting him get close enough to the cliff to push Becky off. I'd have to calculate the moment just short of that when Blake was the closest to me. Then I'd go for him. Somehow I had to get that knife blade away from Becky's throat. And somehow I had to get my hands on Blake long enough to let Becky get away.

I was about twenty-five yards from the cliff now. I slowed my pace, hoping that he'd get closer without quite noticing. It might help if I could distract him.

"How can you do this to Becky?" I asked. "And why the

hell did you agree to treat her in the first place?"

"I didn't want to," said Blake, with something that sounded like real pain in his voice. "Christ. The daughter of the woman I'd killed? But I didn't see how I could refuse Janet without looking suspicious. I was going to pass the case on to someone else, but I began to feel really sorry for Becky. It wasn't fair that she should suffer for her mother's sins. In a way, I suppose, helping her was a kind of atonement. Everything was going fine, too, until she began having those dreams, and I realized she'd seen me. I'd had no idea. After that, I kept getting signs that she was beginning to remember. I'm sorry, I really am. But I'm just not willing to give up my life for hers."

The cliff was about fifteen yards ahead. Peripheral vision from a slightly turned head told me that Blake and Becky had closed to within ten yards of me.

"You burned your own files?" I asked.

"I had to get rid of that file on Becky. After Ann's death I was afraid the court would check my original notes for tampering. They didn't, but I couldn't take that same chance again. Not with all that dream material I'd written down before I understood what it meant. And I figured if anyone started focusing on Becky's therapy, the fire and fake break-in would explain how others could have known what we'd discussed."

It was less than ten yards to the base of that minuscule peninsula that jutted out from the cliff like a deadly diving board. In another moment I'd have to risk lunging for Blake. I felt my stomach knot up, felt fear for Becky clog my chest. Please, I begged, don't let him cut her; let me get to him first.

"That Angel doll was you?" I asked.

"And the phone call—which I made from my office. It got Becky into my hands. And it provides a nice story. Even though I tried to hide Becky away, somehow Angel found us. I tried to protect her, but I'm not much of a fighter. And neither, unfortunately, was the brave, crippled detective . . ."

I don't know if Blake made his move because he saw me

making mine, or whether this had been his timing all along. Just as I started to turn, he shoved Becky into me with violent force, sending us both tumbling, one over the other, onto that small jutting piece of cliff. Suddenly, in the shock of surprise, I was trying all at once to locate the edge of the cliff, keep myself from falling, and grab for Becky. I landed facedown, my head a foot from the edge, felt Becky go tumbling over me, heard a small cry, and reached up desperately, feeling blouse, then arm, bracing myself, grabbing and holding on, seeing her legs dangling over the cliff, pulling at her, dragging her back—all the time expecting Blake to be on us any moment. But as I rolled away from the edge with Becky, I saw that Blake had held back, hoping perhaps that the shove would take care of one or both of us—maybe fearing that he could get tangled with us and fall.

I got to my knees and looked around. The peninsula we were on was perhaps twelve feet long, narrowing quickly from a ten-foot base to a stubbed point three feet wide. The drop from every side was sheer and deep; I could see boulders torn from the hillside sitting a hundred feet below us.

Blake was standing just back from the base of the peninsula; Becky and I were kneeling together about two-thirds of the way out. Blake seemed to study the situation, considering his options. He looked at the knife, then at the cane, then at a softball-sized piece of rock lying on the ground near his feet, the only sizable rock I could see anywhere near us. He folded his knife and put it in his pocket. Then he stepped back and bent for the rock. I maneuvered Becky around behind me, telling her to duck down and grab on to my belt. Her breaths were pure panic, but I could feel her do as I'd said.

The rock was going to get thrown at us from a distance of maybe eight feet. I knew I had to protect my head, because if I blacked out, Becky was dead for sure. I watched Blake jiggle the rock in his hand, then rear back to throw. As his arm thrust toward me, I put my hands up in front of my face; instead the rock caromed off my left forearm into my ribs, making my left side go numb. My vision darkened, and

I had trouble catching my breath for a moment, but I willed myself to stay conscious. Blake had shifted the cane to his right hand and took a step toward us, the cane raised. I could feel the rock on the ground just in front of me, by my left hand. I tried to hurl it at him backhand, but something ripped in my left side at the moment of release, and the rock floated past him, rolling uselessly away.

"Becky," I whispered, "let go of my belt. When I grab him, run and keep running."

I made a move on my knees toward Blake, fearing for my balance if I tried to rise. He seemed desperate, excited, and frightened all at once, building himself up to that first swing. Suddenly he gave a little cry, and the cane came at me, bouncing off my raised left forearm, numbing it, then at me again, cracking something, so that I cried out and dropped the arm. Blake was in a frenzy now, sensing he had me, and he took a step forward to get his whole body into the swing. I threw myself forward, thrusting my right fist with everything I could get behind it into his left knee, seeing the knee buckle, seeing the cane come out of his hands and go tumbling away. He came down on both knees, and I went at him, throwing him backward, crawling up over him, pressing my weight down on him, as I screamed for Becky to run. Blake began to buck furiously, pushing at me, trying to get me off. Blake was strong, and I didn't have the legs for this kind of wrestling. I didn't know how I could hold him long enough for Becky to get away, but I knew I had to—I just had to.

As my head got jerked to the side, I saw with disbelief that Becky hadn't moved. Then I saw what was wrong: Blake was kicking a foot out at her as he struggled with me; there wasn't room for her to get by. Desperate, I tried the only thing I could think of: I tightened my hold on Blake and tried to roll us both off the cliff. Blake let out a scream and wrestled us back from the edge, but that moment had given Becky the space she needed. Out of the corner of my eye I saw her slip by us and start to run.

Blake's bucking became more furious, but he couldn't shake me, so he began grabbing at my head. Fingers tore at the wig, began gouging at the hole in my skull. I pressed the left side of my head against his chest to protect the soft spot, but then he started pounding on the exposed skull, and I couldn't protect that too.

My vision began to darken. In my mind's eye I could see Becky running away, and I knew if I could just hold on, she'd make it to a life that would finally be happy, a life like the one Amy never had.

I've got to give her that life, I've just got to.

As I feel myself losing consciousness, I strain for a grip that will hold even in death. Then, slowly, my head begins to fill with a terrible clattering noise and with a darkness lit by furnace fire. There's a small boy in that darkness, and he has wrapped himself around his father's ankle with all his strength, and he refuses, he absolutely refuses to let go, no matter how hard the man tries to shake him off, no matter how hard the man beats at his head, because the boy can see now that his sister has made it down those stairs, and he knows she can get away if he'll just hold on, and he has to hold on because he loves his sister, and because a brother is supposed to protect his sister, no matter what the cost.

▽

25

I TRY TO fight my way out of the darkness, but the darkness is so heavy and I'm so tired. I smell something like fresh flowers, feel something soft brush against my face, hear someone whisper my name. I struggle up toward the voice, and I begin to see light and blurred faces, and the first face I make out is Janet's, and I say, "Becky?" and she says, "She's all right, Dave, thank you," and I can tell she's crying. And then there's another face—it's Deffinger's—and I say "Blake?" and he says, "He's dead—you cracked his skull with a rock," but I can't make any sense of that because I remember the rock, and it was so far away. Then I see Becky, and there are tears in her eyes, and something else, some fear, and I reach out a hand toward her, and suddenly her head is against my chest and she's sobbing. I whisper to her, "Oh, Becky, you should have run," and she says, "I couldn't leave you like that," and I say, "You're such a brave girl," and she says, "I didn't tell them," and I say, "I won't either," and she says, "I love you," and I say, "I love you too." I want so much to stay there with them, but everything's getting dark again, and I ask, "Am I . . . ?" but I can't stay to finish the question or find the answer, because the darkness is sweeping over me, and anyway there's something I have to do.

Down there in the darkness, the boy is still holding on, his eyes pressed shut against the tears that leak from beneath the lids. His loneliness and his desolation are almost total. He desperately needs someone who loves him to kneel down next to him and say, "I'm here"—to pry his arms loose from penance, and lift him up, and clutch him as he cries, and tell him that whatever there was to be forgiven is forgiven.

And then, as the flames die out and the darkness thickens, to hold him against the night.